blame

blame

a novel

tony
holtzman

CLOUD
SPLITTER
PRESS

Cover design by Eva Cohen   .

For individual orders, contact your local bookstore or www.amazon.com

For more information visit www.cloudsplitterpress.com

ISBN-13: 9780692746134
ISBN-10: 0692746137

TABLE OF CONTENTS

I never blame myself when I'm not hitting. I just blame the bat and if it keeps up, I change bats. After all, if I know it isn't my fault that I'm not hitting, how can I get mad at myself?

—Yogi Berra

FOREWORD

*B*lame is a work of fiction about scientists and science. It is not *science fiction* in the usual sense of the term. True, there is no memory gene capable of preventing Alzheimer's Disease, but the science is accurate and the methods I describe were in use at the turn of the twentieth century when experimental human gene therapy was a lively pursuit, albeit with little success. The death of Jesse Gelsinger in a gene therapy trial, which I mention, actually occurred. Amendments to U.S. patent law in 1980 and Supreme Court decisions on affirmative action in 2003 are described accurately. The scientific papers reporting that a single copy of the apolipoprotein-e4 gene variant did not increase the risk of Alzheimer's disease in African-Americans actually appeared in *Archives* *of Neurology* in 2003, although that finding has been disputed. Data on African-American admissions to U.S. medical schools, including trends and graduation rates as well as rates of faculty appointments reflect actual data. Myriad Genetics Inc. had a monopoly on a breast cancer gene, as the inventors in *Blame* hoped to have on the memory gene, until the Supreme Court declared it unconstitutional in 2013.

My entire professional career has been spent at Johns Hopkins where my clinical and research interests related to genetics. Colleagues and patients at Hopkins and contacts with people from other institutions— academic, governmental, commercial—provided a rich tapestry from which I plucked the characters in this book. No character represents a single person; several are composites of people I have known.

My career spanned years in which academic biomedical research moved from an unalloyed quest for knowledge to greater emphasis on fortune, and to a lesser extent, fame, not only among researchers but among the colleges and universities that hired them. Commercial interests have increasingly intruded the ivory tower. My career also paralleled the crescendo in the civil rights movement and the recognition that African-Americans continue to be mistreated, including in academic research. I try to meld these two themes in this novel.

One problem in writing about science is the use of scientific language, or jargon. Intentionally, I waste no time in introducing the one word of jargon I use. An *allele* is an inherited variant of a gene, usually arising by mutation many generations ago and passed from one generation to the next by reproduction. Readers will have to trust that I use correctly the names of modern genetic techniques, such as Southern Blot and Sanger Sequencing, without defining them.

THE INTERMENT

By the time Janice Polk arrived at the cemetery, thirty cars were parked on the left shoulder of the lane leading to the gravesite. A light rain had started on her way from the airport and after parking behind the last car she fastened a plastic kerchief over her hair and trudged up the lane in a drizzle that shrouded the earth, softened the path, and deposited coalescing droplets on the cars. The car in front of Janice's rental was a Ford Falcon, with rusting rocker panels and fenders. In front of it, a gleaming BMW whose luster reflected the raindrops. Next, an older Corolla, popular with the faculty, then a faded Mazda Miata, its securely bolted black vinyl top holding the raindrops, and at the crest of the hill a shiny black Lexus SUV. Reaching it, Janice gazed down through the mist at twenty more cars behind one sleek gray limo and the hearse. No red Lamborghini was among them. Starting down, she was glad she had worn slacks and flat shoes that stood up to the mud better than heels.

A temporary tent had been erected over the grave, but as she descended, the sea of open umbrellas in front of the tent drew her attention. All black, their uniform size and texture obscured the diversity of the crowd: rich and poor, black and white, learned and unschooled. As Janice crossed the lane toward the mourners, a gentleman in a black suit and dark tie handed her his umbrella, then reached into a barrel and unfurled another for himself. Standing on the periphery, she heard a murmur of "amen" spread through the crowd. Susie Matthews scattered the first handful of dirt onto her mother's coffin, followed by Reverend Johnson and others, and soon the gravediggers were heaping in shovelfuls from the mound they had created earlier in the day. The umbrellas parted to make a path down which Susie, her arm linked to the minister's, trod toward the limo. When she saw Janice, she smiled, left Reverend Johnson, and grasped her arms. "Thank you for coming," she said quietly. "I thought now that mama's dead and the story is finished you wouldn't care anymore." Awkward as it was with the umbrellas, they hugged. For once, Janice had no words.

Reverend Johnson stood by patiently and when the two women separated he escorted Susie to the limo. In clusters of two or three, members of her mother's church clung to each other, dabbing handkerchiefs at their teary faces, then separating reluctantly to enter the cars immediately in back of the limo. Theirs were not the fancy ones.

The President of the University and the Dean of the Medical School formed a knot with their entourages, somber but tearless. Audrey Meacham, Gertrude Brierly, and Gus McAllister stood together, dry-eyed, under their umbrellas. Brierly and McAllister both had parts in the tragedy that had engulfed Audrey's husband, Jason Pearce.

Someone touched Janice's sleeve and she turned to find Richard Piper smiling sadly at her. They had met on the day Janice's story about Pearce broke. Piper had given her a lift to the airport for her flight back to Chicago. They returned their umbrellas and walked back to their respective cars, Richard reaching his first, neither knowing what to say.

The rain fell steadily, forming rivulets along the earthen lane. On the one-way lane, Janice drove up to the crest then down past the gravesite. The tent had already been collapsed and the workers were packing up their shovels and arranging fresh flowers by the grave. They would soon be a sodden blur of colors. She turned on to the highway heading back to the airport, hoping she would be as lucky as that morning: flying stand-by on the day before Thanksgiving.

As she drove out of the cemetery, the rain turned torrential and Janice began to cry uncontrollably. Even after she switched the windshield wipers to high, her vision blurred. She pulled onto the shoulder, shifted into park, and drew a handkerchief from her bag. Since first visiting the city exactly three weeks ago in response to a press release from the Bates-Bronsted Medical School, she had not let her emotions interfere with investigating why Betsy Matthews had developed leukemia while participating in Pearce's clinical trial. As she brought her breathing under control, she realized for the first time since starting the assignment that she was sad and angry about Betsy's death. Despite the intensity with which she had worked, and what she had uncovered, she could not apportion blame.

PART I. BEFORE THE INTERMENT

Chapter 1

HEAR, HEAR!

"Do the mice that carry one allele of the deafness gene show any abnormalities?" Professor Julian Goodrich asked. Jason Pearce had just concluded his first colloquium since joining the faculty at Bates-Bronsted Medical School in Virginia. His work had path-breaking potential, yet he had presented it diffidently, letting the results speak for themselves, omitting the brash claims that increasingly had become the mantra of aspiring young faculty doing genetics research. Students and faculty alike admired his modesty, his gentle humor, his willingness to admit that he might be wrong in his interpretation of the data on gene regulation, and his good looks. Unusually, the audience had applauded.

"As a matter of fact," Pearce replied directly to Professor Goodrich, "they do, and it helps us distinguish them from the normal mice that lack a deafness allele altogether." Addressing the audience, he reminded them, "It takes the presence of two deafness alleles, one inherited from each parent, for the mouse not to hear. We know they're deaf because when they run the maze we constructed they don't hear a buzzer that warns of an electric shock. Consequently, they get shocked much more often than the mice with either one deafness allele or none; they hear the buzzer and learn to turn around before they get shocked." He turned to look directly at Goodrich. "But compared to the mice with no deafness allele, those with one allele forget how to run the maze. It takes the same number of shocks for the mice with one deafness allele as those with no deafness allele to learn to take the alternate pathway. But on successive days, the mice with one deafness allele hear an increasing number of buzzes and then get shocked, eventually receiving as many as on the first day, before they learn to take the alternate path to find the cheese at the end of the maze. The mice with no deafness allele hear the buzzer and remember to turn around before getting shocked."

A few others asked questions and then Goodrich raised his hand again: "From what you said about the maze, Jason, it sounds like your mice with one deafness allele could be a model for Alzheimer's Disease?"

Pearce thought for a while. "I doubt it. There is no association with hearing loss in patients with Alzheimer's so far as I know. And as I recall, the common, late-onset form of Alzheimer's involves environmental factors and several genes." He paused, thinking of other reasons. "Also, inbred strains of mice are a far cry from humans and more knowledge will be gained by studying gene regulation."

"Hear, hear!" Professor Bert Chapman shouted. In his eighties, he was the only emeritus faculty who came to the monthly departmental conference, usually sitting among the students, from whom he took sustenance. As the audience dispersed, he introduced himself, telling Jason, "It's unusual these days that I hear skepticism about the practical applications of one's own work." Chapman's papers in the 1960s were classics on genetic variation and Jason blushed momentarily as Chapman shook his hand. "Why don't you join me for lunch one day next week where we can talk more of your work and I can tell you what I've been up to?" Jason said he'd be honored and they quickly made arrangements to meet in Chapman's cubbyhole of an office. Their lunch the next week, in the autumn of 1994, inaugurated a monthly routine that continued until the end of 1996, when Chapman died in his sleep.

At their first lunch, Chapman presented Jason with his book, which had just been published, *Patents and Profits—The Demise of the University.* "It may be a cliché," Chapman went on between bites of his sandwich, "to call the university an ivory tower, but its mission through the ages has been to pursue knowledge, not commerce. Now its walls are being breached, just as elephants are being destroyed for their ivory." He finished his sandwich and produced an apple from his brown paper bag. "Enough of the ranting of an old man; tell me how you're going to pursue gene regulation." They talked science for another half hour until Jason glanced at his watch and realized he was late for an appointment with a student. He left in such a hurry that he left the plastic tray on which he had carried his lunch from the cafeteria. Chapman placed it on top of a bookcase. It was the first of many that Jason would leave.

By their second meeting, Jason had read *Patents and Profits.* "I hadn't realized," he told Chapman, "that allowing universities to patent discoveries that its faculty made with government support would be so far-reaching."

"Yes," Chapman replied. "That change in the law in 1980 led to an enormous increase in patents assigned to universities, often jointly with private companies. Take Julian Goodrich. He and Bates-Bronsted and the company Goodrich started hold a patent on a discovery of Julian's that improved the efficiency of gene cloning. The University and Julian share in the royalties from the sale of the company's products and from licenses that they give to others."

"You know, it's interesting you mention Professor Goodrich. My students tell me that the students working in his lab are sworn to secrecy. He warns them not to discuss their research until it's published."

Chapman smacked his hand on his desk angrily. "That's just what happens when you contaminate the quest for knowledge with the desire to make more than your salary provides."

"Do you think there's a risk," Jason asked, "that as companies spend more money on university research—research from which they can profit—Congress will appropriate less?"

"Highly probable," Chapman replied. "And research like yours, for which practical applications are not foreseeable, is likely to suffer."

———

Before their last monthly meeting in 1996, which turned out to be their last ever, Jason phoned Chapman to ask if he could bring along Audrey Meacham who was eager to meet him. Chapman was flattered and acquiesced.

Jason had met Audrey a few weeks before at the first meeting of the Committee on Faculty-Industry

Relations convened by the President of the University
to which Bates-Bronsted Medical School was attached.
Fall colors had passed their peak, and as Jason walked
toward the administration building on the brisk sunny
afternoon of the meeting, dry brown leaves skittered
ahead of him. On the steps leading up to the main
entrance he passed a young woman and, on reaching
the door, held it open for her. Inside, he stopped, trying to orient himself. The woman turned back. "Can
I help you?"

"The President's Conference Room?"

"That's where I'm heading." Silently, they walked
side-by-side up the broad curved staircase and into
the empty, double-doored conference room. The
room's centerpiece was a highly polished oval mahog-
any table, in which the woman could see her reflec-
tion as she set her briefcase down at one end. Twenty
cushioned armchairs, inlayed with red leather, encir-
cled the table. Jason took a seat at the opposite end of
the room. Suspended over the table, a multi-lamped
chandelier illuminated the table in a soft light sufficient to read by. Jason had been so busy with his
research, often spending eighteen hours in his lab, that
he seldom had time for thoughts of romance. Now he
admired the woman who was wearing a red suit that
went well with her auburn hair as she removed papers
and a legal pad from her briefcase, arranging them on
the table.

Several older men entered as she did so. One of them immediately approached her. "Audrey Meacham?" he asked. She nodded with a smile, and he introduced himself as the Dean of the Medical School. A few weeks earlier, he had phoned Audrey, inviting her to attend the meeting. "I will be presenting the University's proposals," he had told her, "but I'll need your expertise, Ms. Meacham, in order to get approval without a fight." The twenty seats were quickly filled and the Dean, who sat to Audrey's left, called the meeting to order, asking the members to introduce themselves, beginning with the man to his left.

On the top sheet of her yellow legal pad, Audrey quickly drew a diagram of the seating arrangement and filled in names, ranks and departments. The man she had come in with was Jason Pearce, an associate professor promoted to that rank in his second year on the faculty.

When it was Audrey's turn, the Dean preempted her. "I'd like to introduce Ms. Audrey Meacham, representing the Administration." Referring to the paper in front of him, he informed the committee that in law school she had been Editor of Law Review and, on graduating, had clerked in the United States Court of Appeals for the Federal Circuit, researching cases on patent infringements and intellectual property. "She joined the University's legal staff last year." He turned to her. "Welcome, Ms. Meacham. Would you please give us the legal basis for why the University's position on patenting has changed?"

Audrey began by tracing the University's changing policies on patents. From Chapman's book and their conversations, Jason was familiar with the topic. He listened carefully to learn whether Audrey offered an opinion on the merits of the changes. "The change in the patent law in 1980," she continued, "contributed to the rise of the biotechnology industry; a company could obtain an exclusive license on research a university had patented without fear of competition. Although federal grants comprise the largest source of our research revenues, they are not keeping up with the explosion of research. If Bates-Bronsted Medical School is to continue in the top ranks it must seek new sources of revenue from the private sector, especially the biotech industry. Fees from licensing and royalties can fill the void."

"Thank you, Ms. Meacham." Jason wondered whether she was simply stating the University's position, realizing the dangerous precedent it was setting, or whether she favored the new policy.

Halfway down the table, a hand shot up. "Yes, Richard." Audrey consulted her seating chart. Richard Piper, assistant professor of political science; dark beard, brown curly hair. He and Jason were by far the youngest members on the committee. Richard was the only one with an open collar and no tie. "I am not a scientist in the sense that you gentlemen are. I have no laboratory and my funding comes mostly from the University. It seems to me that patenting could steer the faculty away from basic research in the hope of garnering greater remuneration."

Immediately several hands went up. The Dean started to call on one, but Piper, his voice rising, said, "Just a minute. I'm not finished."

The Dean conceded, but admonished him to hurry up. "I worry, gentlemen, not only that the direction of research will be skewed, but the air of free inquiry, the *sine qua non* of a university, will be stifled as faculty members funded by companies keep their research findings secret in the hope of gaining an advantage."

The Dean called on Julian Goodrich. He was a dapper man with gray hair parted in the middle, neatly plastered down, and a moustache tapering to points. He spoke slowly with restraint. "This University, Mr. Piper"—Goodrich reserved the title of Professor to full professors with tenure—"has a long and honorable history of seeking truth, and the faculty are honorable men not susceptible to financial temptation as you perceive." He smoothed his moustache. "If we were to make scientific discoveries and not patent them we could be denying the public great advances in its well being; hiding our light under a bushel so to speak. If we receive royalties, that is our just desert." Several others expressed variants of Professor Goodrich's argument.

"Just what exactly is the University proposing, Dean?" someone asked.

"I'm glad you asked," he replied as he pulled a sheaf of papers from his briefcase and handed them to Audrey. She took one and passed the rest to the faculty member on her right. While the document was circulating he announced, "Here's a preliminary draft for your perusal. In the next few weeks we'll be circulating it to the entire faculty."

After the last person received a copy, the Dean remained silent long enough for everyone to read it. He looked at Richard Piper. "So you see, Mr. Piper, the University recognizes your concerns and has put limits on commercially supported research."

PRELIMINARY DRAFT   NOT FOR CIRCULATION

ADMINSTRATION PROPOSAL FOR FACULTY-INDUSTRY RELATIONS

- Faculty wishing to obtain patents on their work will do so through the University, which will be a joint patent holder.

- All licenses for and royalties from such patents will be paid to the University. The proceeds will be divided equally among the University, the faculty patent holder, and his/her Department.

- Companies providing research support to faculty will have no more than six months to review papers emanating from the faculty's research before they are submitted for publication.

- No company will provide more than ten percent of any faculty member's salary.

- No faculty conducting research supported by a company will be allowed to receive or hold equity in that company.

Goodrich raised his hand. "By and large, Dean, these seem like balanced proposals except for the last one. I and a few others in this room hold equity in companies that support our research." This admission shocked Jason, but he listened intently as Goodrich continued. "Will the University expect us to divest?"

"That's an interesting question, Julian," the Dean replied. "What would you do if divestment became University policy?"

Smoothing his moustache Goodrich answered, "I might sever my ties with the University and work entirely for the company."

"You see," shouted Piper without being recognized. "You start down this road and the Professor wants to blackmail the University; if you fetter him, he'll take his expertise, his accumulated wisdom, and leave. In the interest of the integrity of the University I think the only patents the faculty should hold are, as in our illustrious past, those that are freely available. It's the position taken by our most distinguished Professor, Bertram Chapman, in his recent book."

Jason, slouching in his chair, sat up straight when he heard Chapman's name and raised his hand for the first time. "Yes, I was wondering, Dean, why Professor Chapman was not invited to join this Committee. He has vast knowledge of the history of the University and has studied the matter of patenting."

"Yes, Professor Pearce, we are well aware of Professor Chapman's position. In putting this committee together, the President, the Provost, and I felt it would be better to appoint faculty whose minds were *not* made up."

Turning to Goodrich, the Dean spoke. "So far as holding stock equity, the Administration is not wedded to the draft proposal. We hope to have a final recommendation at the next meeting." The Grandfather clock on the side of the room softly chimed the hour. Ignoring Audrey's presence, the Dean announced, "Gentlemen, our time is up. Because of the holiday recess, we'll skip December and meet on the fourth Monday in January, that would be the twenty-seventh." Several men penciled the date into their pocket calendars.

Jason sat quietly while others stood in groups of twos and threes, continuing to talk heatedly about the issues raised. Then, shyly, he approached Audrey as she was putting her pad back in her briefcase. "You know, Ms. Meacham, the Administration should read Professor Chapman's book. Have you read it?"

"As a matter of fact, I have, Professor Pearce." She glanced around furtively. No one was paying attention to them. "It is brilliant," she said in low tones.

Jason grinned, pleased to hear her opinion. "I think so too!" He hesitated as Audrey closed her briefcase. "Uh, I wondered if you would care to have dinner with me the week after Thanksgiving? We can talk about it." He had not asked a woman for a date since high school, preferring, when he socialized at all, to go out in groups.

Audrey was caught off guard. Her professional work had engaged her so fully that she had not gone out with anyone since coming to the University, having turned down several invitations. His gaze—so earnest—suggested to Audrey that he'd be crushed if she refused. "That would be lovely. Wednesday a week?"

Jason broke into a childish grin. "Great!"

They agreed to meet at a cozy French restaurant on one of the avenues that converged on the campus. Audrey arrived first and stood shivering under her umbrella, fending off the sleet, wondering if Jason had forgotten. Two minutes later, he rushed up, bare headed in a tan raincoat, apologizing profusely.

Only one elderly couple was inside. Jason helped Audrey out of her coat and stood for a moment admiring her, wondering whether he should pay a compliment. She was wearing a high-necked sheath dress of black silk with a single strand of pearls around her neck. Hesitantly, he said, "You look lovely." She thanked him as they were shown to a table near a crackling fire. Introducing himself, their waiter told them they still had several bottles of *Beaujolais Nouveau*. Audrey looked wistful. "My father always reserved a case just before Thanksgiving."

"Do you have it by the glass?" Jason asked. "I have to go back to the lab after dinner--sober."

"I'm sorry, *Monsieur*. Only by the bottle."

Jason turned to Audrey. "Shall we get a bottle?"

"As you like," she replied.

"We'll get a bottle," Jason told the waiter who returned shortly with the *Beaujolais* and went through the usual ritual.

"I don't know much about wine," Jason admitted when the waiter started to pour a sample into his glass. "You taste it, Audrey." It was the first time Audrey heard him say her name and it made her blush. After sipping the wine, she nodded, and the waiter half-filled their glasses, leaving them studying the menu. Jason was still bent over his when Audrey raised her eyes. His blonde hair was not combed but fell naturally toward the sides and back of his head. He had broad shoulders, an aquiline nose, and when he finally looked up, clear blue eyes, full lips, and a firm chin. Audrey's mother would say that such a chin indicated strong character. Audrey was surprised that his eyes were level with hers; he had started to slouch, the only shortcoming Audrey had noticed. *Both it and the indoor pallor of his skin are remediable*, she thought.

"It's warm in here," he said as he stood to remove his blazer, hanging it over his chair. About five foot-eight, he was wearing a blue button-down shirt—open at the collar, no tie—and khaki slacks without a sharp crease; probably his standard work attire. When he sat back down, she raised her glass and smiled, "Cheers."

Jason quickly clinked.

"I think I'll have two appetizers instead of an entree," she told him.

"As long as it's not because you don't think I can afford more."

"No. As a matter of fact, I expect to pay for my own dinner."

"But I invited you."

"It wouldn't be a good idea for you to pay."

Puzzled, he thought for a moment, then his eyes brightened as he said with a broad smile revealing perfect teeth, "Conflict of interest! Since we're on different sides—maybe even opposing—on the Faculty-Industry Relations Committee, we must avoid even the appearance of a conflict of interest."

"That's it," Audrey smiled. They clinked and sipped their wine. *What if I fell in love with this guy?* she wondered. *What would happen to the conflict of interest then?*

"You know, Audrey,"—her name on his lips thrilled her again—"getting rich is furthest from my mind. I have a living wage and I'm being paid to study gene regulation. It's not going to save any lives, but it's what I love to do. That apparently isn't enough for some of the faculty who receive commercial support, like Julian Goodrich. You heard him threaten to quit if he couldn't keep his stock in Generich. Faculty like him want their cake and eat it too: equity in the companies that contribute to their salaries, and the stimulating arena of the university."

"So far the Administration doesn't approve of their receiving equity."

As the waiter refilled their wine glasses for the second time, Jason said, "I find it disturbing that the President didn't appoint Professor Chapman to the committee."

Audrey twirled the stem of her wine glass, not answering immediately; Jason wondered whether she was hesitating to tell him something. "You know, Jason, I sat in on the meeting that decided the membership of the committee. When Chapman's name came up, the President laughed scornfully. 'Chapman's old guard. He's way past his prime in his science and his politics. Obsolete.' The Provost and Dean laughed along with him."

"That's disgusting," Jason replied angrily. "I can tell you that Chapman's grasp of science is not obsolete and so far as his politics, if the President was referring to University politics, Chapman takes it more to heart than he and the Dean do." He paused as the waiter arrived with their plates. "You know, Audrey, "I have lunch with Professor Chapman once a month. You'd enjoy meeting him."

Audrey, slightly tipsy, was regarding her escargots. "This is a high class restaurant," she chuckled. Jason regarded her inquisitively. "They don't put the snails back in shells."

Jason was surprised. "Are there restaurants that do that?"

"Oh yes," she giggled, "not only do they stuff them into empty shells but when the empty shells come back to the kitchen, they recycle them."

"I hope they wash them first."

She chuckled. "Depends on the quality of the restaurant."

"Have you done a survey?" Jason asked jokingly.

"No, but after college I took two years off to study cooking in Lyon."

"Were you planning to be a chef?"

"I didn't know what I wanted. The guy I'd been involved with for four years found someone else and I was devastated. I went to Lyon as a sous chef and cooked myself out of misery. When my hands got raw from all the washing and scraping I decided I wanted them smooth, and went to law school."

"Surely more than rough hands got you to law school?"

"Oh, Jason, I'm giving you the wrong impression." She put her fork down and lay her right hand on the table, palm down. After a moment's hesitation, Jason tentatively put his left hand over it. "Well, it certainly is smooth now," he said with a smile.

"That's not the reason I went to law school. While I was in college, I volunteered to work in a shelter for the homeless. I became personally aware of injustice. The law seemed a way to do something meaningful."

"And you ended up working for the University."

"It's better than a corporation, don't you think?"

"I suppose. At least it's not for profit."

After eating quietly for a few moments, Jason asked, "How'd you like to join Professor Chapman and me for lunch next week?"

"You'll probably be talking science and I'll just get in the way."

"Not at all. We cover a wide range of subjects, even poetry. We meet in his office on Tuesday at 12:30 and bring our lunches. I'll bring one for you."

"Well then, I'd love to."

"I have to warn you, he can be a little harsh; tells you exactly what he thinks. And his attire is unusual; a black bowtie and pink socks, seldom takes his suit jacket off."

Parting outside the restaurant with a handshake, Audrey said, "See you next Tuesday."

They arrived simultaneously at the squat red brick building, one of the University's few historic structures retained in the construction boom. *Ad virtutem per sapientiam* was carved above the door: To virtue through wisdom. "I bought a tuna and a ham and Swiss," Jason greeted her. "You can have your pick."

"It doesn't matter. Did you tell Professor Chapman I was coming?"

"Yes, he's delighted." Jason chuckled. "Of course, that was after I told him what you thought of his book."

They reached his door and Jason knocked loudly. Audrey heard an incomprehensible grunt from the other side, signaling Jason to open the door. Seated at his desk, sandwich in hand, Chapman turned to them. When he saw Audrey he put his sandwich down on a deflated brown paper bag, stood, and came forward in a courtly manner, offering his hand as Jason introduced her. He was taller and thinner than Jason, which, based on Jason's reverential description, did not surprise her; his voice, slightly higher pitched and nasal, did. For a man in his eighties his face was remarkably unlined and his pliant grey hair was neatly combed with a part to one side. He gestured to his sofa; Jason set the lunch tray between them as Professor Chapman sat and swiveled his chair around. "I can hardly imagine, Ms. Meacham, that anyone in the Administration would be interested in what an old fogey like me has to say about patents. History is for the past, they believe."

"Until this morning, Professor Chapman, I might have argued with you."

"Why? What happened this morning?" Jason asked.

"Chief Legal Counsel informed me that the President will ask the University's Board of Trustees to allow faculty to receive equity in companies that are contributing financially to their research."

They were all quiet for a moment. "That's one more nail in the coffin," Chapman said. "First, the administration encourages the faculty to patent so it can protect its rights to the invention. Then it grants exclusive licenses to the highest bidder. That's enough right there to impinge on free inquiry. Now it's letting faculty hold equity. Soon the universities will be working for the companies."

"Yes," replied Audrey. "They make the university less, less—pristine."

"Indeed. I'll bet my old friend, Julian Goodrich," he spoke sardonically, "went to his buddy, the President, and told him that if he couldn't receive equity, he'd give up his professorship and work exclusively for the Generich company that he helped start and still pays part of his faculty salary."

Audrey and Jason looked at each other. "That's exactly what he said at the Faculty-Industry Relations Committee meeting," Jason reported.

Chapman's phone rang. "Excuse me," he said to his guests. "Yes he is," he said into the phone. "Okay, I'll tell him." He turned to Jason. "Apparently, a student had an appointment to see you."

Jason looked at his watch. "I forgot all about it." He excused himself, telling Audrey he'd call her, and left.

"I should be going, too," Audrey said.

"What's the hurry? You haven't finished your sandwich and I still have my apple." He reached into his brown bag for the fruit. "Quite a bright young man you've got there, Ms. Meacham."

She blushed. "He's not my young man."

"No, I suppose not. Not yet anyway. He likes you, you know."

"How do you know?" she blurted.

Chapman laughed. "I've been around long enough. He hardly took his eyes off you the entire time he was here. He didn't want to leave."

"I like him too," she confided in Chapman.

"He's a good catch. It's rare to find a young scientist these days who's not lured by money or fame. His work on gene regulation isn't going to win him a Nobel Prize but it's important for understanding how genes interact. Do you know Ms. Meach—"

"Please, call me Audrey."

"We need scientists like Jason who are not easily lured away from basic science in hope of fame and glory."

Audrey took the empty tray that had contained their lunch, put it on the stack of trays on Chapman's bookcase, and picked them up. "That's all right," Chapman stood, taking them from her. "I'm not too feeble to return them to the cafeteria myself." He smiled at her. "I hope to see you again soon, Ms., uh, Audrey. Goodbye."

A month later Professor Chapman died in his sleep, stunning Jason to whom he had become a father figure. The University arranged a memorial service for Chapman a month after his death. Audrey picked up Jason and they went together in her car. After the singing of a hymn that Chapman was reputed to have liked, and bland comments by the University President who pretended to be a good friend who frequently sought his advice—although as Chapman wryly had told Jason, seldom took it—members of the audience were invited to speak. Julian Goodrich was the first. "Professor Chapman and I did not always see eye to eye. He tried to argue me out of forming the Generich Company, but when he moved into the new genetics building he complimented me on the Company's generosity in making its construction possible—" he paused for a second and added, "although begrudgingly." A few of those who knew Chapman, including Jason, chuckled. When Jason had told him that Goodrich reputedly admonished his students to keep their work secret, Chapman replied that he rued the day he ever set foot in the building. "But," Goodrich continued, "Bert Chapman and I shared a dream." Jason was perplexed. "We saw the forward march of genetics, heralding the day when humankind would be free of internal diseases. We could not stop accidents or wars but with the tools to clone genes and replace defective ones we foresaw the eradication of heart disease, cancer, diabetes, Alzheimer's, and other mental illnesses. Professor Chapman's early work made all this possible and for that I and my colleagues here at the University and at the Generich Company owe him a great debt."

Jason's heart started to pound as he stood and walked to the podium; nothing like this ever happened when he gave a lecture. He was angry at Goodrich's presumption that Chapman shared his dream.

"After the first seminar I presented at Bates-Bronsted," Jason began, "Professor Chapman invited me to lunch. I didn't expect we'd eat in his office—he ate out of a brown bag—and I had to go fetch a lunch from the cafeteria. We repeated that routine monthly until he died."

"At one of our recent meetings he read Oliver Wendell Holmes' poem, *the Deacon's Masterpiece,* to me." Jason paused, then continued, "Professor Chapman did not believe that scientists and doctors could ever eliminate human disease, that at a ripe old age we would go *"to pieces all at once, All at once, and nothing first, Just as bubbles do when they burst,"* he recited from Holmes' masterpiece. Chapman was much more enthralled with learning how our genes and their products first worked to develop us, then how they sustained us in a hostile environment, and finally, how they programmed our senescence. If, along the way, geneticists made lives better, that was a good thing, but to have the hubris that we could end disease, Chapman believed was an illusion." He left the podium and resumed his seat beside Audrey.

On their way back to her car, Jason dejectedly told Audrey, "I don't think my eulogy impressed anybody."

"Let's go back to my house," said Audrey. "I'll throw a light supper together and then I can drive you home." They drove to a quiet tree-filled fringe of the city where Audrey lived in the small white colonial-style house in which she had grown up. Her father, a lawyer, had died suddenly of a heart attack three years earlier. Not prepared for widowhood, her mother needed company and Audrey, having just been hired by the University, needed low-cost housing. With Audrey's companionship, her mother regained her vitality and became active in civic organizations. She was fearful of driving into the center of the city and moved into a new high-rise condominium downtown, leaving the house, by this time free of mortgage, to Audrey. Now it was in the most affluent neighborhood in the city, its value having risen more than tenfold since Audrey's parents had bought it in the 1960s.

She led Jason in through the small vestibule, then turned to face him, put her arms around his neck and kissed him for the first time. After a few moments, they were on the couch, petting and kissing until finally Audrey rose, led him by the hand to her bedroom upstairs, where she folded the bedspread back and slipped off her shoes as Jason removed his jacket and tie.

After an hour, they lay on their backs, gazing sidewise at each other. "Can we take a time out for supper?" Jason asked. "I haven't eaten all day."

Six weeks later they were married in a private ceremony at which only their mothers were present. Jason's had taken a bus all the way from Kearney, Nebraska.

Preparing for the birth of their first child was lots of fun. They shopped together for baby furniture and other infant accouterments. Jason was as thrilled as Audrey when he put his hand on her belly and felt the baby kick. When the students and fellows in Jason's lab organized a rafting trip in the spring of 1997, Audrey, feeling it was a little risky in her condition, encouraged Jason to go without her, but he did not want to leave her alone and stayed home. Rachel was born in November, right on schedule.

Chapter 2

THE THIRD MILLENNIUM

Waiting to speak to Jason Pearce while he and Professor Chapman made arrangements for their first lunch, Laura had prepared her introduction. Now she delivered it: "Professor Pearce, my name is Laura Mittelman. I'm a graduate student here, just passed my prelims, and I wonder if it might be possible to do my doctoral thesis on gene regulation in your laboratory." Pearce's eyes locked on hers; they did not wander fleetingly over her body, as did those of many males, including professors. Some women liked that sort of admiration. Laura, an attractive blonde, perceived it as a disrobing fantasy.

"That's certainly possible," he replied. "Why don't you come by my lab next week and we can discuss your interests."

Pearce's discovery of gene regulation was based on his observation that in matings between hearing mice with one allele for deafness and deaf mice with two, the ratio of deaf offspring to hearing mice was consistently less than the expected one to one. Pearce hypothesized that a gene separate from the one that accounted for deafness was in some way inhibiting expression of the deafness gene in the excess of hearing mice. Laura's task was to see if there were mice with one allele for deafness who consistently gave birth to an excess of hearing offspring.

The white mice were cute, but before Laura mastered picking them up by their tiny bodies or the very proximal part of their tails, she was bitten and clawed a few times. Except for the scratches she had nothing to show for her effort: no mice consistently conceived an excess of hearing mice. In fact, and to her and Pearce's surprise, the excess of hearing mice in successive crosses between deaf mice with two deafness alleles and hearing mice with only one was diminishing, approaching one to one. It occurred to both Jason and Laura that maybe there wasn't a regulator gene, but neither shared this idea with the other. She also confirmed the observation that Jason had mentioned in response to Julian Goodrich's question at Jason's first seminar: that mice with one deafness allele seemed to forget how to run the maze.

Laura participated in the friendly banter in the lab, from undergraduates doing electives, the other predocs, and on to the postdocs, but when any of the males came to close, she made it clear by withdrawal, a scowl, and words if necessary, that she did not enjoy being touched. The men learned to keep their physical distance.

She worked long hours, apparently with no outside interest or pleasures, and despite the setbacks with the regulator gene, she had one success. In anticipation of isolating a regulator gene she developed a technique for fine mapping short segments of DNA. The paper describing the method, with Laura as first author and Jason as senior author, was published in _Genomics_ in 1998 and within months was used and cited by other researchers.

Laura wrote up the gene regulator and fine mapping experiments for her Ph.D. thesis, but not the "forgetful" mice observations as they were nothing new. She sailed through her oral examination and despite the negative results of the search for the regulator, her committee, chaired by Julian Goodrich, unanimously recommended awarding the doctorate, primarily on the strength of her methodology.

Jason's research, including support for pre-doctoral students, was funded by an NIH program project grant that would expire in December 2000 unless Jason successfully applied to get it competitively renewed.

Laura Mittelman was the brightest young scientist Jason had ever encountered, and he hoped she would join the faculty at Bates-Bronsted. Even before she had been awarded her Ph.D. he urged her to apply for an NIH research grant to improve methods to search for the regulator of the deafness allele. He was beginning to worry that he might not get his competitive renewal unless his lab could provide more evidence for the regulator.

So in addition to preparing for her thesis defense, Laura spent the first half of 1999 writing the application. She met often with Jason for his input. He listened to what she had to say, read drafts of her proposal, almost always saying he couldn't improve on what she'd written. Once Laura submitted the application, she almost forgot about it, so sure it would be approved and funded, launching her on a successful career in biomedical research with her own laboratory, contributing to knowledge, and eventually having her own students and postdocs.

Jason and Audrey threw a New Year's Eve party to welcome the third millennium, inviting Audrey's colleagues in the Legal Department, Jason's in the Department of Genetics, and his entire laboratory crew. They rolled up the rug on their living room floor. Audrey had prepared a mixtape of pop hits, including some Lenny Kravitz, Eagle Eye Cherry, and, of course, Prince's classic with the refrain, "Tonight I'm gonna party like it's 1999." Most of the guests drank beer and wine until five minutes to midnight when Jason popped a few bottles of champagne. Two-year old Rachel slept through it all.

Laura hadn't felt much like going. The paralegal she was living with was out of town visiting relatives, but more depressing, she had just learned that NIH had not given her grant application a high enough score to be funded; she faced the prospect of being jobless in a year. The news sent her mood into a well of gloom, and her lab co-workers had to pull her out to the party.

Although Laura was ready to leave shortly after midnight, the friends who brought her were having a great time and in no mood to go. Everyone else was dancing, even Jason and Audrey. Audrey was a good dancer, but Jason just went through the motions. Laura slunk into the empty kitchen, absently filling a small plate with shrimp, cheese and crackers. A few moments later Professor Goodrich came in and stood next to her, filling his plate. "It's nice to get away from all that noise," he said as Laura, plate in one hand, pulled out a kitchen chair with her free hand. She smiled in agreement. "Do you mind if I join you?" he asked, pulling out another chair and placing it at a right angle to Laura's. Having little choice, she smiled wanly, not imagining they'd find anything to talk about.

"You know, Laura, your Ph.D. thesis was one of the best I've ever read. No one on your committee had any doubts. You should have a great future ahead of you."

"Thank you," she said politely. She was not ordinarily buoyed by past accomplishments.

"Have you ever thought of working for a biotechnology company?"

A month ago her answer would have been *No*, but since her grant was turned down, she had considered everything, even that. "Yes, I've thought of it."

"The Generich Company—I'm on its Board of Directors—is eager to get into the gene cloning business. From your thesis, and the paper you've published, that should be a snap for you. If you're interested, you should visit the Company. The labs are not far from the Medical School. Come and meet the people I—uh, we've—already recruited."

"Thanks very much, Professor Goodrich, I'll give it some thought," she replied.

On a bitterly cold morning a few weeks into the new millennium, Julian Goodrich phoned Jason to ask for a lift to work; his new BMW would not start and he had an important ten o'clock meeting at the Generich Company. Goodrich lived close to the Pearces and ten minutes later he was sitting in the passenger seat of Jason's trusty old Corolla.

Merging onto the highway leading downtown, they encountered a major traffic jam and to pass the time started talking about their families and their common neighborhood. Then Julian asked, "So, how's your work going, Jason?"

Jason admitted that his efforts to find a regulator of the deafness allele were not bearing fruit. As the caterpillar of cars inched forward, paused, inched forward again, Goodrich was surprised how openly Jason talked.

"Is that the same gene that you were working on when you gave the seminar shortly after you arrived at Bates-Bronsted?" Jason nodded. "The one I suggested might be a model for Alzheimer's Disease?"

"I remember," Jason said. "Mice with one deafness allele seemed to forget how to avoid the shock."

"If your money's running out it might be prudent to follow that up. A major breakthrough in Alzheimer's has eluded investigators for a decade. You might be sitting on a gold mine."

Jason took his eyes off the road to glance at Goodrich. "Well, I'll think about it. My renewal application is due June first. I'm still chasing down a few leads on the regulator. But thanks, Julian, for reminding me of the Alzheimer's possibility."

"If you decide to pursue it, let me know. The venture capitalist that helped start Generich might be interested in helping you."

The traffic began to move, then stalled again. Julian changed the subject. "How's Laura Mittelman doing?" he asked. "I had a nice chat with her at your New Year's Eve party."

"Quite well. She's busy writing grants. If I don't get my renewal I'll have to let her go."

"A very attractive young woman. Sexy."

Jason shot Julian a glance. "I wouldn't know."

"You wouldn't know that she's beautiful?"

"She's beautiful I suppose. I wouldn't know how sexy she is."

"If she was working for me I'd have a hard time keeping my hands off her. She must have a boyfriend."

"If she does, I've never met him," Jason said.

At five minutes to ten, as they reached the downtown exit, the traffic sped up and within two minutes they were at the entrance to Generich's combined offices and labs.

Goodrich's question about the deafness gene preoccupied Jason as he walked from his parking spot to the genetics building. That afternoon he pulled up a stool to chat with Laura who was writing up an experiment at her bench. The post-docs, including Laura, and students in his lab, all of whose livelihood was at stake, had noticed his anxiety about finding a regulator of the deafness allele and were working literally night and day on a variety of leads. She was surprised when he asked, "I wonder, Laura, if you would look more closely at the learning deficit in the mice with only one allele of the deafness gene."

"'Learning deficit.' What do you want to know?"

"I want to know why they don't retain their knowledge of how to avoid the electric shock to reach the cheese. Maybe their hearing was impaired and that interfered with their memory."

"But they did learn that the buzzer warned them of the shock, so it seemed their hearing was okay," Laura replied. "They just seemed to forget."

"Well, I'd like to document it. Besides, we don't know if age has anything to do with their forgetting."

She looked at Jason curiously. "That doesn't seem a promising lead for finding the regulator," she remarked. "Why do you want to know?"

He had always encouraged Laura and the others in his lab to 'talk back' to him. This time he was evasive. "It's just a hunch."

"You know, Jason, I'd rather be working at the molecular level than fooling with live mice again. Maybe you should get a psychology student to do this."

He shrugged. "Unless you've got a brilliant idea for finding the regulator," he said sarcastically, "why don't you humor me? You can continue to fool with the regulator problem in your spare time, but I'd really like to know more about the mice's forgetfulness."

※

"What did you and Julian talk about this morning?" Audrey asked Jason at dinner that evening.

"Nothing much." He chuckled. "Julian thinks Laura's a very sexy woman."

"What do you think?"

"How would I know? She is beautiful, I suppose—" He realized he might be offending her and put his hand over hers "—One beautiful woman is enough for me," he said soothingly.

Ignoring Jason's compliment, Audrey said contemptuously, "Julian Goodrich can't keep his hands off women."

"What do you mean?"

"At our New Year's Eve party he gave me more than a cursory hug, got really close and had his hand on my bottom."

"He was drunk," Jason quickly insisted.

"Maybe, but so were a lot of other men and they didn't touch me like that." For a few moments they ate quietly then Audrey asked, "Was Laura all that you and Julian talked about?"

"Julian thought maybe my mice with one deafness allele might be a model for Alzheimer's."

"Alzheimer's?" She looked puzzled. "That's not an area of expertise for you, is it?"

He slouched in his seat. "No, but I can learn."

"Does Alzheimer's have anything to do with regulators?"

"Not so far as I know."

"Then why even think about it when you've got to apply for a competitive renewal of your grant?"

He bolted upright and surprising even himself, he snapped, "I don't need you to remind me." Throwing his napkin across his plate, he stomped into the living room. Audrey cleared and washed the dishes, chores they usually shared.

As they prepared for bed, Jason apologized for snapping and said he'd try to explain. She sat on the side of the bed and he faced her in a comfortable armchair.

"You know, Audrey, "Serendipity plays an important role in science: Archimedes spilling water out of the bathtub, Fleming finding penicillium mold killing his culture of staphylococcus. So I'd be foolish to ignore that the gene I've been working on for totally different reasons impairs memory in mice." By the time they went to bed Jason had almost convinced her that some good might come from shifting the direction of his research.

After the NIH's failure to fund her grant, Laura was losing confidence in her own scientific intuition. *Maybe Jason knows best,* she thought after he asked her to study the forgetful mice in January. She went to work on the problem, beginning by repeating the maze experiment in mice of different ages. For young mice she found no significant difference between normal-hearing mice without the deafness allele and those with one deafness allele in the number of shocks they sustained on the first day of the experiment, or on subsequent days, before hearing the buzzer and turning to the shock-free alternate pathway to the reward. The results, however, were different for mice that did not run the maze until they were older. As with the younger mice, both older groups learned equally rapidly how to avoid the shock on the first day and get the reward. But on successive days the hearing mice with one deafness allele sustained progressively more shocks than the normal mice lacking a deafness allele before they avoided the shock. In other words, they seemed to forget how to avoid the shock. The older the mice were when they first ran the maze, the more shocks it took on successive days for those possessing one deafness allele to remember how to avoid them.

It was May by the time Laura followed a sufficient number of mice of various ages for ninety days after they first learned the maze to be convinced that the differences were reproducible. She presented her findings to Jason. From then on, he stopped referring to the "deafness" gene, but instead called it the "memory" gene.

Laura took the occasion to tell Jason that she had decided to work for Generich.

Jason did not take nearly as much interest in Audrey's second pregnancy as he had with the first. A month after David Leon was born in July, Jason announced to Audrey that he had been invited to fly out to Chicago to make a presentation on his work to Donald Sharp, a venture capitalist.

"A venture capitalist?" She asked skeptically. "What are you doing with a venture capitalist?"

"Look, Audrey, the trail to the regulator has run cold. In my competitive renewal application to NIH I made an abrupt shift, pointing out that the mouse gene I had been working on might be a model for Alzheimer's Disease. The reviewers are likely to have the same reaction you had back in January."

She instantly remembered: *That's not an area of expertise for you, is it?*

He went on, "If I were the reviewer, I wouldn't fund it. Even though I have tenure, the medical school won't pay my salary for more than a few years, and they won't pay for my lab expenses or my post-docs.

I'll just be twiddling my thumbs. I've got to look for alternatives."

"The venture capitalist is interested in Alzheimer's Disease?" Audrey asked. Jason nodded.

—∞—

He returned from Chicago happy. "They're going to give me $100,000 as soon as the University signs off on it. The only string is they don't want to pay for post-docs— only technicians.

A month later he asked Audrey to look at the contract that Ventures Unlimited, Ltd., Sharp's company, had sent for his signature. When she finished, she told Jason, with some trepidation, "As the contract is written you're selling your soul to Donald Sharp and his company."

"But we need the money."

"Let me finish. Yes, we need the money, but the contract gives Ventures Unlimited unlimited power. With the help of the University, you need to renegotiate it."

"What should the contract say?"

"First that if any of your work is patentable, Ventures Unlimited will have to file jointly with Bates-Bronsted and you. That's in accord with University policy. Second, rather than giving the company veto power over your publishing, it should have a maximum of six months to review any paper before you submit it."

"I hope that doesn't quash the deal and blow $100,000."

She smiled, laying her hand on his arm. "They've got the best and the brightest in Jason Pearce. They'll come around." He offered her one of his biggest smiles in months.

Ventures Unlimited, Ltd. agreed to the requested modifications. The medical school signed off on the contract, receiving the $100,000 check for Jason's research just before Thanksgiving 2000. In December, Jason was informed that NIH would not fund his competitive renewal. The main reason given was that he had no experience in Alzheimer's research, an already crowded field.

In the years that followed Ventures Unlimited Ltd. was very generous to Jason Pearce enhancing his salary, giving him very low interest loans for personal use, and, finally, stock and stock options in Ventures Unlimited.

Chapter 3

JANICE POLK'S FIRST FEATURE STORY

Shortly after Janice Polk received her Master's degree from Northwestern's Medill School of Journalism in 2001, her grandma Bertie was transferred to the Alzheimer's unit in an assisted-living facility in Chicago.

Janice's mother fled from her abusive husband when her daughter was in kindergarten, taking Janice with her, and went to work fulltime to support the two of them. After school Janice went to grandma Bertie's house, having milk and cookies, doing her homework, practicing piano on Bertie's Baldwin spinet, and if any time was left, playing before her mother picked her up. Bertie had taught music in the Chicago public schools and gave Janice her first piano lessons. In high school and afterwards, Janice hardly ever saw Bertie, but she remembered the after-school visits to her house and when told of her incarceration in the Alzheimer's unit could not believe that Bertie wouldn't recognize her.

On her first visit, Janice took careful note of the assisted-living facility in which the unit was housed. The place was posh—carpeted floors, wooden planters filled with colorful flowers, soft music in the public areas, lots of people on walkers or sitting in plush lounge chairs watching television—but little conversation. The Alzheimer's unit was locked and Janice had to give her name, relation to Bertie, and home phone number. Having passed the admissions test, she was buzzed into a common area filled with people, a few shuffling around but most sitting, staring, and hardly talking over the drone of the television. Bertie sat on a sofa with two other women; none of them were doing much of anything. She had barely changed in appearance in the years since Janice had seen her. Her cheeks were unusually smooth and unlined for a woman of seventy-five, but her sparkling blue eyes had turned languid. As Janice walked briskly toward her, Bertie glanced at her and then stared across the room. Janice stood in front of her. "Hello Bertie."

Bertie smiled politely when she heard her name and then gazed away.

"Bertie, it's me, Janice." Again, Bertie glanced at her. Janice knelt down, took her grandmother's hands and gazed into her face. "Bertie, Grandma, it's Janice, your granddaughter. I used to come to your house everyday after school."

Again the polite smile but no recognition.

Maybe I've changed, Janice finally thought. In fact, she had changed less than many girls as they mature. Her growth spurt had been slight; she was only five feet tall. And her face still bore the innocent charm of childhood. As on most days, she wore no make up and her loose fitting blouse and slacks obscured her mature features.

Exasperated, Janice noticed an upright piano against one wall of the room. "Let's play the piano," she said softly. She helped Bertie stand and, with her arm around her grandmother, walked her to the piano.

"Are you going to play something for us, dear?" Bertie asked.

"No, Bertie. I want you to play. You're a very good pianist. You gave me lessons."

"I'm sorry, dear, I don't know how to play. But if you took lessons, then you play." They sat side by side on the bench. Janice thought of the pieces Bertie had taught her and almost automatically her fingers played *The Wild Horseman* from Schumann's *Album for the Young*. By the end of the piece, Bertie was keeping rhythm and had started to hum along. When Janice finished, Bertie put her fingers on the keys and actually played a few measures.

Janice was thrilled. "You see, Bertie, you can still play! Now do you remember me?"

Bertie stared at her blankly. "I'm sorry, dear, I don't think we've met before." Bertie stood as Janice repeated a few measures. "That's very nice, dear, but I think it's time for me to be going. It was nice meeting you. Have a good day." With that, Bertie shuffled back to her seat on the sofa and resumed staring across the room. Janice had never imagined that someone who outwardly seemed unchanged could have literally lost her mind.

Janice had been a shy quiet child, often withdrawing rather than facing conflict, possibly a result of witnessing the fights between her parents when she was very young. Having always read a lot, she excelled in English in high school. Invited to join the school newspaper by the faculty adviser, she became editor-in-chief in her senior year. By that time her face had cleared of acne, and her experiences interviewing students, faculty, and sometimes people outside the school for newspaper stories built up her confidence. She was accepted by her brainy peers and asked out on dates, but never had a steady boyfriend. Her other interest was science; she had won prizes in her school's science fairs.

Coming on the heels of 9/11, her visit to Bertie reawakened Janice's feeling of helplessness in the face of all the madness in the world. Working as a stringer

for the *Chicago Sun-Herald,* she floundered trying
to find something interesting to cover other than
the attacks. Her mother suggested she write about
Alzheimer's. Janice's first reaction was to run away
from it, to blot out Bertie's deterioration, at the same
time fearing that some day everything might be blotted
out for her. No one else in the family had been diagnosed with Alzheimer's, but Bertie was their oldest
relative. Janice mentioned her mother's suggestion to
the Science editor at the *Sun-Herald,* who encouraged
her to pursue it. "As a matter of fact," he told her, "I've
heard that a Chicago Company, Ventures Unlimited, is
beginning to invest in Alzheimer's research." He gave
Janice the address and phone number, but suggested
she learn more about current research on Alzheimer's
before contacting the company.

So she took her own crash course, frequenting
the libraries at Northwestern and Pritzker, piecing
together what was known, and enrolling in a community college natural science course to gain more
background. She was relieved to learn that although
genetics played a role in late-onset Alzheimer's, it was
not like some of the very rare early-onset forms for
which the chance of inheriting it, if you had a parent
with the disease, was one out of two. She went back to
Bertie's Alzheimer's Unit several times and observed
the behavior of the patients, but more rewardingly
talked to their visiting relatives, mostly daughters,

sons, and siblings. The horror of what had happened to their relative, and what they themselves might face, haunted them as it did Janice.

Searching the PubMed database she kept abreast of scientific papers on Alzheimer's and quickly became adept at tracking down sources and interviewing experts. She found papers by Jason Pearce describing a memory disorder in mice that mimicked Alzheimer's Disease, noticing that some of them acknowledged the support of Ventures Unlimited. She made an appointment to see the company's President and CEO, Dr. Donald Sharp.

∼∼∼

The company had a suite of offices in the Sears Tower. Dr. Sharp's secretary invited Janice to sit on the leather sofa in the reception area and offered her coffee. Modern paintings adorned the walls; business magazines Janice had never heard of were strewn on the coffee table in front of her. As she flipped through one, Donald Sharp emerged from his office, extended his hand and greeted her warmly. Unaccustomed to such luxury, Janice felt like an imposter.

Sharp's voice was higher pitched than she expected. He towered over her. A six-footer with a slight paunch, his resemblance to the corporate prototype stopped there. He was wearing a navy blue turtleneck with a polished malachite pendant hanging from a gold chain. His heavy-heeled cowboy boots were shiny and elaborately tooled. Pouring himself coffee, he refilled Janice's cup and led her into his office. She was somewhat surprised to note that his glossy black hair was tied in a long ponytail.

Janice began by telling him she had read the papers about the memory defect in mice that acknowledged his company's support and by describing her personal interest in Alzheimer's.

"You should join a nonprofit organization we've contributed to, Relatives of Alzheimer's Association." He handed her the group's card.

"Do you think Pearce's work will help reveal more about Alzheimer's Disease in humans?"

He gazed at her for a few moments before answering, making her nervous. She thought her question was neutral. Finally, he smiled and said quietly, "Do you think this company would be investing in Professor Pearce's work if we didn't think so?"

"So Professor Pearce is working on memory loss in humans with Alzheimer's."

"I didn't say that."

Janice asked her first stupid question. "Is he?"

He seemed to scan her body, wondering—or so Janice thought—whether she was fully matured. She had to resist pulling her skirt over her knees. Putting his cup down on the round table that separated them, he said, "Let me give you a tip, young lady: When someone responds evasively, don't put him on the defensive by insisting on greater precision." Janice felt heat in her face. Smiling benevolently, Sharp picked up his cup and took a sip. "Just between the two of us, why do you think I won't answer your question?" Before Janice could reply, he added, "If I said, 'I don't know,' I'd be lying."

From Journalism 101, Janice knew that this intimate preface meant that whatever his response, it was off the record, not for attribution. Janice, her confidence ebbing, felt like a schoolgirl being interrogated. "It's a secret?" she replied with hesitation.

"Now why would I want to keep it a secret?"

Her first reaction was to say *because you don't want anyone to know.* But that was a tautology. *I have to be more specific.* "Because you don't want competitors to know." This time she didn't ask; she stated it. He smiled like a teacher proud of his student giving the right answer.

"Is there anything else I can help you with, Ms. Polk?"

Regaining some confidence, she asked, "Do you think people will want to know if they're going to get Alzheimer's?"

"Wouldn't you?"

"Not right now. I want to develop my career, maybe get married, have kids——"

"But if you knew you were at high risk for Alzheimer's and then when you're pregnant you could have your fetus tested and avoid having a kid who would get Alzheimer's Disease, wouldn't you want to do that?"

Janice stared at him incredulously. *Only a man could come up with such a scenario.* It was beginning to feel like an argument, not an interview. Her journalistic sensibility was starting to kick in, telling her to back off. But she didn't. "By the time my kids are old enough to have Alzheimer's, surely a treatment will be available."

"Okay," he conceded, "let's leave the kids out of it. What about your mother? Does she want to know if she'll get it?"

"We've talked about it. And I've talked to others my mother's age that have a parent with Alzheimer's. Most want more information—information Professor Pearce might be able to provide someday." She paused, getting angrier. "But you're not willing to give them any encouragement by telling me whether Professor Peace is extending his research to the human disease or not."

He looked genuinely offended. "If I tell you what Jason Pearce is working on now, and you blab it to the world, will the people at risk for Alzheimer's be better off? What if Pearce's mice are not a model for Alzheimer's? You'd be misleading them."

Janice had no rejoinder and Sharp seemed to have nothing more to say. Thinking that he had terminated the interview, she set her cup down and was collecting her purse when he started speaking slowly. "There's something else you should know, Ms. Polk. When Jason Pearce started to work on the mouse memory gene, he applied for an NIH grant to fund it." He paused, perhaps waiting for her to ask, but then supplied the answer. "NIH turned him down, said he had no expertise in the matter. His previous work, looking for a gene regulator, had foundered after a brilliant start. Had he not come to Ventures Unlimited when he stumbled across the memory gene, he would be driving a taxi today.

"If you think Ventures Unlimited invested in Jason Pearce because they saw a pot of gold at the end of the rainbow, you're partially right. But if there is such a pot it will be because Pearce will find either a cure or a means of preventing Alzheimer's. My job is to give him every advantage in what will surely be a race to the pot. Perhaps now I have answered your question—off the record of course."

Sharp stood, smiling graciously. "You're an engaging young woman, Ms. Polk. I hope what you write will help advance research in Alzheimer's as much as what we're doing here at Ventures Unlimited." He offered his hand and shaking it, Janice felt that maybe the interview had not been a total failure.

Her first brief story on Alzheimer's appeared in the *Sun-Herald* under the headline, "Glimmer Of Hope For Preventing Alzheimer's." She did not mention Donald Sharp or Ventures Unlimited. She focused on Pearce's papers on the memory gene—there would have been no story without them—and his response when she had talked to him by phone.

She had planned carefully for the interview to avoid the unpleasantness of her conversation with Sharp, and vowed that she would not get sidetracked. Pearce started off with flat, short answers. His speech picked up timbre as they proceeded and he warmed to the topic, realizing that the reporter he was talking to knew something about Alzheimer's. He had a pleasant tenor-like voice without any regional accent that Janice could detect. Janice's contralto voice made her sound older than she was, unlike her physical persona.

After her desultory conversation with Donald Sharp, talking to Pearce was a pleasure. Although he hadn't told Janice in so many words, she was pretty sure he was working on Alzheimer's. In the first story, she wrote:

Professor Jason Pearce at the Bates-Bronsted Medical School has found that injecting the normal mouse memory gene into the brains of young mice destined to forget how to run a maze maintains their ability to run it through old age. Undertaking this experiment in humans is fraught with difficulty, but it might still be undertaken if the human memory gene differs between patients with and without Alzheimer's Disease.

While working on other stories over the next few months, Janice maintained her interest in Alzheimer's. The card that Dr. Sharp had given her contained the address of the Relatives of Alzheimer's Association, a well-appointed suite in another high-rise office building in the Loop. She met with the Chairperson, a woman in her late fifties who wore heavy but tasteful jewelry over her ample frame. Proudly, she showed Janice a reprint of her Alzheimer's story; she had circulated it to the organization's membership, which had just passed the one thousand mark and was growing rapidly. "One of our missions," she told Janice, "is to make sure that when the human memory gene is isolated the FDA will hear loud and clear that clinical trials on Alzheimer's prevention must go forward."

"Do you think it will be long before that happens?" Janice asked.

"A year maybe. Pearce and Don Sharp don't like to talk about it."

Janice knew she was stirring a kettle of fish but this time she thought she'd get a meaningful response. "Why not, do you suppose?"

"They want to be the first," the Chairperson replied. "Could be a Nobel Prize for Pearce and a pot of gold for Sharp and his company."

Janice could not have asked for a more meaningful response. "Do you think such secrecy is best for an organization like yours whose members are waiting for a cure or prevention?"

The Chairperson looked at Janice carefully for the first time. She could almost hear the older woman's brain thrum, *who is this twerp?* Finally, she said, "I've known Don Sharp a long time and I trust that his reason for not wanting to talk about it is in the best interest of advancing Alzheimer's research. He told us Jason Pearce was the best scientist around and so far he's been right. Don has also been very generous to us."

Maybe he's using you, Janice thought though she said nothing. "I'd like to interview some of your members from different parts of the country." The Chairperson was delighted and said she'd compile a list and e-mail it to Janice. They shook hands cordially. The Chairperson patronized her, "Keep up the good work, dear."

Janice wanted to write a story on the attitudes of relatives of Alzheimer's patients who were at risk for developing the disease. Her editor was willing to put up money for her to go north by bus to Milwaukee and south to St. Louis but little more. Many of her contacts were made through the list from the Relatives of Alzheimer's Association. But she suspected they might be biased in favor of being tested for the memory gene; they were mostly upper middle class people who could afford to contribute to the Association and to be tested if an aberrant memory gene were to materialize in humans with the disease. So on her trips she made a point of visiting community centers that cared for poor elderly people with Alzheimer's, often meeting their close relatives.

In a May 2002 issue of *Science,* Pearce and his colleagues reported that patients dying with late-onset Alzheimer's Disease had an increased frequency of a "forgetful" allele in their "memory gene," confirming that he was indeed working on Alzheimer's in humans. She phoned Pearce again. His group had isolated the analogous gene in humans, he told her, but found that it was not associated with deafness. A variant allele, however, was present in three times as many patients dying with Alzheimer's than in age-matched controls dying of something else. "Even more surprising," he went on, "when the e4 allele of another gene, apolipoprotein-e—already known to increase the risk of Alzheimer's—was present together with the 'forgetful' allele of the memory gene, the chance of getting Alzheimer's jumped to eighty percent compared to less than a third for the presence of either allele alone."

"Are you proposing to inject the normal memory gene into humans at high risk for Alzheimer's—the same sort of experiment you did in mice?"

The line was silent for a few moments, as if the blunt question caught Pearce off guard. "The FDA won't let us proceed until we can prove it's safe."

"Is there a way to do that?" she asked.

"We've gotten an IND—"

"IND?"

"Investigational New Drug approval from FDA to inject the memory gene into neurosurgery patients without Alzheimer's who are going to have a hole drilled in their skull for tumors or other serious conditions and consent to have the normal human memory gene injected into their brains through the hole. They call it a Phase I trial. We'll follow them carefully for at least a year looking for unexpected complications."

"Such as?"

"Well," he started tentatively, "It might disrupt the function of other genes." He paused. "But that's unlikely because we're injecting the gene directly into the brain and it would have to cross the blood-brain barrier to get into other cells. It sounds riskier, but because of the barrier it's actually safer to inject into the brain."

Still, Janice was puzzled. *Couldn't the injected gene disturb brain function?* She used Google, then in its infancy, and medical databases to look up "gene therapy" in humans. There were very few instances in which it had been tried, and none by an injection into brains. One case in particular disturbed her. In 1999 an eighteen-year-old young man, Jesse Gelsinger, who had an inherited enzyme deficiency, became acutely ill and died within days after his blood was injected with the normal gene for the enzyme. Two others participating in the experiment had become ill but neither had died. However, monkeys given similar treatment had died. Janice noted that both the Principal Investigator and the University of Pennsylvania, where the experiment was performed, were reported to have financial stakes in the research.

Janice called Pearce to ask him about it. He pointed out that Gelsinger's death was attributed to the virus used to encapsulate the gene. "Fair question, but we're not using viruses," he declared. "We're making a few modifications in the gene's DNA so it will attach more readily to the target brain cells. That should reduce the chance that the injected DNA will get into other brain cells. The Phase I trial should tell us whether it's safe."

Janice's second story appeared in June 2002 in the *Sun-Herald*'s Sunday magazine.

Depending on the outcome of what's called a "Phase I trial," middle-aged people who have a relative with Alzheimer's Disease may soon be able to participate in a clinical trial to see if the disease can be prevented by the injection of a memory gene into their brain.

If she has the opportunity, Tanya Bornstein would volunteer. Forty-nine years old, Bornstein does not want the same fate as befell her mother, who is locked into an Alzheimer's unit in a St. Louis assisted-living facility. Tanya's mother first showed signs of the disease when she was sixty-seven, wandering away from home and unable to find her way back. Now, at seventy, she does not recognize Tanya or her younger brothers. Tanya, who teaches high school history and has two children of her own, is willing to take the risks of gene therapy to reduce the odds of losing her memory if she's found to be at risk.

Fifty-nine year old Jack Bailey, a healthy computer programmer in Chicago whose older brother has Alzheimer's, told *The Sun-Herald,* "I hope I'm still healthy when and if the clinical trial gets underway. If I were found to be at risk, I'd get the injection if it helps prevent me from suffering my brother's fate.

Next, the article summarized Pearce's research and described the Phase I trial about to begin, and then continued:

The subjects will be followed for at least a year. "If there are no complications," Pearce said, "we can proceed to a clinical trial in which healthy middle-aged people at high risk of Alzheimer's consent to have either the normal memory gene or the same liquid without the memory gene injected into their brains."

Those eligible to participate in the clinical trial will have to have one "forgetful" memory allele as well as the apolipoprotein-e4 allele." The simultaneous presence of these two variants increases the risk of developing Alzheimer's Disease to about eighty percent according to Pearce. They will also have to be old enough to develop signs of Alzheimer's in the next ten to fifteen years. Based on his research in mice, Professor Pearce does not believe that injection of the memory gene can arrest or correct the memory loss of Alzheimer's Disease once it begins, but he hopes it could prevent that process from developing.

In 1999, a gene therapy trial at the University of Pennsylvania, involving a disease unrelated to Alzheimer's was halted when a young man died after a gene encapsulated in a virus was injected into his bloodstream. The virus was believed to be the cause of his death. The memory gene that Pearce and his colleagues will use is not contained in a virus but has been modified to gain entry into certain brain cells.

The Bates-Bronsted Institutional Review Board approved the Phase I trial. Under Federal regulation, IRBs are charged with protecting human subjects in research. The Bates-Bronsted Board felt that that subjects who were going to have a hole in their skull drilled anyway incurred little risk from the procedure of having the memory gene injected through the hole. Following the IRB recommendation, the Food and Drug Administration designated the human memory gene as an Investigational New Drug, clearing the way for the Phase I trial.

Even if safe, a big question is whether injection of the memory gene will prevent Alzheimer's Disease. One geneticist unaffiliated with the trial doubted that normal memory genes injected into the brain could be inserted into the correct place in the genome. "But if the injected normal gene doesn't have to be correctly incorporated, it might work," she said.

The Citizens Watchdog Group, a nonprofit organization concerned with consumer safety, cautioned that the one-year follow-up required in the Phase I trial is not long enough to detect all of the harmful effects of the gene injection. The Group urged continuing surveillance of those who receive the memory gene after any clinical trial ends.

Not everyone who has Alzheimer's in their family is as ready as Bornstein and Bailey to take part in a clinical trial. Sarah Jackson, living in a shelter for homeless people, whose older sister died of Alzheimer's, says it's "God's will. If I'm gonna get that disease so be it. I don't want no scientists experimenting on me. What I hope right now is to get me a job and get out of this shelter."

Others are not sure they would want to know their risk of developing Alzheimer's, or undergo gene therapy if they were found likely to get the disease. Harold Trent, an auto-worker in Detroit, told the *Sun-Herald*, "Before I get a gene injected into my brain I want to be sure it's safe. I'm not going to volunteer to be a guinea pig. People stronger, or maybe crazier than I am, can take that chance, and if they survive and don't lose their minds, then maybe, if I'm still around I'll think about it. But until I know that gene therapy works I'm not going to have a test just to find out I'm at risk; if there's no treatment I'd be worse off knowing I was at risk. I don't think my wife and kids would be better off either."

The Relatives of Alzheimer's Association, a nonprofit group whose members, as their name indicates, have someone with Alzheimer's in their family, has been clamoring for FDA to approve a clinical trial in patients at high risk for Alzheimer's as soon as the Phase I trial concludes, assuming it does not show harmful effects within one year after the injection. "Every year of delay means that thousands of minds will be lost unnecessarily," the group's brochures and posters say.

Professor Harold Wise of the History of Medicine Department at Northwestern Medical School noted that improvements in education, nutrition, and public health, and some successes in medicine, have enabled more people to escape dying from infections, heart disease, and some cancers, allowing them to live into their eighties, nineties, and even the early hundreds. As a result, the prevalence of diseases of the elderly, like Alzheimer's, have increased. "But even if scientists can prevent Alzheimer's," Dr. Wise said, "those lucky enough to grow old without it will die of something else; they'll live longer but who knows whether their quality of life will be better."

Should injection of the gene be shown to prevent Alzheimer's—an endpoint it may take years to reach—the cost of the procedure may send it out of reach for many people. Preparation of the gene for injection, the neurosurgical intervention, and long-term follow-up are all expensive. Medicare might cover the injection in eligible people who are sixty-five and older. One private insurance executive told the *Sun-Herald*, "Until we know whether the gene injection prevents Alzheimer's, and what the costs are we can't speculate on whether our company would cover it."

Unless they qualify for the pending clinical trial, Tanya Bornstein and Jack Bailey may have a long time to wait. Bornstein lamented, "I hope by the time the trial shows that gene therapy works, it won't be too late for me to benefit." Bailey remarked, "I hope I can afford it when the time comes." To Sarah Jackson and

Harold Trent, the clinical trials won't make any difference.

The *Sun-Herald's* readers nominated Janice's story for the best feature story for 2002 and she subsequently became a salaried Science/Health reporter for the paper.

Chapter 4

LAURA SURPRISES AUDREY

One morning in the spring of 2002, the legal department's secretary buzzed Audrey to say that a Laura Mittelman was on the phone and urgently wanted to speak with her. "Ask what it's about," Audrey said and put the phone down, but she could not get back to work.

"She says it's a personal matter," the secretary buzzed back. Audrey remembered how jealous she had been of Laura's access to Jason when he first introduced her as one of his graduate students. When they were looking for an *au pair* for Rachel, Jason had interviewed a few candidates during a trip to Germany for a seminar, hiring one of them. When Hannah arrived, Audrey was stunned by her resemblance—in face, figure, and deportment—to Laura Mittelman.

"Audrey Meacham."

"Audrey, this is Laura."

"Yes?" Audrey replied coldly.

"Laura Mittelman. I'm sure you remember. I worked with Jason."

"Yes, of course. How are you?"

There was a moment of silence as Laura grappled with how to begin. "Audrey, I need your advice. Would it be possible for us to get together for lunch today?"

What sort of advice could Laura need? Is this a pretext for telling me she is having an affair with Jason? Torn between curiosity and not wanting to hear more, she said, "I'm afraid I have a lunch engagement."

"How about a drink after work then?"

"No, I have to pick up my kids."

"I really need to talk." Laura sounded as if she needed help.

"Can we do it over the phone?"

"I'd rather not."

Curiosity won. "Let me see if I can rearrange my schedule. Give me your number and I'll call you back."

She notified the Chief Legal Counsel's secretary that she wouldn't be attending the weekly staff lunch and called Laura to arrange a time and place. Before leaving the office, she gave her hair a thorough brushing and put lipstick on. *If Laura was having an affair with Jason, why would she tell me?* Jason spent evenings at home when he was in town, loved the kids and spent almost as much time with them as she did. They didn't make love as often as before the kids, but still, it was passionate. The one thing that did trouble her was his recent purchase of a red Lamborghini. Don Sharp must have lent or given him most of the $200,000 he put down on the car. *Was Jason trying to impress someone?*

They met at a small bistro a block off campus. It was unseasonably warm for April, with the trees blossoming and jonquils in planters on a low wall in front of the café adding a splash of yellow. Laura was sitting at a table for two on the sidewalk next to the wall. She was not wearing lipstick and her hair was slightly askew. She stood when Audrey approached and held out her hand. "I really appreciate your changing your schedule." They ordered salads and iced tea and Audrey nervously rearranged her silverware waiting for Laura to begin. "I need a lawyer, Audrey. That's why I called you."

Audrey breathed a sigh of relief. *An unlikely gambit if she's my husband's mistress.* "I don't handle personal matters unless they relate to the University."

"Well, this might," she said cryptically. "Audrey," she began hesitantly, twisting her paper napkin and tearing off bits, "I thought a woman lawyer would be more understanding than a man. If there's a fee..."

Audrey's attitude changed as she realized she was listening to a young woman in distress. For the first time since she had met Laura, she felt sorry for her. Reaching across the table, she touched Laura's sleeve. "Don't be silly. There's no fee or even a professional relationship. There can't be until you tell me what this is about."

The waiter placed their salads and a basket of bread on the table and asked if there was anything else. They shook their heads.

"I'm being harassed—I think that's the proper terminology."

How stupid of me. Of the possibilities Audrey had considered, harassment was not one. *And it couldn't be Jason.* "By whom?"

"Julian Goodrich. I've been working at his company for almost two years.

Relieved, Audrey nodded. She was not too surprised. They both paused to eat. "Do you have evidence of harassment?"

"If you mean in writing—like a love letter—no. Julian's too smart for that." She thought for a moment. "At first, I didn't realize what was happening. He invited me out to lunch several times and I was flattered; the conversation was pleasant—a mix of talk about our research and personal stuff, you know, where we came from, brothers and sisters, vacations. Then when he came back from a trip to France he gave me a gift of expensive perfume. That was about a year ago. When he started to stroke my back, fondle my bottom—he doesn't do that with anybody else—I began to catch on."

"Do you do anything he might construe as encouragement?"

"No. I move away as quickly as I can. One of the other women noticed and told me if it bothered me I should stop dressing 'provocatively.' I wore what I was comfortable in—maybe it looks good on me—but I don't wear it seductively."

You could have fooled me. Audrey thought back to when she first met Laura in Jason's lab—she'd been wearing a tight T-shirt, with a double helix unraveling down her chest to her exposed navel, "Scientists Have More Fun" printed on the back, and short shorts.

"So I've started to dress differently at work." Audrey hadn't really paid attention to Laura's high-necked, loose-fitting white blouse and baggy slacks. "I've had to rebuild my wardrobe."

"Anything else Julian does?"

The waiter collected their plates and they ordered coffee. Last week when he took me out to lunch he reached for my hand across the table and said he'd like to have an affair." She stopped, looked directly into Audrey's eyes. "That's when I decided I needed help.

"What did you say?"

"I pulled my hand away and told him it was impossible."

"Why impossible? You're not married, right."

"But he is. That's one reason. Another is that Julian's thirty years older than me. Also, there's nothing about him I find attractive. He's a good scientist"—she paused and smiled—"a better businessman, except he can't sell himself to me."

Audrey was watching Laura closely. "Anything else?"

Laura hesitated, then looked directly at her. She picked up what was left of her shredded napkin. "I'm gay."

All Audrey could think to say was, "Do you have a partner?"

"Yes. I've told her about Julian. She just laughs and says, 'Well, you are good looking.' I could swat her. But look, even if I were straight, I wouldn't want to be mauled. You don't see women pawing over men at work."

That's for sure, Audrey agreed silently. "How do you think I can help, Laura?"

"I could file a complaint with the University; I'm no longer a University employee but Julian is."

"Harassment is not my specialty. Besides, as a lawyer for the University I'd be obligated to defend the employee, Julian in this case." She decided to herself, *If Chief Attorney asks me to defend Julian, I'd recuse myself; my allegiance is to Laura.*

"Can't you give me advice?" Laura asked, almost pleading.

Audrey poured cream into her coffee. "I'm not sure the University would do anything about it, especially since you're not on the payroll."

"Really? When I was there we got memos about sexual harassment, urging anyone who was harassed to report it promptly."

"Yes, I'm aware of those memos." The federal government imposed them primarily because harassment at other universities had received publicity. She picked up her cup but didn't drink. "The Administration won't be eager to act against Julian, I can tell you that. His patents bring in more royalties than any other faculty member's. The University also gets stock from his company." Laura's face darkened. "Can you complain to the Generich Company?"

Laura shook her head. "Julian's the most powerful man in the company. I'd get the same response you're predicting the University would give." The sun peeked out from the awning that had shaded the diners and shone directly on Laura's face. She had to shield her eyes in order to see Audrey. "What else can I do?"

"You could tell him to stop, threaten him with exposure if he doesn't. That might be enough, especially if you put it in writing and have the letter witnessed."

"Would you witness it?"

"No. I'm not your lawyer—and I work for the University. Maybe your partner could be the witness."

The waiter brought the check. Immediately Audrey picked it up. "I'm afraid I haven't been of much help. The least I can do is pay for lunch."

"Thank you," Laura said distractedly. "You know, working's become so unpleasant I'm thinking of quitting."

"That's always an option. You probably should tell Julian why. Not that you're gay, I mean, but that you resent his behavior—let him know you view it as harassment; that might tone down his philandering."

The check paid, the women rose and turned towards each other without the sun in either's face. What Audrey said next never would have occurred to her that morning, but now it was clear Laura posed no threat to her marriage. "You know, Laura, Jason's work on Alzheimer's is going great guns. There might be a job in his lab if you're interested. Even a faculty appointment, I suppose."

"Seriously? Can you mention me to Jason?"

"I'll tell him we had lunch together, that Julian has been harassing you and you're thinking of quitting." Audrey looked at Laura directly. "That's *all* I'll tell him. Unless Jason calls you, which I doubt, you'll have to call him."

"That's great, Audrey. I'll call him tomorrow." As they left the bistro together, Laura said, "I hear Jason's driving a Lamborghini."

Audrey said with a laugh, "Boys will be boys. He has Ventures Unlimited, or its CEO, Don Sharp, to thank for that. And that's not all. We just took a mortgage on a ten-acre plot outside the city. I grew up in the house we live in now, but it's not good enough for Jason. He wants our kids to grow up in the country. He's promised Rachel a pony and he plans to build a swimming pool. God knows what else he'll want." As they parted, she thought to add, "Please don't tell Jason we talked about his plans. He'd be annoyed."

Laura hugged Audrey and kissed her on the lips as they went their separate ways. Audrey wouldn't have given a second thought to the kiss, except that now she knew Laura was gay.

—

That evening she told Jason about her lunch with Laura, saying no more than she had told Laura she'd say.

"I sure would like to get her back."

The next day Laura called Jason. She said she was eager to have a role in elucidating the mechanism by which the gene he had identified influenced memory. "From partial sequencing," he told her, " it looks like both the mouse and human memory genes might resemble presenilin." It was a gene implicated in one form of inherited early-onset Alzheimer's. "That would be a good starting point for you. I think I can get you an appointment as Assistant Professor. The paper work will take a few weeks. Besides, you have to give Julian notice, don't you?"

Laura agreed, immediately thinking what she would tell him.

In July 2002, paid for by funds coming from Ventures Unlimited, Ltd., Laura's appointment came through and she started working at the University. She decided that her reputation as a scientist would be enhanced by an NIH grant. Besides, she didn't want to be tied to Jason's, or the company's, apron strings. The NIH Study Section gave her application to study the presenilin-like activity of the mouse memory gene a very high priority score. She was awarded the grant, commencing in June 2003.

Chapter 5

BETSY MATTHEWS

In November 2003, when Professor of Neurology Gus McAllister interviewed Betsy Matthews for the Alzheimer's gene therapy trial neither of them remembered that they had had a brief encounter thirty-three years earlier when McAllister, an intern at City Hospital, diagnosed lead poisoning in her comatose two-year-old son.

"We've got to get out of that lead-loaded rat trap," Betsy had said to him after he explained how the boy had been poisoned. "That'll make him all right, won't it, doctor?" she pleaded.

"First we have to admit him and get the lead out of his body. Then we'll see," Gus said evasively. He arranged for the admission and shook hands with Mrs. Matthews. Her son never awoke and Gus did not see

Mrs. Matthews again until she was considering the gene therapy trial.

A year after their son died, Betsy and her husband moved to a neighborhood where houses, though small and a bit rundown, were lead-free. They had a daughter, Susie, in 1980 when Betsy was thirty. Four years later, her husband was killed on a construction job; the rope holding the scaffold on which he was standing severed, plunging him seventeen floors to his death. Betsy was left with very little money and a mortgage. She got a job as a clerk in a local grocery store. Before long she was promoted to handling the cash register. When Susie was in high school, Betsy became active in church affairs.

Until she started school, Susie stayed with a neighbor who ran a small daycare center from her home while Betsy worked. Once in school, Susie had to check in with her mom at the store on her way home before going to aftercare. From the third grade on, she was a latchkey child, letting herself in and learning to be self-sufficient. Not allowed to play in the street, Susie amused herself at home with a few raggedy dolls and then with books, which she read voraciously.

Betsy's older sister, Martha, moved in with Betsy and Susie after her husband died in 1995 and helped with the mortgage payments. The sisters were very close; their mother had died when Betsy was thirteen. Martha, twelve years older and still at home, took care of her younger sister, making sure that Betsy graduated from high school. When she moved in, Martha was working as a teacher's aide, but two years later, when she was sixty, the school let her go, saying that the quality of her work had deteriorated. Betsy fretted over her sister's forgetfulness. Martha was a great knitter but sometimes she couldn't remember where she put her knitting, or her glasses. Soon her knitting looked like Swiss cheese. Once when Betsy returned from work, Martha was not at home. Betsy waited until 9 o'clock. Still no Martha. She called the police who told her they had found a woman wandering the streets with no identification who fit her description.

Betsy quit her job to care for her sister, but her meager savings ran out and she feared eviction if she did not meet the mortgage payments. Susie was a senior in high school, getting up at dawn to catch the school bus that brought her across town where she was in the half of her class who was black, and returning home after dark. Just as Martha had seen to it that Betsy finished high school, Betsy had no intention of pulling Susie out to care for Martha. A neighbor said she'd take Martha in during the day, and Betsy was lucky to get her job back at the grocery store.

A friend suggested to Betsy that maybe her sister had Alzheimer's Disease. Betsy had never heard of it. Not having a doctor, Betsy brought Martha to the Emergency Room at City Hospital, where they sat for hours; after all, Martha's problem was not urgent. Finally, a nurse told Betsy to take Martha to the Neurology Clinic and was kind enough to make an appointment for her six weeks later, the earliest available. In the clinic it did not take long for the doctors to diagnose Alzheimer's Disease. Betsy was counseled to have Martha admitted to an Alzheimer's facility at a public nursing home. Reluctantly, she agreed. Although Martha's social security covered part of the expense, Betsy had to pay the difference, adding to her financial burden.

⚬

At the beginning of 2003, Donald Sharp suggested to Jason that he start to identify subjects for the clinical trial. "But the IRB hasn't approved the trial yet," Jason replied. "They only approved the Phase I trial."

"That's not a problem. You won't be signing them up until the trial is approved."

Jason scratched his head. "What if the trial isn't approved?"

"You tell the subjects what happened. But if it is approved you'll be ready to start the trial almost immediately. You don't want to waste time, do you, Jason?"

"No, I suppose not."

Jason discussed Sharp's suggestion with Gus McAllister. To help plan the Phase I trial and present it before Bates-Bronsted's Institutional Review Board, he had asked Gus, Chief of Neurosciences at Bates Bronsted as well as Professor of Neurology, to join him as Co-Principal Investigator of Alzheimer's research in humans. Gus had a reputation for making sure his patients and research subjects understood their condition and what could be done to help them. Impatient younger physicians didn't like making rounds with him because he actually stopped to talk to the patients. Under Gus's guidance the protocol for the Phase I trial sailed through the IRB.

"I think we should check it out with Gertrude Brierly," Gus told him. Brierly was executive secretary of the Bates-Bronsted IRB.

"I don't see the point, but if you think so, go ahead."

Gus spoke to Gertrude by phone. "The media have already described your proposed trial," Gertrude told him. "As long as you're not asking for a commitment to participate, I think you can go ahead."

※

In March 2003, Betsy had received a letter from the Neurology Clinic at City Hospital inviting her to learn about a study soon to get underway on the prevention of Alzheimer's Disease in relatives of patients with the disease. After Martha had been diagnosed, Betsy worried she too might eventually get the disease.

Every time she forgot something, she feared it was Alzheimer's. But in the ensuing years her memory did not deteriorate.

The letter said that if she was interested, she should attend a meeting at the Bates-Bronsted Medical Center on April eighth. On the seventh, a freak spring snowstorm was forecast for the following day, but Betsy was determined to go to the meeting. As the temperature dropped and the wind started up on the morning of the eighth, she walked two blocks to the bus stop and waited patiently for the bus to the Medical Center.

A hundred others had also defied the forecast, filling the meeting room. Gus called the meeting to order and introduced Jason Pearce who described his mouse experiments and the study he and Dr. McAllister were proposing. In order to participate, Jason told them, they had to have at least one parent or sibling who had Alzheimer's.

The storm never materialized. As soon as she got home after the meeting, Betsy sat at the enameled kitchen table to write to her daughter. Susie, a recent graduate *cum laude* of the University of Wisconsin, was working in a bookstore in Madison, trying to earn enough money to go to graduate school. "I went to a meeting at Bates-Bronsted today to learn about a study to prevent Alzheimer's Disease," Betsy started, "the disease your Aunt Martha has. Professor Pearce, the Director, a very nice young man, told us that the meeting was just for informational purposes, that they were not asking us to participate at this time. When the study officially begins, they will go over every-thing again and get our consent if we're interested. He emphasized it would be our choice, but I'm not so dumb to believe that he won't try to persuade us to sign on. He seems to be fair in his presentation, tell-ing us things that might go wrong and that only half of those who choose to participate will get what he calls 'the memory gene' injected into their brains through a small hole drilled in their skull. The other half, the 'controls,' will get an injection of a liquid that doesn't contain the memory gene. The participants won't know which half they're in.

"Professor Pearce said that if we wanted to volun-teer we'd have to be tested to show that we weren't yet losing our memories. I don't think I am, but maybe I should find out. I can still make the cor-rect change from the cash register. He said that once memory loss begins, receiving a normal memory gene wouldn't work. If the test shows that my memory is okay, I could decide not to participate; I haven't signed anything yet." She ended the letter by asking Susie whether she should sign up for the clinical trial when the time came.

The letter horrified Susie, especially the part about drilling a small hole in the skull and injecting something into the brain. She would have immediately e-mailed her mother, but Betsy did not have a computer. Calling long distance would add substantially to Susie's phone bill, so she immediately wrote her mother a letter, saying that the procedure didn't sound very safe. The letter arrived a few days before a second meeting at Bates-Bronsted for people who were still interested in participating. Betsy went, surprised that many fewer people attended than the first meeting despite better weather. Betsy was the first to ask about the safety of injections into the brain. As soon as she got home, she wrote Susie what she had learned.

> Dear Susie,
> At the meeting I went to this morning, Professor Pearce and Dr. McAllister told us that inserting a needle into the brain is not dangerous. Twenty patients without Alzheimer's have been injected with the memory gene and none of them have had problems a year after the injection.

The letter did not alleviate Susie's concern. She thought back to the first grade when she wanted to be the first African-American girl astronaut. Her mother had bought her a child's space suit for Halloween and Susie wore it to school the following

January on the day when the Challenger was launched with teacher Christa McAuliffe on board. With her classmates, Susie watched the launch on television, witnessing the explosion that killed all seven crew-members, white plumes streaking the sky. When the teacher, taking her cue from the television, told the class what happened, Susie cried, wondering exactly when they had died and what Christa and the others must have thought at that instant. Susie never wore her space suit again. Years later, she read that a scientist had pointed out that there had only been twenty-four manned space flights before that Challenger, not much to inspire confidence that nothing could go wrong. True, it was the only launch in subfreezing temperatures and, as the sci-entist showed, the O-ring in the solid rocket booster couldn't withstand the cold. Picking up her mother's letter, Susie thought, *rockets are more similar to each other than humans, and the human environment differs by more than hot and cold. So following twenty people who had the injection for a year doesn't convince me that noth-ing can go wrong.*

Betsy's letter also said that she would have to have a genetic test to see if she had a forgetful memory gene and another gene variant called apo-e4. "They also would want to test Martha for those genes."

The last thing Susie wanted was to frighten her mother. *Bates-Bronsted is one of the top medical schools in the country,* she thought, *and surely an experiment like this could not go forward unless it's safe. But how can the medical school know for sure?* One other thought lingered in her mind. *Mom would have told me if Pearce or McAllister is black. Mom is black, poor, and she never went beyond high school. Are they taking advantage of her?*

Susie decided to visit a young black professor at the University of Wisconsin whose course, The Politics of Health Care, she had taken. It included several lectures on inequality in health. His office was a tiny cubicle in North Hall, the oldest building on campus. He was just getting ready to leave for a class when Susie entered unannounced. Recognizing her as a former student, he invited her to walk with him. As they crossed the campus, she told him about the proposed clinical trial to prevent Alzheimer's Disease and that her mother had asked for her daughter's opinion before deciding whether to participate if it came to be.

"Where is the trial being conducted?"

"Bates-Bronsted Medical School."

His eyes lit up. "I've got a good friend who's on the faculty at the University there. Let's talk some more. Coffee this afternoon?"

They met in the Memorial Union where Susie told him what she knew.

"Has the IRB approved the trial?" he asked.

"IRB?"

"Sorry, the Institutional Review Board. Every medical school has one." He explained the function of IRBs and told Susie that before the study could recruit subjects, the Bates-Bronsted IRB would have to approve it.

"According to my Mom, she's just received information. She hasn't signed anything yet.

"My friend, Richard Piper, in Political Science at the University there, has been studying IRBs. The federal government created them after the Tuskegee experiment to protect human subjects."

"Oh yeah, I remember. You assigned us reading about the Tuskegee syphilis experiment."

"The IRB reviews the scientific merit of a study, which must outweigh the risks or harms to the subjects. So the Board expects the investigator to indicate all foreseeable risks and communicate them to potential subjects."

"Who's on the Board? Are they qualified to review merits and risks?"

"Usually other scientists from the same university or medical school review the scientific merit and—"

"Don't they have a conflict of interest?" Susie interrupted.

"What do you mean?"

"Well, they might be friends of the investigator—colleagues, you know."

"It's true, IRBs have been criticized for that. Although, scientists are highly competitive and scrutinize each other's work very carefully, it's not a perfect system by any means." He greeted a faculty member who passed their table, then continued. "The informed consent that subjects must sign isn't perfect either."

"How so?"

"The IRB wants to make sure that subjects being recruited into the study understand the risks and benefits." He paused, sipped his coffee. "The trouble is that the disclosure forms used for informed consent can be difficult. They should be written so that the people being recruited into the study, some of whom may not have gone beyond eighth grade, can understand them."

"My Mom graduated high school."

He smiled. "To have raised a daughter like you, I'm sure she's got smarts." Finishing his coffee, he said, "I'll tell you what. I'll e-mail Richard Piper and tell him about our conversation. How can I contact you when I hear from him?" Susie scribbled the information on a napkin, and as they shook hands, he smiled. "You'll be hearing from me."

After leaving the professor, Susie wandered along Lake Mendota, thinking about how to advise her mother. The spring afternoon was sunny and warm, the trees beginning to bud, and the wind stirred whitecaps on the lake. *Do I want Mom to participate? If I said 'do it' and something bad happened to her, would I be to blame? If I told her no, and she listened to me, and then she developed Alzheimer's, would I be to blame if it turned out the gene injection prevented the disease? What if I said, 'Mom, it's your decision'? Would I be shirking my responsibility as her daughter?* Sailboats were leaning into the stiff spring breeze, the sailors hiking out over the side of their boats, hanging on to the lines that made their sails taut. *Why am I so upset about this?* Slowly it dawned on her that she had something at stake in her mother's decision. If Mom has the memory gene defect, I have a fifty-fifty chance of inheriting it. *Here I am in my midtwenties. Do I want to know that I've got a high chance of getting Alzheimer's? When I meet Mr. Right would I tell him our risk of having a child who would get the disease? We'd probably both be dead before that happened. It seems ridiculous to worry about, but knowing I might get Alzheimer's could hang over me like a sword of Damocles. On the other hand, if the trial showed the disease could be prevented, couldn't I and thousands of others breathe easier?* Turning, she headed back to the Union. She'd tell her mother that it was her own decision.

Chapter 6

THE CLINICAL TRIAL

Publication of Pearce's research was delayed until Ventures Unlimited and the University had jointly filed patents on the mouse and human memory genes. Finally appearing in *Science* and *Nature* in 2002, the reports attracted considerable attention. Headlines like, "Dementia Prevented in Mice," and even "Cure for Alzheimer's in Sight," appeared in *The New York Times, U.S.A. Today* and other leading papers in the U.S. and abroad. Interviews with Jason appeared in several papers and magazines, together with his picture. He became a scientific celebrity overnight. Audrey worried he would be seduced by the limelight if not by some attractive science reporter. Neither happened.

In September 2002, the twentieth subject was recruited into the Phase I trial. None of the previous nineteen had shown any deleterious effect so far, but only after September 2003 could the next phase begin—if the twentieth subject survived without complication. As that month drew near Jason and Gus notified Gertrude Brierly of the Phase I results and submitted their protocol for the next phase. She scheduled the IRB review for the Board's meeting in late September.

Gus defended the proposal before the IRB. "How are you going to recruit patients for the clinical trial?" Richard Piper asked McAllister. As a political scientist, Piper was studying IRBs and regularly attended Board meetings as an observer. "Will you recruit from University Hospital or City Hospital?"

"Why do you ask?" Gus asked.

"As I'm sure you know," Piper replied, "the City Hospital patients are almost all poor and mostly African-American." He paused and smiled. "Different from the composition of the University Hospital patients."

"And that's why we'll recruit from both," Gus replied. "It will make the study group more representative. Thank you for bringing that up."

"What if one of the participants gets a complication from injection of the gene?" a Board member asked. "Who will pay for his treatment?"

"The consent document states that if complications arise, the Medical School will bear the expense of treating them."

"What if the subject suffers irreversible damage?" Piper interjected

"That's highly unlikely."

"But if it happens, can the subject or his or her next of kin sue the Medical School?"

"I'm not a lawyer, so I can't respond." Gus thought for a moment. "I would think that by consenting to participate, having been made aware of the risks, subjects would waive their right to sue."

Audrey Meacham, an ex-officio member representing the legal department, answered the question. Disgusted with the University's promotion of commercialization, she had requested and received reassignment to the medical school and University Hospital after David was born. In her new position she became involved with managing adverse events and possible negligence. "There's no sentence in the consent document that says subjects waive their right to sue. And if you put such a waiver in the disclosure it will dissuade people from participating."

When there were no more questions, Gus withdrew and the Board deliberated. The fact that none of the twenty in Phase I had any harmful effect from the drilling of the hole and injection of the memory gene through it reassured the Board of its safety.

One scientist on the Board, concerned about adverse effects of the injected memory gene, thought that the injection should be tried in primate animals first. The other members argued that this would cause too much delay before it could be learned whether Alzheimer's Disease could be prevented. After prolonged discussion, the Board unanimously approved the clinical trial.

More people volunteered than Jason and Gus anticipated. If the volunteers were still interested after reading and signing the consent form—most were—they had to have the inside of their cheek swabbed so that their DNA could be analyzed in Dr. Laura Mittelman's lab for the presence of the forgetful memory allele. If she found the forgetful memory allele to be present, that subject's DNA was sent to another lab to determine the presence of the apo-e4 allele.

Within a month, Laura and her technician had examined DNA from over one hundred eligible subjects and found nineteen whose genomes contained both the apo-e4 and the memory gene variants.

Jane Sharples, the genetic counselor with the project, brought the buccal swabs to Laura's lab for DNA extraction. Jane had applied to medical school but didn't get in and instead of reapplying she decided to get a Master's in genetic counseling; the science aspects interested her most and she was thinking about an advanced degree in genetics instead of medicine. She was not altogether happy with genetic counseling whose basic tenet is objectivity: presenting the pros and cons but not venturing an opinion. "How am I supposed to be non-directive when we're trying to recruit eligible subjects?" she asked Laura.

"You tell them the risks and benefits, don't you?"

"Yeah, but it's not as simple as that. First of all, the people are all older than I am, more than twice as old as a matter of fact. I'm just a kid to them. Some are so eager to get the gene injected—they don't want to end up like their relative with Alzheimer's—I'm not even sure they're listening when I tell them the risks."

"Then you don't have to worry about recruiting them."

"You're right, but I feel guilty. Sure they'll participate, but what if something goes wrong? Unless I shake them by their lapels to listen, they're not making an informed decision. And if something does go wrong, they might say I never told them."

On another occasion, Jane brought in a specimen, shaking her head. "This specimen belongs to a nice lady, Betsy Matthews. She listened to me attentively, asked a few good questions, ending with, 'What would you do if you were me, Miss Sharples?' I told her it was her decision. Mrs. Matthews shook her head wistfully. 'I asked my daughter, Susie—she graduated from the University of Wisconsin—and she told me the same thing.' We went through the risks and the benefits again. Finally she said, 'Well, I guess I'll sign the consent.' Then she asked, 'I can still decide not to get the injection, even if I'm eligible?' 'Yes you can,' I told her."

Recruiting volunteers, like Betsy Matthews, for the clinical trial began in October and injections of the memory gene or placebo in qualified, consenting patients began in December 2003. Gus McAllister was in the operating suite for each injection, but Jason decided not to go, worried that he might pass out, he told Laura half jokingly.

———

In November 2003, Betsy Matthews was notified that the trial was about to start. She quickly consented and underwent the requisite tests. A few weeks later she was notified that she and her sister Martha had both the apo-e4 and forgetful memory alleles, that she had passed all the neurological and psychological tests and consequently was eligible to join the clinical trial. She quickly decided to continue in the study, but was still troubled that she would not know whether she'd be in the group that received the memory gene or in the control group. She told Susie, "Dr. Pearce and his colleagues worry that if we knew what we received our behavior might be affected, and if the doctor examining us knew, their examinations might be influenced.

'Neither the doctors nor the subjects will know which of us received the gene. Only the statisticians will know.' They call that 'double blind.' I guess that's reasonable, but it's creepy."

Now that her mother had decided to participate, a momentous decision, Susie offered to come home when Betsy was to receive the injection in December at University Hospital's Clinical Research Unit. She would be taken to the neurosurgery operating room for the injection, observed for twenty-four hours, and then if all went well, sent home. A week before the operation was scheduled, Betsy made a rare long distance call to Susie to tell her that she'd become good friends with some of the other people in the study. "Just as I helped one of the women who already received the injection, she and a few others will help me," she told her daughter. "They'll make sure I can get around and they'll fix my meals when I first get home. You'll only complicate matters if you come, Susie. Of course, I do love you." So Susie stayed in Madison.

Betsy had the injection without incident. A week later she was back behind the cash register at the grocery store. She took time off to make her monthly visits to Dr. McAllister as part of the clinical trial, for which her bus fare was reimbursed and she received a small stipend, almost enough to make up for her lost wages and bus fare.

By January 2004, nineteen subjects had received the injection into their brains. According to the statistician, ten received the memory gene and nine the control liquid. Neither Jason nor Gus knew which was which. All had done well and most were able to leave the hospital after one post-operative day. For the first year, Gus examined every patient monthly. They also underwent psychological tests every six months. The subjects were all between fifty and sixty-two years of age and it was unlikely any of them would show even subtle manifestations of Alzheimer's for at least five years.

With all the publicity, relatives of people with the disease across the country called or wrote Pearce asking if he could test them for the aberrant memory gene. On the advice of Don Sharp he declined. "Once the human memory gene is patented," Sharp told him, "Ventures will invest in a commercial lab to offer the test for it."

Laura was surprised when Jason told her about the lab for testing. "What will people do when they learn they've got the mutation?" she asked. "Until you know whether injection of the memory gene prevents Alzheimer's there's nothing they can do about it except worry."

Jason stared at her blankly. "That's their problem," he said, abruptly shutting down the conversation.

In January 2004, the Patents and Trademark Office issued a patent jointly to Pearce, Bates-Bronsted

Medical School, and Ventures Unlimited on "the human memory gene and all variant sequences hitherto or hereafter discovered." A few weeks later, the University held a press conference at which Jason, Donald Sharp, the President of the University, and the Mayor announced that the construction of a new commercial laboratory funded by Ventures Unlimited, with tax benefits from the city, was underway on public land just outside the campus. The clinical laboratory would be the exclusive provider of tests for the memory gene and its variants. At Jason's invitation, Laura attended the press conference.

One of the journalists asked if 'exclusive' meant that they would not license the test to other scientists or laboratories. Jason replied that scientists could obtain the gene for research purposes only. "All clinical testing will be performed in the new lab." The journalist followed up, "Do you mean people anywhere in the world who want this test would have to arrange for their specimen to be sent to your lab?"

Jason replied that by limiting the test to one laboratory he could assure the quality of testing and be able to search for more than the currently known forgetful allele. He gestured toward Laura. "Professor Mittelman is searching the memory gene for rare mutations that might be even more strongly associated with Alzheimer's Disease than the common one. The lab will have the capability of testing for them.

Because Bates-Bronsted holds the patent on the memory gene, other labs won't be able to do that."

The way Jason described her work surprised Laura. She also thought that the attempt to monopolize testing was not in the best interest of people who might have forgetful alleles. If, as seemed to be the case, people would clamor for the test, the new commercial laboratory could set the price as high as the traffic would bear and make a fortune in testing.

Dismayed, that evening she told her partner Amanda, "Jason doesn't seem bothered by questions like, 'What will people do if the test shows they have the forgetful allele?' When I went to work on my Ph.D. with him, he railed against the Genetics faculty members who had commercial ties and held their work tight to their vest. The man he was closest to on the faculty was Professor Chapman whose last book deplored universities' policy of filing patents not for the public good but for making money from exclusive licensing. Since Jason's taken money from Ventures Unlimited he seems to have changed his views. The company's been very generous to him. There's no other way he could be driving a Lamborghini."

Chapter 7

THE CRASH

As on her previous visits, Betsy Matthews waited for her ten-month visit with Dr. McAllister in a windowless examining room whose fluorescent lights gently hummed. The nurse's aide who led her to the room took her blood pressure, pulse, and temperature, and asked her to take off all but her underpants, handing Betsy a flimsy gown with a single tie at the back of the neck. After the aide left, Betsy did as she was told, and tied the gown with difficulty, leaving most of her back and buttocks exposed. Using the small step stool, she ascended the steel-rimmed examining table, its cushion covered with lightly waxed white paper that crackled as she sat. Feeling adrift, like an iceberg in a cold and hostile sea, she gazed at the stark walls, adorned only with black and white diagrams of the brain and the vertebral column. A knock on the door, and before Betsy could answer, Dr. McAllister entered in his long white lab coat, his name inscribed in heavy blue thread over the breast pocket. Extending his hand, he said, "Good to see you again, Mrs. Matthews. You're looking well. How are you feeling?" To Gus, the imbalance between the white-coated physician and his scantily clad patients did not fortify the doctor-patient relationship, much less the researcher-subject relationship. He had urged the Hospital Administration to make the rooms warmer and more humane, but they never changed.

Gus and Jason had decided that Gus rather than junior neurologists would perform the initial and follow-up clinical examinations in order to maximize the chance of picking up subtle changes in the cognitive function of trial participants. Kept busy with administrative duties and teaching, Gus hadn't performed as many complete neurological examinations for several years as he did after the start of the trial.

Seeing them once a month for the first year after injection of the memory gene, Gus got to know the subjects as well as, if not better than, doctors get to know their regular patients. On their first visit, many of the subjects, including Betsy, told Gus they were sure they had received the memory gene and were eager to show him that their memory had not deteriorated. Again and again, he had to tell them that he didn't know whether they had or not. By the sixth exam, they were getting on with their lives, becoming more philosophical about the study, some of them saying they were glad they had participated—contributing to the advancement of knowledge—even if they hadn't received the memory gene. Gus found no evidence that any of them had any memory loss. Since they were all under sixty-three that was to be expected.

"I just have a little cold," Betsy replied to Dr. McAllister's greeting.

"Are you feeling all right otherwise?"

"I seem to tire easily. Ordinarily I'd walk up here to the third floor, but today I took the elevator; I'd have been late if I walked. It's probably this cold. When I get colds lately they take longer to clear up."

"That's aging," Gus replied. "Even if the memory gene works, it won't help that aspect. Have you had your flu shot?" She assured him she had.

Gus hadn't peered down people's throats for a while, but Betsy's looked a little red. Her neurological exam was completely normal. He reassured Betsy she'd get over the cold and arranged to see her in a month as specified in the trial protocol.

Sitting in his office three weeks later, Gus got a call from the Director of Emergency Services at City Hospital. "I'm calling you because we'd like to admit Mrs. Betsy Matthews who says she's a patient of yours."

"She's not a patient of mine but a subject I've been following for the Alzheimer's prevention trial. What's the problem?"

The Director proceeded to tell him that Betsy had dragged herself into the City Hospital Emergency Room that morning. After two hours of waiting she got up to get a drink of water and collapsed, bringing her at last to the attention of the nurses. She was immediately brought into a cubicle, revived, examined by a doctor, and an IV started. "We worked her up and it looks like she's got AML."

Gus had been away from internal medicine so long that it took a few seconds for the acronym to register. "Acute myeloid leukemia?"

"Yeah. She's got an enlarged liver and spleen and easily palpable cervical and axillary lymph nodes. Her hemoglobin is five, and on the smear, there are hardly any platelets and over twenty percent of white cells are blasts or juveniles. We'll have the platelet count tomorrow."

Gus broke into a cold sweat.

"We're ready to admit her, but I thought I'd call you first," the Director said.

"Who is the attending on the Heme-Onc service at City this month?"

"John Gilman."

"Good. He's on the faculty of Bates-Bronsted and on the staff at University Hospital. Let me try to reach him."

"Okay. We've typed and cross-matched her blood; I don't think we should wait too long before transfusing her."

"I understand, but don't transfuse her yet. I'll call you back within fifteen minutes." He immediately paged Dr. Gilman.

The cold sweat persisted. He sat at his desk, staring ahead. *Why didn't I do a complete physical on Mrs. Matthews when she complained of a cold and tiring more easily? Maybe I didn't feel competent; it's been twenty years since the last one I did. Of course, I should be able feel a big liver and spleen. Am I such a narrow-minded specialist that I can only think of neurological problems? Maybe we should have gotten an internist to do complete physicals periodically. How could I have been so shortsighted?*

John Gilman responded quickly and Gus explained the situation.

"Do you think the leukemia could be related to her getting the memory gene?" John asked.

"I don't even know if she got the memory gene. But if she did, there's the possibility that some of the DNA we injected escaped the blood-brain barrier and inserted itself in a marrow stem cell. I haven't yet told Jason Pearce; he'll be the one to orchestrate whether the memory gene is responsible."

"What do you want me to do, Gus?"

"Mrs. Matthews would be closer to us if she was admitted to University Hospital." He didn't have to tell John her care would be better there.

"No problem. Tell the ER to page me in a half hour. By then I'll have arranged a bed for her and transport."

"That's very good of you, John. Please have your secretary call me when Mrs. Matthews has been transferred and tell me what floor she's on."

"Did the ER say they'd told her the diagnosis?"

"They didn't tell me," Gus said. "If not, I think it would be better if you, Jason, and I told her together,"

"I agree. I'm available this evening. We can tell her then, draw blood for additional studies, do the bone marrow aspiration, and then transfuse her. It's not in her best interest to wait until tomorrow, but we can't transfuse her before the aspiration; it could confuse the picture."

Gus called the ER Director, told him to page Dr. Gilman to arrange the transfer to University Hospital, and not to transfuse Betsy. "Have you given Mrs. Matthews the likely diagnosis?"

"No. I checked with the residents. No one mentioned leukemia to her."

"Good. We'll tell her. And thanks for letting me know."

"No problem," the Director replied, and then asked how to bill for her ER visit.

"Does she have insurance?"

"No. She's not old enough for Medicare; she might be eligible for Medicaid."

Gus was getting impatient. "Just bill the way you would if she wasn't in a study. If the leukemia's related to the trial, Bates-Bronsted will pick up the tab," he added without authorization.

Gus called Jason. "Are you sitting down?" Jason said he was. "I just got a call from the City Hospital ER that one of our study patients, Betsy Matthews, probably has acute leukemia. She dragged herself to the ER and fainted while waiting to be seen."

"Did you break the code?"

"No. I thought you should do it."

"Okay. I'll call the statistician and tell her we need to know whether Betsy received the memory gene." Jason was silent for a moment. "Isn't Betsy Matthews African-American?"

"Yes," Gus replied.

"Have you told anyone else, Gus?"

"John Gilman. He's head of the Hematology-Oncology Service at University Hospital. He's arranged to have her transferred from the ER at City Hospital to University. And please, Jason, let me know as soon as you hear from the statistician"

"Sure."

Shortly after his conversation with Jason, Gus received a call from Dr. Gilman's secretary, telling him that Mrs. Matthews had been transferred to the third floor of University Hospital, and adding that Dr. Gilman would meet Gus there at eight o'clock. Gus puttered around the office, waiting for Jason to call back. At six o'clock, just as he was about to call him, the phone rang.

"Mrs. Matthews received the memory gene." Gus sagged. "It's too late to notify anyone today," Jason continued, " so let's sleep on it."

"We've got to tell Mrs. Matthews this evening. John Gilman wants to aspirate her bone marrow and transfuse her afterwards; she's very anemic, probably explains why she fainted. Waiting for tomorrow could be dangerous. You'll want to get marrow cells for DNA analysis before the transfusion."

Jason did not immediately answer. Finally he exclaimed, "Damn! Audrey and I are having dinner with the President of the University at eight o'clock."

"Considering what's happened, it might be better if you canceled your engagement, Gus replied. "I'm going to meet Gilman in Mrs. Matthews' room at eight o'clock. I hope to see you there."

John Gilman was reviewing Betsy Matthews' chart at the nurses' station when Gus arrived promptly at eight. "Is Jason going to join us?"

"I'm not sure," Gus answered. "He and his wife were supposed to have dinner with the President tonight." They chatted amiably until the clock above the nurses' desk showed five past eight. "Let's go in without him. I know you need to get the consent for the marrow aspiration," Gus said.

John nodded. "We've got a couple of units of blood ready to transfuse."

Betsy was pleased to see a familiar face. "Dr. McAllister, how nice of you to visit. Maybe you can tell me what's wrong. Nobody else has."

Propped against her pillow on the high hospital bed, Betsy looked gaunt compared to the last time he had seen her. Her brown skin had not changed but her fingers, lying limply above the blanket, showed no color in her nail beds. "That's why I'm here, Betsy." Gus introduced Dr. Gilman. "He's a specialist in blood diseases. You do know that you fainted because you're very anemic, don't you?"

"Yes, they told me that. But why am I anemic?"

Gus turned to Dr. Gilman to explain. "What we think, Betsy, is that your bone marrow is not making red blood cells, as it normally does, but another kind of cell that interferes with red cell production and also with the production of platelets, tiny cells that help your blood clot. You may have had some internal bleeding as a result; that would contribute to your anemia."

"Sounds like leukemia," Betsy said, startling both doctors. "I forget which magazine I read it in."

Gilman continued. "That's possible. We can't be sure until we examine your bone marrow. With your permission, we'll stick a needle in your hipbone and remove some marrow. We'll numb the area but it will be uncomfortable for a moment." She was looking at him fixedly. "We need your consent."

"I can bear the pain. Where do I sign?"

"I'll get the forms and make arrangements," John said as he left the room.

Shortly after, there was a knock at the door of Betsy's room and Laura Mittelman entered carrying a small Styrofoam box. "Dr. Mittelman, I didn't expect to see you here," Gus said.

"Jason called me a little while ago. He asked if I could bring over some vials for a sample of Mrs. Matthews' bone marrow." Laura looked at Betsy and smiled warmly as Gus introduced her as an associate of Dr. Pearce.

"Dr. Gilman's just gone out to get the form and arrange for the aspiration," Gus told Laura. "You're just in time." Lowering his voice, he asked her, "Do you happen to know whether Jason is coming?"

"He called me from home, asked if I'd mind collecting some marrow cells," she replied quietly. "He said he had another engagement."

John returned with the form and a nurse came with a wheelchair to take Betsy to the treatment room. After signing the form, Betsy looked at Laura. "Do you think this could have anything to do with Dr. Pearce's study? You know, I received that injection into my brain." The nurse was helping Betsy into the wheelchair.

Dr. Gilman and Gus looked at Laura. "I don't know, Mrs. Matthews," she began. "Dr. Pearce is very concerned about your health and wants to make sure that whatever your trouble is that it's not related to the study." She paused, pointing to the Styrofoam box. "He asked me to take a small sample of your marrow to see if there are signs of the memory gene in it."

"That means I did get the memory gene, is that right?" Once again, the doctors looked surprised.

"Yes, Mrs. Matthews," Gus said. "We broke the code this afternoon and found that you did receive the memory gene."

"I hope it's not related. Dr. Pearce is such a nice man, trying so hard to prevent Alzheimer's. For his sake more than mine I hope he succeeds." The nurse started to wheel her out.

"Would you like to join us in the treatment room?"
Dr. Gilman asked Laura. "If not, I'll fill the vials for
you."

"No, I'll go with you."

The treatment room was like a mini operating
room with a large round circular light that could be
swiveled to focus on a particular field, and a faint
smell of disinfectant. The nurse helped Betsy get up
onto the procedure table, then had her sit, her legs
hanging down below her short hospital gown, not
touching the floor. "Dear," said the nurse, "I just want
you to hold tight to me. Dr. Gilman is going to prep
over your hipbone."

"Oh, that's cold," Betsy said as Gilman swabbed
the area.

"Mrs. Matthews," he said from his seat on a chrome
stool in back of her, "you're going to feel a little prick
as I anesthetize your skin so it won't be too painful."

She winced. "Ouch."

Wearing latex gloves, Dr. Gilman turned to the
prep stand alongside his stool and picked up a large
syringe with a long large bore needle. "You're going
to feel some discomfort now." He plunged the needle
into her pelvic bone as she groaned and shuddered, the
nurse holding her tightly. Watching intently, Laura
noted that Betsy's ribs were visible against her skin,
gauntly, like a concentration camp victim. "That's the
worst of it," Gilman said as he slowly pulled up on the

syringe plunger, bloody marrow rushed in. He pulled the needle out, pressed a gauze pad over the wound and had the nurse come round, hold and then tape it. Laura removed the vials from her Styrofoam box, rubbed their rubber tops with alcohol wipes, and held them as Gilman injected marrow into the vials. "My lab will examine Betsy's cells for chromosome abnormalities associated with AML," he told her. "If you send over a fluorescent probe for the memory gene we can see whether it's out of place." Laura told him she'd bring it in the morning.

When Dr. Gilman finished filling the vials, Laura placed them back in the box, put the lid on and headed out, calling "Goodbye, Mrs. Matthews," from the door. "I hope you'll feel better, now." As she walked back to her lab, Laura thought *what a stupid thing to say*; of course *she would feel better after the needle was withdrawn. She's going to suffer a lot more. Why couldn't I have said something more comforting?*

Chapter 8

THE SLAP

When Jason came home about seven that evening, Audrey was at her dressing table, preparing for dinner at the President's house, putting on the pearl necklace and earrings he had bought for her fortieth birthday.

"Sorry, I'm late dear." Jason came up behind, kissed the back of her neck, admiring her tight fitting black satin dress with its Mandarin collar. "Gus McAllister called this afternoon to tell me that one of our subjects has leukemia."

Putting down the earring she had not yet fastened, Audrey turned to face him. Familiar with the protocol, she asked, "Did you break the code?"

"Yeah."

"And?"

"She received the gene, but," he quickly added, "I doubt her leukemia's related. The memory gene DNA would have had to cross the blood-brain barrier. Besides, leukemia's not rare in her age group. Even so, Gus is freaking out."

"What's being done for the poor woman?"

"Gus had her transferred from the ER at City to University Hospital. I'm not sure why. He and the oncologist are meeting with her at eight. I told him we had a dinner date with the President."

Jason started to change his shirt.

"Is it that important that we go?"

"The President wants to show off his star faculty in hope of extracting more money from the trustees."

"Don't you think you owe it to uh—your subject, uh—"

"Mrs. Matthews. Betsy Matthews."

"—to visit her in the hospital?"

"Gus'll be there. He's been following the subjects more closely than I have."

As attorney for Bates-Bronsted, Audrey had managed enough adverse events to know that the best way to head off a patient's, or a relative's, anger was to acknowledge the problem and placate the family. This coincided with what was right ethically. "I don't see it that way, Jason. Everyone will be better off if you visit Mrs. Matthews this evening."

He removed a new shirt from his bureau. "You may see it that way, but I don't," he said, unwrapping and unbuttoning it. Suddenly, he stopped. Laying the shirt on their bed he exclaimed, "Oh, damn it." He pulled out his pocket directory, then picked up the phone on the night table and dialed. "Laura, it's Jason." He repeated what he had told Audrey. "Look, Audrey and I have an important engagement this evening. Can you go to the lab, pick up some vials and bring them to Betsy Matthews' room at University Hospital to collect bone marrow cells?" He put it as a question but it sounded like a command. "Gus and the oncologist are supposed to meet there at eight. If you leave now you can get to the hospital before they do the marrow aspiration." He listened. "No. I don't think I should break my engagement to be there." He looked at Audrey. "Audrey seems to think so, but I don't." He listened again. "Thanks, Laura. You're a doll."

"'An important engagement?' Why is it so important we visit the President?" she asked.

"I told you. He wants to milk more money out of these rich trustees by having them hobnob with his star faculty."

"You've got all the money, all the recognition you could ask for. The President is using you. I don't see our going as important as taking care of a woman who put her trust in you."

"Trust?"

Audrey stopped and turned to face him. "You talked her into participating in your trial, having a hole drilled in her skull, a needle stuck in her brain, and a foreign substance injected. Doesn't that entail trust?"

He shrugged, put the new shirt on and started to button it.

"From what you told Laura it sounds like Mrs. Matthews' leukemia might be related. Is that true?"

"I'm just covering all the bases."

Audrey sighed. "Let's play out one scenario, Jason: We go to dinner with the President. Laura gets the cells, discovers that the memory gene in Mrs. Matthews' marrow cells has triggered her leukemia. You can't keep that quiet."

"So?"

"So tomorrow, or whenever Laura finishes her analysis, the President is notified, as he surely will be, and he thinks back to tonight's dinner and says, 'Hmm, Jason was at my house, drinking my wine, smoking my cigars, instead of attending to his subject.' Will that endear you to him?" Audrey stopped, not sure she had made her case, but then she thought of something else. "Jason, just ask yourself one question, What would Professor Chapman say?"

"What does he have to do with it?"

She sat on the edge of the bed. "Do you remember when you invited me to meet him at lunch in his office? It was shortly before he died. You were called back to your lab before we had finished, and he invited me to stay. You were still working on the regulator gene. He said, 'It's rare to find a young scientist these days who's not lured by money or fame.' We both admired you for that, Jason. I hope you're not changing."

"Of course I'm not changing. This clinical trial means everything to me."

"Then call the President and tell him what's happened."

"I can tell him when we get to his house."

Obviously, she hadn't gotten through to him. She stood and walked toward him. "You have changed. Your ego's as big as a balloon and one of these days——" Shuddering, she didn't finish the sentence. Instead, she opened the night table drawer and pulled out the University Directory, bent over it, running her finger down the first page until she found the number for the President's official on-campus residence. Then she picked up the phone.

"Who are you calling?"

"The President, to tell him we're not coming."

Jason grabbed the phone from her and smacked it back on its cradle.

"Of course we're going," he shouted. "This has nothing to do with my ego!"

Very quietly she said, "Jason, I really think you should go to University Hospital to see Mrs. Matthews." She dropped the directory on the bed.

"Why? What's my presence going to add?"

"It's your experiment. Aren't you concerned that you might—might—be responsible for the leukemia, that she might die?"

"Die? She's not going to die, Audrey. This is the twenty-first century. We can cure her leukemia."

"Can you be sure?" Still facing him, she reached over her shoulders to unzip her dress, pulling it over her head, then she went to her closet for a housecoat.

"What are you doing?"

"If you want to go to the President's dinner, you'll have to go alone."

Jason took a step toward his wife, his face choleric, the blue of his irises reduced to a thin rim around his black, dilated pupils. His arms shot out, pulling her toward him, but she pushed him away, gathering the top of the housecoat around her throat. She had never seen such rage—*hatred*—in his face as he glowered at her, their eyes inches part. Through clenched teeth he said, "Put your dress back on. *We*" (he emphasized the word) "are going to the President's for dinner." She turned away but with his right hand he spun her around.

When Audrey played the scene back in her mind—many times—it was always in slow motion, as if she could analyze every frame, halt the action, and snip out some of the frames.

Jason took a step back, raised his left hand and slapped her hard across the face, his wedding band striking the cheekbone just below her right eye. Too stunned to move, she stared at him as he staggered backward and sat on the bed.

Frozen in time and space neither said a word. After a minute Jason said meekly, "I'm sorry."

Her face burned. Gingerly, she touched the skin below her eye. No blood. *Was this Jason?* She realized she had been holding her breath and exhaled slowly, trying to breathe normally. He rose, approached her and tenderly tilted her face to examine it carefully. A red welt had formed under her right eye. He bent and kissed it. "I promise, I will never strike you again."

Audrey stepped back. *Wasn't that what wife abusers said until they struck again?*

Jason looked at his watch: a quarter to eight. "If we leave now we can still make it."

Still facing him, Audrey sat on the bench in front of her dressing table and finished buttoning her house-coat. She stared at her husband in disbelief, unable or unwilling to speak to him. *Did he realize what he had just done? Did he think a kiss would heal everything?*

Jason came to sit beside her but she immediately left the room, closing the door behind her. He heard her yell for their children from the hall, "Rachel, David..."

Burying his head in his hands, elbows on his knees, Jason sat quietly for a few minutes. Slowly, he got up, retrieved the Directory Audrey had left open on the bed, and dialed the President's residence. The President's wife answered, and he said, "This is Jason Pearce. I've had some serious trouble that will keep me in the lab quite late. I'm afraid Audrey and I can't make it tonight. Please forgive us. Some other time, I hope."

It was nine o'clock before Jason got to University Hospital. Betsy was asleep in her hospital room. McAllister, Gilman, and Mittelman had departed.

⸺

When Audrey left their bedroom, she walked downstairs, wrapped a clean cloth around some ice cubes and applied the pack to her cheek. She called Rachel and David who were playing with Hannah, their *au pair*. "Time for bed, children."

"Mommy," Rachel asked, "What happened to your face?"

"Oh, I wasn't looking where I was going and walked into the edge of daddy's bureau."

Rachel moved Audrey's icepack away. "Doesn't look too bad. Keep the ice on it," she said in her best professional tone. "Will daddy tell us a story?"

For a moment Audrey didn't know what to say. Finally, "What if I tell you a story, or read you one? Will that do?"

"If it's got a surprise ending like Daddy's," David said.

"I'll see what I can do," Audrey replied with some trepidation, a new unease fomenting inside her. She propped the book on a pillow, holding the icepack against her cheek while Rachel, who could read, helped turn pages.

The next morning Audrey and the children were having breakfast when Jason came downstairs, announcing that he would take Rachel to school in the Lamborghini. Audrey regarded him suspiciously, but before she could say anything David piped up. "Why can't you take me to school, too? I don't want to ride in Mommy's big black ugly SUV."

"You know the Lamborghini only holds one passenger," Audrey told him gently. "When you're big enough, Daddy will give you a ride, too. Children your age have to ride in a back seat."

Pouting, Davy stirred his cereal with his baby spoon, but said nothing more. The kids finished eating and left to brush their teeth and get their jackets while their parents sat silently at the table. Finally,

Audrey said, "You think it's a good idea, taking her in the Lamborghini?"

"She's been clamoring for a ride and she's big enough to be protected by the shoulder belt." He finished his coffee. "Her friends will be surprised when she pulls up in a red sports car."

It is his ego, she thought. "You're spoiling her, Jason. Do you want her to grow up thinking she's rich?"

"Well she is. At least her parents are. Why shouldn't she?"

Rachel flew down the stairs. "Come on, Daddy, let's go or I'll be late."

The topic of wealth reminded Audrey of Ventures Unlimited. As she helped Rachel with her coat and Jason put on his jacket she asked, "Have you let Don Sharp know of the new development?"

"You mean Betsy Matthews?"

"Is there another new development I don't know about?"

"No." With Rachel pulling his sleeve, Jason said over his shoulder, "I plan to call him this morning."

Chapter 9

AUDREY MEACHAM

Jason's slap and their short dialog at breakfast gnawed at Audrey as she drove David to daycare in her "big black ugly SUV." *Why shouldn't Rachel grow up thinking she's rich?* Audrey's parents had been well off for as long as she could remember but they had never flaunted their wealth. She smiled as she recalled their evasiveness when, as a little girl, she asked, *Are we rich?*

Parking in the daycare's lot, she unbuckled Davy's seat belt and walked him into the school. "Mommy loves you," she shouted after him as he ran off to play with his friends.

Heading back to her car, she couldn't help comparing her upbringing to Jason's: *She had grown up solidly in the middle class and was content to be there. Jason* had grown up poor and now seemed dazzled by wealth and prestige.

Audrey drove to the Medical School, smiling as she recalled the first years of their marriage.

On the strength of his work on the gene regulator in mice he had advanced to full professorship in record time. While running a busy lab with two technicians, eager graduate students and post-docs, he still had time to play with Rachel and be a caring and loving husband. Bringing in all his salary and support with grants from NIH, he was the darling of the Bates-Bronsted-Administration, which garnered over half of what he received as overhead from the federal government. But then as the expiration of his major grant approached, their marriage had become tense.

As she stopped for a red light at the entrance to the campus she pinpointed when their relationship had changed—it had been the icy day in the first month of the new millennium when Jason gave Julian Goodrich a lift to work. That evening they had fought about switching his research to the memory gene. She recalled subsequent milestones—her fury at the terms Ventures Unlimited wanted to impose on his contract, his drunken return from Chicago in the spring of 2001.

A liveried chauffeur had whisked Jason out of the house into a sleek black Lincoln Town Car. "If you have a chance, darling," Audrey yelled after him, "call to let me know how your presentation went." The chauffeur drove Jason on to the airport tarmac, where he boarded Ventures Unlimited's private Leer jet. He did not call Audrey. The next day, when she had returned from work after picking up Rachel and Davey at daycare, she found him fumbling at the front door trying to get his key in the lock. "Didja change za locks?" he slurred. She opened the door with his key, leaving him to stumble into the house while she unbuckled Rachel and Davey from their car seats and led them to their makeshift playroom, returning to the living room to find her husband prostrate on the couch. "Cum eer," he commanded.

"No. Maybe there's a good reason why you're dead drunk, but I'm not getting near you while you are." She headed for the kitchen and said over her shoulder, "I'll get you a cup of black coffee, then I've got to attend to the children."

Jason reappeared in the kitchen after the kids were asleep while Audrey was preparing some left-overs for herself. "Would you like a bite to eat? It'll probably be good for you," she had remarked.

"That would be nice," he said soberly. Sitting at the kitchen table, he explained how he more than made up for his abstinence on the outbound flight,

on which he was the only passenger, on the way back. Putting his hands on his forehead, trying to press out the ache, he groaned, "What a hangover. I'll never be tempted to do that again."

"Let's hope not," Audrey had said, almost to herself. As Jason described his conversations with Don Sharp after he had presented the results of the mouse gene therapy experiment, Audrey became more concerned than ever that her husband was on the road to perdition.

"If Don has anything to say—and his money talks—he'll have the University endow a chair for me and jack up my salary to match the highest paid faculty member, probably Julian Goodrich. And pretty soon, Audrey, we'll be on Easy Street."

"I thought our life was pretty good already."

"This house is too small for us."

She felt a pang; it was the house I grew up in.

"Rachel and David will each have their own room and they'll be able to go to private school."

Wait a minute, Audrey had thought, I went to public school and the schools in this neighborhood are still good.

"We're still driving the cars we had before we were married; we can soon afford new ones."

She had stood up impatiently, not waiting to hear Jason's other plans.

Reaching the Medical School, Audrey asked herself, *Are we really rich or could the whole edifice crumble like a house of cards if the memory gene is implicated in Betsy Matthews' leukemia?* Swiping her ID card in the reader at the entrance to the staff parking lot, she waited for the gate to swing up, then drove through. She stopped to let a car pull out and then eased her Lexus SUV into the spot, picked up her bag, locked the car and walked to her office. *Big ugly SUV.* Jason had surprised her with it on their fifth anniversary, shortly after his drunken return from Chicago. A few months later, with a personal loan from Donald Sharp, he had bought the red Lamborghini.

Busy with meetings and phone calls the rest of the morning, Audrey put her personal problems out of mind until that afternoon when Gertrude Brierly announced at the regularly scheduled IRB meeting that a subject in the Alzheimer's clinical trial had been diagnosed with leukemia. Audrey was sitting next to Richard Piper and when the meeting concluded he turned and looked at her. She felt self-conscious and flustered, involuntarily touching the tiny bruise on her cheek. "How's Jason managing with this?" he asked, apparently oblivious of the blemish.

"Oh, fine," she answered blithely and left the room.

When she arrived home Jason was going over the mail. He glanced up, smiled winsomely, and chucked the mail aside. "Too many bills," he muttered.

"How'd Rachel like her ride to school?"

"I don't know, Audrey. Maybe you were right. She was snobby, tried to be nonchalant when the other kids gathered round. I could almost swear she walked into school with her nose up in the air." He paused. "I'm not going to make a habit of it." Audrey didn't reply and Jason changed the subject. "I stopped in at Laura's lab this morning. She's the one who's looking for a connection between the memory gene and Mrs. Matthews' leukemia. By Monday, she hopes."

The children barged in and the conversation did not resume until they had gone upstairs and the couple was dining alone.

"I did speak to Don Sharp today. Told him about Mrs. Matthews. He was quite upset."

"I'm glad to hear he's compassionate."

He looked at Audrey, surprised. "When I told him, his first comment was, 'Can't her own doctor take care of it?' I told him that the Emergency Room at City Hospital noticed she was a subject in our trial and called Gus McAllister who notified me."

So Don was more interested in his investment than another human being.

"What upset Don was that I had notified the IRB before I called him."

"You did the right thing."

"I had to do it. After I broke the code, I asked Gus not to tell anyone else. This morning Gus said if I didn't notify Gertrude he would."

"Were you thinking of *not* notifying Gertrude?"

"It crossed my mind, just like it crossed Don Sharp's."

"Did Sharp show *any* remorse?"

"About Betsy Matthews?" He thought for a moment. "No, not really. The only remorse he showed, and I can understand it, was that if the memory gene is implicated in her leukemia, Ventures' investment in the commercial lab that would test for the memory gene will not pay off."

"Not to mention his investment in you."

"What do you mean?"

"If the memory gene is implicated in Mrs. Matthews' leukemia, do you think Ventures is going to continue to fund you? Who do you think is going to volunteer to get a gene injected in their brain if they risk getting cancer? He'd be throwing good money after bad."

Chapter 10

BETSY MATTHEWS' DNA

From the nurses' station outside Mrs. Matthews' room, Gus called Gertrude Brierly, apologizing for the late hour. "Something has happened you should know about. Do you mind if I come over for a few minutes?"

"No problem," Gertrude answered. She put on the kettle for some tea and took out a package of Oreos, the only sweet in her townhouse apartment. The kettle whistled just as Gus arrived in his sport coat, the knot of his tie pulled loosely down to the second button of his shirt, his collar open. They sat on opposite sides of the dining room table, Gertrude's back to the galley kitchen. She let the tea steep in the pot before filling their cups.

"I've just come from University Hospital, seeing one of the subjects in the Alzheimer's study." He paused as Gertrude slid his cup and saucer toward him and he took an Oreo from the small plate she had set out. "She has leukemia," Gertrude stopped pouring her own cup, resuming as he filled in the details.

"How terrible. Do you think the memory gene——"

"Jason sent Laura Mittelman—you know who she is?" Gertrude nodded. "She put some of the marrow in vials for DNA analysis." Gus took another Oreo.

"Jason wasn't there?"

"He and Audrey were supposed to have dinner at the President's house this evening, although from what Laura told me, Audrey wasn't too happy about going." He took another sip of tea and an Oreo.

"Are you still recruiting subjects?" Gertrude asked.

"Not many, but yes."

"You can't put anyone else at risk—at least not until the memory gene is exonerated." She refilled his cup from the teapot, then answered, "As of right now, the study is suspended."

"I don't feel quite right that it's me and not Jason telling you this."

Gertrude went back to the galley and put another half dozen Oreos on the plate. "Then I think what you should do, Gus, is call Jason when you get home or first thing tomorrow and tell him to give me the news. I won't say anything about our talking."

They chatted for a few minutes before Gus stood. "I don't want to take any more of your time, Gertrude. Thanks for the tea and cookies; they were my supper!" He thought for a moment. "If Jason refuses, I'll tell him that I will tell you."

###

At its regularly scheduled meeting, Gertrude informed the IRB that Professor Pearce had informed her that one of the subjects who received an injection of the memory gene into her brain ten months ago had been diagnosed with leukemia. A collective gasp went up. "Professor Pearce and his colleagues have obtained a sample of the subject's bone marrow and will attempt to learn whether the injected memory gene played a role in her leukemia. The Medical School is obliged to suspend the trial until it can be certain that the leukemia is coincidental. Also, as required, we will notify the FDA of the suspension." The group was silent for a moment.

Then one of the physicians on the Board asked, "Where is the patient now?"

"Dr. McAllister arranged for the patient to be admitted to University Hospital on the Oncology service under the direction of Dr. John Gilman, Bates-Bronsted's leading oncologist. If it had not been for enrollment in the study the subject would have been admitted to City Hospital. That's where the leukemia was diagnosed. University Hospital and the Medical School have accepted Drs. McAllister and Gilman's recommendation that it would be inappropriate to transfer the subject back to City even if the DNA analysis is negative."

"What is the patient's prognosis?" a scientist asked.

"I did not discuss that with Dr. Pearce."

"What if the memory gene is implicated?" another asked.

"Then the FDA will undoubtedly shut down the trial, pending an investigation."

"Who's going to pay for the patient's treatment?" asked Richard Piper.

"The University will assume full cost of the patient's admission, including diagnostic tests and treatment, regardless of whether the memory gene is implicated."

"Can you tell us the patient's name?" asked Reverend Henry Johnson, the community member of the IRB. "A few members of my congregation are participating in the study. Perhaps I can—"

"I'm sorry, Reverend Johnson, the Director of the Hospital and the Dean thought it best that until we have more information and the next of kin has been notified, we cannot release the patient's name." After that the room was silent.

"Well," Gertrude concluded, "if there are no more questions, let's get on with our regular business."

After the meeting, Reverend Johnson entered Gertrude's office, closing the door behind him. "Henry, I'm glad you stopped by," Gertrude greeted him. I'm sure you understand why I couldn't name the patient in front of everyone. We also want to protect uh, her, from being hounded by the press. But I will tell you in strictest confidence that the patient is Betsy Matthews, who lives in the City not far from your church." The Reverend flinched at the name. "I thought you might know her."

"Indeed I do. And her sister and her daughter, too. Can I visit her?"

"If you're her minister, I can't stop you. But please—"

"Don't worry, Gertrude, I won't even tell my wife."

"Thank you, Henry."

Later that day, Gertrude spoke to John Gilman. Betsy had received two units of blood and a platelet transfusion, he told her, and was looking and feeling much better.

"Can her leukemia be cured? I'm out of touch with the advances."

"It depends. If the memory gene is implicated, all bets are off. We'll be dealing with something unprecedented. For that reason she'd be excluded from some of the experimental chemotherapies; they have rigid criteria for enrollment."

"When do you and Pearce expect to know more about her cells?"

"My lab and Dr. Mittelman's are working overtime on it. I'd hope by the beginning of next week." He paused for a moment, shifting gears. "You know, Dr. Brierly, Mrs. Matthews is eager to go home. And her home may be a safer environment than the hospital, where she's more likely to contract an antibiotic-resistant infection. She tells me that she's got a daughter in Wisconsin, although she hasn't yet told her about her illness. I'd feel better about discharging Mrs. Matthews if I knew a responsible adult would be at home to care for her, at least until we decide on a course of treatment and readmit her. Betsy's daughter would be ideal, but Betsy told me she's working hard on the Kerry-Edwards campaign and doesn't want to distract her."

"I may be able to help you. I can't say any more, but perhaps by tomorrow Betsy's daughter will know her mother is sick. Whether she agrees to come home is another matter."

⸻

"I was planning to visit Betsy after dinner this evening," Reverend Johnson told Gertrude when they spoke again shortly after Gertrude's conversation with John Gilman.

"Actually Henry, her doctors would like to discharge her, provided she has someone to care for her."

"Susie, uh, Betsy's daughter, is just the one."

"According to Dr. Gilman, Betsy hasn't notified her daughter of her condition."

"Okay, I get the picture, Gertrude. Let me see what I can do."

Henry called Gertrude that evening to say that he and Betsy had both spoken to Susie by phone from the hospital room. "Susie's first question was whether the memory gene injection had anything to do with her mother's leukemia. I just told her what you told us at the IRB meeting. Susie said she would be here tomorrow evening."

"Thanks, Henry. I'll notify Dr. Gilman. Remember, not a word about this to anyone else."

Susie returned on Thursday evening and on Friday morning, she brought her mother home from the hospital.

—※—

Gertrude was pleased that she was able to provide some comfort to Betsy Matthews, whom she had never met, by bringing her home from the hospital in the care of her daughter, but the turn of events troubled her greatly.

She traced her interest in medical ethics to her father, also a physician. Before she was born in 1947, he had served in the U.S. Army Medical Corps in Europe. Fluent in German, he was liaison to the British forces that had liberated the Bergen-Belsen concentration camp in April 1945. Only a flicker distinguished the emaciated bodies of the living from the stacks of corpses that were swept into mass graves. Gertrude's father never spoke about his experience until one day when she was in the sixth grade and brought home *The Diary of Anne Frank*. "They say Anne died of typhus in a concentration camp in March 1945, less than two months before the Germans surrendered," Gertrude announced at dinner.

Her father put down his fork. "At Bergen-Belsen," he said quietly. He told them what he had found at the camp, and about the trial after the war at which some of the horrific experiments Nazi doctors had conducted on the prisoners were revealed. "Before the Nazis," he concluded, "German science stood at the pinnacle of civilization."

Gertrude excelled in science and, with her parents' encouragement, applied and was accepted to Bates-Bronsted Medical School where the vast majority of students were male and white. Her outstanding record, not her looks, earned her an internship at University Hospital affiliated with Bates-Bronsted. During her internal medicine residency there, the

Tuskegee experiments, in which penicillin treatment was withheld from poor African-Americans with syphilis, were exposed. It reminded her of her father's description of Bergen-Belsen and the Nazi doctors, kindling her interest in the relatively new field of medical ethics. She took a year off to get an M.A. in bioethics at Georgetown University, returning to Bates-Bronsted to become the Executive Secretary of the Medical School's IRB. No one else was interested in the job.

Gertrude had a sinking feeling that she would be held partly responsible for Betsy Matthews' leukemia. But she could not escape her duty, notifying the FDA that a patient in the clinical trial had developed leukemia. After discussing the matter with the Dean of the medical school and Audrey, both of whom concurred, she informed the director of Public Relations. "Before FDA announces the problem, it would be in Bates-Bronsted's best interest to issue its own press release. The head of PR said he'd get to work on it.

⸺⸺

After collecting Betsy Matthews' bone marrow samples, Laura walked back to her lab, thinking about the next few days' work. In the morning, she would bring the fluorescent probe of a large segment of the memory gene to Dr. Gilman's lab. It had already been used to locate the memory gene to human chromosome fourteen. With the probe, Gilman's lab could see if Mrs. Matthews' leukemic cells contained the normal memory gene on any chromosome in addition to fourteen. The presence of the memory gene on other chromosomes would suggest but not prove that it had triggered her leukemia. Proof would come if Laura could show that the memory gene had disrupted a normally occurring proto-oncogene, converting it to a malignant oncogene—then the case would be very strong. To learn if this had occurred Laura needed probes that were complementary to known oncogenes. She would get some normal marrow from Dr. Gilman to use as a control.

In the lab, she set up Betsy's marrow cells from two of the three vials in tissue culture, arranging them carefully in the incubator. She refrigerated the third in case something went wrong. At her computer, she browsed the website of a DNA supplier and ordered radioactive probes of oncogenes. She was home by ten-thirty.

Late Wednesday morning Jason came to Laura's lab, gave her a gentle hug, something he had never done before, and said she looked terrific, even in a lab coat— another remark that surprised her. He thanked her for setting up Betsy's cells the previous night. "Are her cells growing?" he asked.

"I think so, but I don't want to harvest them until I'm sure I'll get a good amount of DNA. Besides, there's no point until I get the radioactive oncogene probes I've ordered. They'll arrive on Friday. I'll work the weekend and if all goes well I should have the answer on Sunday."

"Well, there's no point in my sticking around here. You've got everything under control—as usual. I've got an appointment with the architect who's designing our house."

"House?" Forgetting what Audrey had told her a couple of years earlier, she added, " I didn't know you were planning to move."

"With two kids, our 'peasant' house is too cramped. Audrey and I bought ten acres outside the city, hired an architect, and now it's under construction." He looked Laura up and down. "Do you like to swim?"

"I don't get a chance very often, but yes. I was on my high school swim team."

"We're going to build a twenty-five meter pool, big for a back yard, but there's plenty of space for a wooden deck around the pool, exotic shrubs… I bet you look terrific in a bathing suit. You're invited to come out for a swim any time."

"Thanks, but I really can't think of swimming now."

"Yeah, it's been a cold fall. I haven't decided whether we should heat it."

The radioactive oncogene probes arrived on Friday, as expected. Laura harvested Betsy Matthews' cells, extracting a plentiful amount of DNA and enzymatically clipping it into segments of different length, then doing the same with DNA from normal marrow cells for a control. Using the Southern blot technique, she laid unexposed X-ray film over each blot. By Saturday the radioactivity would make a dark band on the X-ray film wherever a segment of Betsy's, or the control's, DNA hybridized with a radioactive probe. She met Amanda downtown for dinner and then they saw *Million Dollar Baby*. It took Laura's mind off Betsy's cells.

On Saturday, she developed the X-ray plates. In the blot of Betsy's DNA, but not the control, the memory gene probe hybridized to a segment of approximately the same length as one of the oncogene hybrids.

While Laura was studying the probes, Dr. Gilman called. "Ah Laura, I thought I might get you at the lab today. Any results yet?"

"I'm just analyzing the Southern blots. I'm not sure, but it looks as if a short sequence of the memory gene has migrated with an oncogene in the leukemic cells but not the controls. Did the fluorescent memory gene probe I gave you hybridize anywhere else than chromosome fourteen?"

"Yes it did. Chromosome eight."

"Just a minute." Putting the phone down, she went to the probe catalog and checked the chromosome location of the oncogene that seemed to be attached to the memory gene probe. She picked up the phone. "Dr. Gilman. The oncogene that seems to be attached to the memory gene is on chromosome eight."

He was silent for a few moments. "Well it looks like the memory gene escaped from the brain."

"I'd like to run my experiments one more time and use Sanger sequencing to confirm that the sequence migrating with the oncogene is from the memory gene. I don't want to disturb Jason or Gus's weekend until I'm absolutely sure."

"I won't either," Gilman replied.

She started the experiments immediately and did not get home until past midnight. Sleeping late on Sunday, Laura did not get to the lab until almost noon. By five o'clock she had confirmed her earlier results. In addition, the Sanger sequencing confirmed that the memory gene sequence was inserted into the oncogene.

She called Jason. Audrey answered. "Jason's playing with the kids in the back yard. We're planning to take them trick-or-treating after an early supper."

"I have some results for Jason to look at."

"Did your experiment show—"

"Either have him call me at the lab or drive down. So long." Laura didn't think it was right to tell Audrey before Jason knew.

Fifteen minutes later Jason arrived in his sweatshirt and jeans while Laura was cleaning up after the experiments. He hugged himself and rubbed his arms. "Winter's coming early this year."

"In more ways than one," she mumbled. First, she told him that Dr. Gilman had found the memory gene hybridized to chromosome eight as well as fourteen. Then she walked over to a view box similar to the one radiologists use and flicked the switch so that the light underneath illuminated the x-ray films from the Southern blots she had clipped to the box. She pointed out the probes that were used on each blot. Instantly, he reached the same conclusion she had. "Shit! What about the Sanger sequencing?"

"The printout shows the memory gene is inserted into the oncogene." Jason was standing very close to Laura in front of the view box. He slipped his arm around her waist, pulling her closer. "What are we going to do?" he said as she struggled to extricate herself.

"*We* are going to do nothing, Jason. Please don't touch me like that again. I am a scientist and your colleague, not a sex object." Jason opened his mouth as if to protest, but said nothing. "You've got plenty to worry about without a charge of sexual harassment." She straightened her lab coat. "You've changed, Jason. I would have given a second thought to call you here if I thought you were going to respond like that." She flicked off the light of the view box.

"I'm sorry. Stress."

"Stress, sure, but hugging me, or whatever else you had in mind, is not going to reduce your stress, believe me."

Jason took a step backward and said quietly, "I'll let the IRB know tomorrow morning about your results. Good bye." He turned and left abruptly. Minutes later, Laura happened to look out the window in time to see Jason climb into his red Lamborghini and drive off.

When Jason returned home he said nothing. After supper, they all went trick-or-treating, strictly limiting the immediate consumption of the candy they had garnered. As they prepared for bed Jason told Audrey what Laura had found.

They were having breakfast Monday morning when the phone rang. "Yeah, hi." Jason listened for a few minutes. "Sounds good. When will it be out? Okay, thanks.

"That was Public Relations," he told Audrey. "They wanted to check that I was okay with the press release." He gobbled up his customary bowl of cold cereal and announced that he was going to call Gus and Gertrude Brierly to tell them what Laura had found as soon as he got to the lab. "I won't be able to take Rachel this morning."

"I understand, and I'll check in with you later."

As it turned out, Jason wasn't the one to keep Audrey informed. She dropped both kids off and drove to her office. Gertrude knocked on her door a little before noon. "The Dean has called an executive meeting for 2 P.M.," she told Audrey. "Jason will tell those who need to know what's happened. It's still hush-hush, but all hell will break loose when it becomes public. You've had experience dealing with medical errors; it would be good if you could provide some guidance."

"Do you think that's wise? Jason's my husband."

"You don't need to remind me, Audrey. You can recuse yourself after you give us your opinion. Actually, I've discussed your participation with the Chief Attorney. He thinks it's important for you to come."

"Is what happened really a medical error? Jason didn't make a mistake, did he?"

Gertrude looked at her sadly. "I don't know. A small minority on the IRB initially thought the trial was premature, that the Phase One trial was not big or long enough to conclude that the injection of a foreign gene into the brain was safe…and that Jason was a cowboy. They went along with the majority."

A cowboy riding a red Lamborghini, Audrey couldn't help thinking.

"I'm afraid that the IRB is going to be blamed."

The Dean's conference room was on the eleventh floor of the main medical school building, commanding a breathtaking view of the city, the river, and the surrounding hills. The last time Audrey had been in it the day had been rainy and blustery and the heavy mauve drapes were tightly drawn. Fluorescent fixtures hung from the ceiling, emitting a soft buzz, but most of the light this afternoon came from outside and those seated facing the splendid window saw nothing but blue. The carpet, the cushions and upholstered arms of the chairs were royal blue; the walls a paler blue, interrupted periodically with full-length portraits of illustrious past deans in full academic regalia, many with purple hoods; the oval table was a dark veneer. Jason took a chair opposite Audrey, his back to the window. She feared—correctly as it turned out—that as the afternoon progressed Jason's slouch would get the better of him—*he might sink below the surface.*

The Dean was the last to arrive. The Associate Dean for Research, the Public Relations Director for the Medical School and Hospital, the University's Chief Attorney, Gertrude Brierly, John Gilman, Jason Pearce, Gus McAllister, and Audrey Meacham were already present. Consummate politician, the Dean paused on the way to his chair at the end of the table to chat briefly with those facing the window. When he reached his chair, the room fell silent. He began by

turning to John Gilman, asking how Betsy Matthews
was doing.

"Not very well, I'm afraid. From the laboratory
data, she has acute myeloid leukemia, and we would
like to begin standard therapy. Now that the memory
gene's been implicated, we can't enroll her in trials of
promising new drugs." He paused. "Mrs. Matthews'
nutrition has not been good, and she is quite frail. I'm
not sure she can withstand repeated bouts of chemo,
or radiation and stem cell therapy, but we have to get
her in remission."

"John," the Dean continued, "I understand that
Mrs. Matthews is African-American. As you know,
the local black community has accused us of ignoring
its needs, or not putting them high on our agenda.
This case could become a *cause celebre*. Please keep
that in mind as you consider your course of action."
He turned to Gertrude. "Dr. Brierly, where do we
stand?"

Gertrude was sitting at the opposite end of the
table from the Dean. She began in such a timid voice
that the Dean had to ask her to speak up, which
prompted more discomfort. She spoke up but sometimes covered her mouth with her hand, and stam-
mered more "uh's" and "I mean's" than Audrey had
ever heard from her before. "Uh, the trial in which
Mrs. Matthews was a subject was approved, uh,
by the Medical School's IRB in accord with federal

regulations. Last Wednesday, Dr. Pearce," she glanced at Jason, "informed me that Mrs. Matthews had, uh, acute myeloid leukemia, and that she had received an injection of the memory gene into her brain. In my authority as Executive Secretary of the IRB I suspended the trial and notified the Administration. As the intervention falls under the purview of the Food and Drug Administration, I notified the FDA of the suspension. That is all I have to say."

The Dean turned to Jason. "What can you tell us, Jason?"

He began fully upright, his interlaced fingers resting motionlessly on the glossy surface. "I'm afraid, sir, that the memory gene that we injected into Betsy Matthews' brain crossed the blood-brain barrier and entered her marrow stem cells. There, it disrupted a proto-oncogene, with the resultant oncogene triggering a malignant transformation." Audrey was pleased that her husband did not beat around the bush or obfuscate by describing Laura's experiments in detail. Jason had been speaking to the table. Now he looked up, "I'm not an authority on tumorigenesis so if there are questions along those lines they are best asked of Dr. Gilman. If you like, I can summarize the experiments that Dr. Laura Mittelman, my colleague, performed that led me to what I have just stated. An experiment performed by Dr. Gilman corroborated Laura's, which he can describe."

No one had questions.

"Sir," the Chief Attorney raised his hand and the Dean recognized him. "As I'm sure you know, this case poses some ethical and legal issues that if not handled properly threaten the integrity of the Medical School and the University. Audrey Meacham," he turned to Audrey, "an attorney in our office, has experience both with commercial aspects of research and, of more immediate concern, with the management of medical errors—mistakes made by our staff. She serves as the Legal Consultant to the Hospital's Risk Reduction Committee. I've asked Audrey to advise us and then recuse herself, since her husband, Jason Pearce, is the Principal Investigator."

The Dean called on Audrey. She smiled at Jason, who had already sunk an inch from his full height above the table and then turned to the Chief Attorney with whom she was on good terms. "First, let me make a slight clarification. We are not dealing with a medical error here but with an adverse event. Some adverse events turn out to be the result of circumstances beyond the medical staff's control and, consequently, are not medical errors. Second, we are not dealing with a patient undergoing routine medical care here but with a subject in a research trial, a trial approved by our IRB. I would argue that the medico-legal concerns are similar to when patients are involved if not more stringent.

"Much as we would like to avoid publicity about adverse events, experience has taught that it is virtually impossible to do so. Sometimes it is the patient or the family that seeks outside legal advice. Sometimes it is a member of the staff who exposes the problem." Audrey turned to Gertrude. "In cases of adverse events in clinical research involving new drugs or biologics, the Food and Drug Administration must be notified, just as Dr. Brierly has done. The NIH, which funded Jason...uh, Professor Pearce in the past and Ventures Unlimited, which funds him now should also be informed. There's no requirement that these agencies keep such matters confidential." She paused for a moment. "My point is that if the Hospital or the University waits until someone else leaks the problem, we will be put on the defensive. Not only will we have to explain what happened but why, seemingly, we kept it secret."

The Dean turned to the Public Relations officer. "I believe your office has drawn up a press release?"

"Yes sir. We worked on it with Professor Pearce and Dr. Brierly."

"What do you think, Audrey? Should we release it?"

"The sooner the better," she replied.

"Before you leave," the Dean commanded, "let's see if there are any questions."

The Associate Dean for Research spoke. "Let me establish something before I pose my question to, uh,

Mrs. Pearce." He turned to Gertrude. "When subjects in the trial consented to participate were they told something could go wrong?"

"Yes, that's a standard part of our disclosure," she replied. "The form Dr. Pearce used states the risks and Betsy Matthews signed it."

"So," the Associate Dean turned to Audrey, "Betsy Matthews knowingly accepted the risk. Why, Mrs. Pearce, are we culpable if everything was done properly?"

"I'm not saying the medical/scientific staff or IRB was culpable," Audrey replied, ignoring the misapellation. "But even if there is no legal concern, there's an ethical one. I believe it will be in the Hospital's and the University's best interest to provide Betsy Matthews the best possible care at the Medical School's expense, as her leukemia would not have occurred without her participation in the clinical trial." Then she added, "And let the world know we are acting compassionately." She paused. "And now I really must—"

"I have another question before you go," the Dean said. "Ventures Unlimited has been very generous to Dr. Pearce and to the Medical School. We have a joint venture in establishing a commercial laboratory to test for mutations in the memory gene. I understand that you no longer are involved with those types of contracts but can they be broken by Ventures Unlimited?"

"The Chief Attorney is better able to give you a definitive answer on that. However, I can tell you that

Jason's, uh, Professor Pearce's contract is renewed every year, and Ventures Unlimited is under no obligation to renew it again." She noticed that Jason had sunk another inch.

The Chief Attorney spoke. "Such contracts spell out the reasons that each party can withdraw, usually after giving due warning. I will have to go back to look at this contract to be more specific. It's possible that if there is negligence, moral turpitude of the Principal Investigator, or some breach of scientific behavior, Ventures Unlimited could withdraw."

"Well, it doesn't seem that any of those possibilities operate in this case so let's issue the press release, give Betsy Matthews the best care available, and let Professor Pearce get on with his research," declared the Dean. Gus raised his hand.

"Dean, if there's going to be a press release and the papers pick it up, the other participants in the trial may worry that something will happen to them. Might I suggest that we notify all the participants and urge them to contact me or their own physician should they become sick?"

Good thinking, Gus, Audrey said to herself as she left.

Such a letter was sent, several subjects came in with various complaints, but none of them was serious or related to the trial.

On Tuesday morning, Election Day, Audrey was downstairs before Jason and the kids. She made coffee and went outside to pick up the newspaper. The article based on the press release was at the bottom of page ten.

Tuesday, November 2 2004. Bates-Bronsted Medical School announced yesterday that one of the subjects in the School's Alzheimer's Disease prevention trial has developed leukemia. The subject had received an injection of normal memory gene into her brain ten months ago. It is unclear whether the injection of the memory gene is related to the leukemia, but Dr. Jason Pearce, Professor of Molecular Genetics and director of the study, and his colleagues are attempting to make this determination as quickly as possible. Until they have an answer, the Medical School has halted the study. Dr. Gertrude Brierly, Executive Secretary of the Medical School's Institutional Review Board that approved Dr. Pearce's study said, "No new patients will be enrolled in the study until it is clear that the injection of the memory gene is in no way implicated in the subject's leukemia." The patient was diagnosed with leukemia at University Hospital last week. Her treatment will be paid for entirely by University Hospital and the Medical School. The patient has the highest regard for Dr. Pearce, the School reported, and hopes that her leukemia would not hinder his work.

Dr. Pearce said it was too early to tell whether the injection of the gene prevented the development of Alzheimer's, but the results so far were promising. Dr. Pearce's research on the 'memory' gene and Alzheimer's has been published in *Science, Nature*, and *The New England Journal of Medicine*. Bates-Bronsted Medical School and Ventures Unlimited, Ltd., a company supporting Dr. Pearce's work, plan to offer a test for the forgetful memory gene in a laboratory currently under construction. Its completion is expected in 2005.

Just as Audrey finished reading, the kids came racing down the stairs, Jason playfully growling like a lion roaring after them. "Kids, quiet down," she begged. "Go play in the living room. Your father and I need to talk for a minute." Jason looked at her quizzically, shrugged, prepared his cereal, and sat at the table. Sitting down opposite, she pushed the paper over to him, folded open to page ten. "You approved this?"

He scanned it quickly. "Yeah," he said warily, "that's what they read me on the phone yesterday."

Audrey thought that maybe she hadn't understood him with his mouth full of Cheerios. "And you let it go through?"

He nodded and took another spoonful. "Why? What's the matter with it?"

She picked up the paper and read a sentence out loud. "'It is unclear whether the injection of the memory gene was related to the leukemia.' That's a bald-faced lie, Jason, or else you were lying when you told me and the committee that Laura found the memory gene in Betsy Matthews' bone marrow."

"I guess I missed that," he said apologetically.

"And what's this nonsense that the 'results so far are promising.' It's only been a year and most of your subjects are not old enough to show signs of Alzheimer's." Audrey stood up to get the kids, "Oh Jason! You should have stayed with your mice and the projects you really wanted to do."

Jason began to seethe. He pushed his chair back and stood. "You forget, my dear——" Audrey stepped back, fearing another attack. His jaw was clenched; he was clearly trying not to raise his voice. "You forget, my dear, there was no money. My grant wasn't renewed. Do you want to continue to live in this chicken coop the rest of your life?"

Audrey lost it. "I grew up in this 'chicken coop'," she shouted, "and if it was good enough for me, it's good enough for my kids." She threw the paper on the table, knocking Jason's spoon out of the cereal bowl, spattering milk across the table and floor, and stormed out of the kitchen. Trying to get as far away from him as she could, she pulled on a windbreaker, and shouted, "I'm going to vote," slamming the door behind her.

Jason retrieved his spoon, read the paper as he finished his cereal and drank his coffee. He went into the living room, calling to Hannah upstairs that he was leaving, and hugged Rachel and David. "Goodbye kids. Daddy loves you. See you this afternoon." Grabbing his jacket and briefcase, he drove down the street in his Lamborghini, passing Audrey on her way to the voting place. Neither waved.

When Audrey returned home, she called Gertrude. "Have you seen the report in this morning's paper about the clinical trial?"

"I read it while I was waiting in line to vote."

Audrey expected Gertrude to say more, but when she didn't Audrey exclaimed, "It's out of date, Gertrude."

"Yes, I suppose it is. Public relations checked it out with me last Friday. When did they check with Jason?"

"Yesterday, Monday morning. They called when he was still at home."

"Then Jason must not have known the memory gene was implicated when he spoke to them."

Then it dawned on Audrey that only three people knew that Jason had learned the results on Sunday:

Herself, Laura, and Jason. And she decided not to relay that to Gertrude.

Still angry, she said to Gertrude, "But after the Dean's meeting yesterday afternoon, Public Relations knew. Why didn't they rewrite the press release, or if they had already distributed it, why didn't they issue a correction?"

Gertrude did not answer right away. Finally she said rather obliquely. "Look, Audrey, the important thing is that we suspended the trial. The press release made that clear. I'm sure the PR department will issue a new release soon."

Had Jason deliberately withheld the news that the memory gene was implicated when PR called on Monday morning? If so, Audrey thought, *what did he think he would accomplish? Or was he just not paying attention when the woman from PR read the release back to him? Or did he not realize the seriousness of Laura's discovery?* She didn't know what to believe.

Chapter 11

INVESTIGATIVE JOURNALISM

Entering the newsroom at the *Chicago Sun-Herald* on Election Day, Janice was stopped by her editor who paged back on his computer screen to the press release from Bates-Bronsted Medical School and printed it for her. She took it to her desk, read it twice, and returned to him. "I'd like to follow this up, but to do the job right I'm going to have to visit Bates-Bronsted."

Twirling a pencil between his fingers, her editor leaned back in his swivel chair, studying her. "Do you think this woman's leukemia came from injection of the memory gene?"

"I don't know but if it did, there's a page one story, and we could be there first."

Her editor, whom she had genuinely impressed despite her youth, gazed at her paternally. "Do you think you can have something for next Sunday's paper?"

"It depends on when they find whether the memory gene is implicated. It shouldn't take long. I'll bet the FDA is breathing down their necks."

He put the pencil down and leaned forward. "Okay, Janice. We'll pay for your flight—economy class—and our usual per diem for three days. I'll need a story by Friday night at the latest." Usually quiet and staid, Janice blew him a kiss.

She reserved tickets on the 6 A.M. flight Wednesday and the return to Chicago on the seven P.M. flight on Friday, and booked a room for two nights at the Holiday Inn near the University.

The rest of Tuesday she spent updating her knowledge of Alzheimer's, making sure she had not missed any publications by Jason Pearce, and plotting a strategy for her visit. Janice's first sortie would be to identify and interview the research subject who had developed leukemia. She thought about calling the Public Relations office at Bates-Bronsted to indicate her interest and obtain the name of the woman, but decided her chance of gaining cooperation would be better if she appeared in person. Even if refused access, she could still interview Pearce, whom she had spoken to by phone for one of her previous stories.

Returning to her apartment about 6 P.M., Janice put a frozen dinner in the microwave and ate in her tiny living room, watching the early election returns. Her journalist friends who covered stories in exotic places had warned her not to check bags; it wasted valuable time and sent you up the creek if your bag was lost. So she threw a wrinkle-resistant blouse and skirt plus a few other items into her rollerboard together with her laptop, by far the heaviest item. She went to sleep just as it looked like Bush would beat Kerry.

The cold hit her as she walked through the airport doors on the way to the taxi stand. She was glad she had brought her winter coat, though the weather was not as blustery as Chicago. The Ethiopian cab driver told her that this time around Bush had gotten a majority of the popular vote and the Republicans had made inroads in the state. When she asked, he said that he had not heard of the woman participating in the clinical trial at Bates-Bronsted who had developed leukemia.

He dropped her off in front of the main medical school building where she went first to the Public Relations office, customary for visiting journalists, to tell them she was covering the story for the *Sun-Herald*, and to request the patient's name in order to interview her. Primed to deal with such requests, the receptionist told Janice she'd have to discuss it with the PR Director. He in turn would have to consult with the Dean, and if the Dean said it was okay, then the PR office would call the patient to make sure she agreed to be interviewed. "Our Director's not in yet so why don't you go down to the cafeteria, get yourself a coffee and a doughnut, or whatever, and come back in half an hour? You can leave your rollerboard here." As she hadn't had breakfast, Janice took the receptionist's advice. When she returned, the Director had arrived and had five minutes before going off to his first appointment. He studied Janice's press pass and glanced at her. "Is this your first assignment?" he asked, assuming Janice was younger than she was.

"No. I've been covering science and health for the *Sun-Herald* for three years and interviewed Professor Pearce by phone a while ago. I have a special interest in Alzheimer's Disease. My grandmother suffers from it," she told him, peering into his eyes intently.

"I'm sorry to hear that." The Director spun his chair so he could buzz his secretary. "Get me the Dean, will you?" Hanging up, he said apologetically, "I'm sorry Ms. Polk, the patient is quite ill and her doctors advise that visitors should be restricted to friends and family. I'm sure you understand that if we allow one journalist to visit, we'd have to allow others. Bates-Bronsted appreciates your interest in our research and we would like to cooperate. My Secretary, Evelyn, can help you with interviews with Professor Pearce or anyone else on our staff. Now, if you'll excuse me I've got to meet with the head of Cardiology." He stood and ushered Janice out, telling Evelyn to give her all the help she needed.

"*Except seeing the patient.*" Janice said to herself.

Evelyn smiled pleasantly. "What can I do for you?"

"I'd like to see Professor Pearce."

Evelyn looked up his phone number and rang him. "Is Professor Pearce available?" Putting her hand over the mouthpiece, Evelyn reported, "He's not available today, but he can see you at nine tomorrow morning."

"That's good," Janice said, somewhat disappointed. Evelyn confirmed the appointment, hung up, and wrote out his room number in the Genetics Building.

"Anyone else you'd like to see?"

"How about Dr. Gertrude Brierly?" Hers was the only other name in the press release. Evelyn looked in the University address book. She's two floors down, room 804."

"Don't bother to call her, I'll find her." She took the elevator and walked to room 804. A tall woman with an ordinary face greeted her.

"I'm looking for Gertrude Brierly," Janice told her.

"That's me." Gertrude smiled and Janice explained who she was and why she was there.

"You should be talking to Professor Pearce, not me."

"I'll be speaking with him tomorrow, but I thought you might give me some background—explain the role of the Institutional Review Board."

Gertrude invited her into her inner office and gave her a detailed description of the IRB's involvement. "Considering that the Phase I trial did not show any harmful effect in the twenty patients followed for at least one year, we did not expect that leukemia resulting from the injection would occur in the clinical trial."

"Is the subject's leukemia related to the memory gene?"

Gertrude realized she was about to lie. "I don't know, Ms. uh—"

"Polk, Janice Polk."

And to temper the lie, Gertrude added, "Nothing is impossible, although leukemia is not that rare in the patient's age group."

"There's one other item in the press release that interested me, Dr. Brierly, the role of Ventures Unlimited. Do you know whether any part of Professor Pearce's salary comes from Ventures Unlimited?"

"I do not know, although..." Her voice trailed off.

"'Although?'"

"Oh nothing. You'd have to ask Professor Pearce or his wife, Audrey Meacham, legal counsel to the

Medical School." The involvement of Jason's wife was news to Janice. "She's just down the hall," Gertrude continued, getting up and pointing the way to the Legal Counsel's suite.

Audrey was just coming out of her office as Janice was telling the secretary she wanted to see her. "I'm Audrey Meacham. What can I do for you?" She was an attractive woman—auburn hair, slim, well proportioned, dressed simply but stylishly—but she winced when Janice stated her purpose. "Have you spoken to Professor Pearce?"

"I have an appointment to see him tomorrow."

"He can answer your questions about Ventures Unlimited better than I can. If you'll excuse me, I have an appointment. *People here have a lot of appointments*, Janice said to herself.

Janice went back to the tenth floor to retrieve her luggage. Evelyn gave her a map of the campus and instructions on how to get to Genetics and to the Holiday Inn. Pulling her roller board behind, she walked to the inn, formulating a plan as she went. The registration clerk said her room was not ready, but she was able to check her luggage. In the public restroom off the lobby she put on lipstick and combed her hair; she wanted to look as mature as possible.

The map Evelyn had given her showed the location of University Hospital and Clinics adjacent to the campus. Walking to the clinic building, she joined the short line in front of a uniformed guard just past the information desk. When she came to the front of the line, the guard asked if she had an appointment. "I'm going to the Oncology Clinic," she answered honestly. The guard handed her a visitor's pass, which she slapped on the front of her coat. She checked the wall directory and took the elevator to the floor on which the hematology-oncology clinic was located. "Good morning," she said pleasantly to the receptionist, quickly adding, "My that's a lovely pendant you're wearing."

"A gift from my son," the receptionist beamed, touching the pendant.

"He's got excellent taste. I wish a man would give me one like it."

"He's twenty-four," the receptionist confided. "Confidentially, I think his girl friend helped him pick it."

Janice showed surprise. "You're not old enough to have a twenty-four year old son."

"He's my baby," she continued. Lifting a framed photograph off her desk, she turned it so Janice could see. "Here's the baby." She pointed out a grown man, "and here's his older sister. She works in the hospital, too."

"A lovely family," Janice observed. She leaned over the chest-high barrier that separated her from the receptionist, reading the name on her ID badge. "Mrs. Johnson, I'll tell you why I'm here," she said *sotto voce*.

"Don't you have an appointment?"

"Not exactly. I read in the paper yesterday about the woman with leukemia."

"Oh yes, I saw that, Betsy Matthews—oops, I shouldn't have mentioned her name."

"I've forgotten it already," Janice lied. "I'll tell you why I came. My brother died of leukemia last year and I read a lot about it. I want to do something to help its victims, you know, donating bone marrow, or something like that."

"Then you'll want to speak to Dr. Gilman. He's her doctor." She opened a large appointment book. "He's not scheduled to be here until next week, Monday afternoon. Shall I make an appointment?"

"Does he have a lab?"

She nodded. "That's where he spends most of his time."

"Well thanks very much, Mrs. Johnson, I'll come back if I can't catch up with him."

In the lobby, Janice located a phone book. As luck would have it, only one Betsy Matthews was listed. She jotted down her address and phone number. Outside, she hailed a cab and gave the driver Betsy's address. "That's an old part of town," he told her. "Used to be posh. The University's been moving out from its hub, buying property and talking about collaborating with the City to build a research park. Folks who could afford to move out have already left. The rest

just hang in there, hoping the plan won't materialize." The driver, obviously well-educated, told Janice
that a few grocery stores had closed, the buses didn't
run as often as they used to, and the houses were less
well kept than in the past. "My family and I were
lucky enough to get out a few years ago, thanks to old
Lizzie here." He patted the steering wheel. Glancing
at Janice in the rear view mirror, he said, "Might not
be too safe here for an attractive, nicely dressed young
woman."

He parked in front of a small, one-story frame
house with paint peeling around the window frames,
wooden steps slightly off kilter, the small rectangular
front yard overgrown with dying weeds. Janice paid
and the driver jotted the fare on the back of a card.
"Here's my company's card—the receipt. If you need
a ride back, give me a call."

A young African-American woman answered the
door; Janice assumed she was a caretaker. "Hi," Janice
said brightly, "I'm Janice Polk, reporter for the *Chicago
Sun-Herald.* I'm looking for Betsy Matthews."

"That's my mother." She stood implacably in the
doorway. "What do you want?"

"I understand your mother is a subject in a clinical trial being conducted at Bates-Bronsted Medical
School.

"Who told you?" she asked suspiciously without
moving.

Janice desperately wanted to establish a friendship with the woman. The best tack was to be honest. "The Medical School wouldn't give me your mother's name, so I went to the University Clinics where a receptionist inadvertently mentioned it." Continuing on her full disclosure approach, Janice said she knew that Betsy had leukemia and that the leukemia might have occurred because of the injection of the memory gene. "What we——"——she intentionally used the plural——"need to find out is whether the trial was properly conducted, whether there was any negligence."

The woman seemed to relent. She stuck out her hand. "I'm Susie Matthews. Let me see if mom will talk with you." Susie entered the house closing the door behind her, returning in a few moments to invite Janice in.

The front door opened directly into the living room. After the bright autumn sunlight, the room was dark and it took a few moments before Janice saw an older woman sitting on a brown velour sofa, its arms and cushions shiny from decades of wear, threadbare in spots. A brown shag throw rug, beginning to fall apart, covered the floor in front of the sofa.

"Terrible day," Susie said as she helped Janice with her coat. Her mother was looking at an old small television perched on a table opposite the sofa. "Another four Bush years," Susie said. "I don't know if we can take it." She introduced Janice to her mother, who started to get up with the help of a cane that hung on the arm of the sofa.

"Please don't get up, Mrs. Matthews. I'm sorry you're not well." She was very thin, with brown wrinkled skin, tight curly white hair, a slight tremor in her hands. The cardigan she wore—one button missing, some moth holes—was a size too big.

"I'm feeling a lot better than last week. They've transfused me with two quarts of blood—".

"Two pints, mom. Not quarts."

"Well okay," her mother replied. "I have leukemia, you know."

"Yes, I know. That's why I came to visit you. The newspaper said you had received an injection into your brain ten months ago and that the scientists thought your leukemia might be related to the injection."

"Can I get you some tea, Ms. Polk?" Susie interrupted. "It's a bit chilly in here."

"That would be lovely. Please, call me Janice." Susie motioned for her to sit on the sofa next to her mother while she went to prepare the tea.

"I spoke to Dr. McAllister last week," Betsy continued. "He helps Professor Pearce with the project, you know. And I met the young lady who took my bone marrow to see if the memory gene was in it. Dr. Pearce and Dr. McAllister are such lovely men, trying to find ways to prevent Alzheimer's Disease. I know it will be a setback if they find the memory gene in my bone marrow." The talking took her breath away and she had to pause. "Dr. McAllister said he or Professor Pearce would call me when they had an answer. So far I haven't heard anything. They say 'no news is good news,' don't they?"

"I hope that's the case." Janice took Betsy's frail hand for a moment before continuing. "If you don't mind, Mrs. Matthews, can you tell me how you learned about the Alzheimer study and why you decided to participate?"

Betsy proceeded to tell Janice about her older sister, Martha. "I finally got her to a clinic at City Hospital and they told me she had Alzheimer's and should be put in a special facility. That's where she is now. She can't dress or bathe herself. She doesn't even recognize me, her own sister."

Susie returned. "Why don't we go into the kitchen? It's warmer there and mama complains of being cold." She helped Betsy stand, putting her arm around her as she guided her mother into the kitchen. They sat in plain wooden chairs around a white enameled table, the bluish undercoat showing at the edges. Susie had put out a plate of crackers spread with raspberry jam. She poured the tea into three mismatched cups, their glaze worn off in some places. A chipped sugar bowl finished the table setting.

Betsy sipped her tea. Susie offered her a cracker, which she refused. "I don't have an appetite, you know." After another sip she said, "So you want to know how I learned about the study."

This lady does not have Alzheimer's, Janice thought.

"I got a letter from the Neurology Clinic. It had been sent, the letter said, because I had a close relative—it didn't mention Martha by name—who had been diagnosed at City Hospital. The letter went on to say that doctors at the Medical School had discovered a gene that might prevent Alzheimer's if it was injected into young relatives of patients with the disease before they showed any symptoms." She paused to catch her breath. "So I went over to the Medical School to learn more about it. That's when I met Professor Pearce and Dr. McAllister. If there was any way I could avoid what happened to Martha, I'd grab it, even if there were risks." She sipped her tea. "When I got home I wrote Susie about the meeting." She took Susie's hand and smiled. "I don't think you were too happy about my participating, but you said it was my choice."

"Did Professor Pearce speak to you individually, Mrs. Matthews?"

"Please call me Betsy. Not at first. I was invited to a meeting, let's see, it was in April last year. There must have been a hundred people there—the room was packed—all of us had relatives with Alzheimer's, some had died, others were still alive. Dr. McAllister introduced Professor Pearce and I remember his first words: 'I'm not here to promise you anything.'"

"So it didn't sound like a sales pitch?" Susie asked.

"No. He told us what he had discovered in mice, what it might mean for Alzheimer's, how he proposed to find out, and what the risks were. He kept emphasizing that he wanted to make sure we understood before we decided to participate, and that when they started to recruit, participation would be entirely our individual choice."

"What had he discovered?"

"He told us about the mice who couldn't remember how to run a maze to get a piece of cheese. I remember him saying, 'Now, that's a far cry from memory loss in people with Alzheimer's.' That got a lot of laughs. 'Or is it?' he continued. 'When a person with Alzheimer's wanders a block or two from her home, she can't remember how to get back even though she's done it thousands of times.' Then he told us that he had found a gene in normal mice that, when injected into the brains of mice that would become forgetful, maintained their ability to find the cheese, but to do it, the gene had to be injected before the mice were old. The 'memory gene' he called it. He also told us that he had found the memory gene in humans."

Susie laughed nervously. "There is a big difference between mice and men."

"Of course there is, Susie, but he also told us that mice who lost their memory had a defect—a mutation he called it—in the memory gene and that some patients with Alzheimer's had this same defect."

"Did he say that this defect was sometimes present in older people who didn't have Alzheimer's?" Janice asked.

"Yes he did, but he said that when a mutation in another gene, apo-e—" she hesitated.

"Apo-e4?"

"That's it, apo-e4. When apo-e4 and the forgetful memory gene were present together, Pearce said the chance of Alzheimer's was about eighty percent." She paused, took another sip of tea and closed her eyes briefly. "When his lab tested us, Martha had two copies of the apo-e4 gene, and I had one. We both had a single copy of the memory gene mutation. That made me eligible for the study."

"What did Dr. Pearce say about the risks?" Janice asked.

Betsy laughed. "The biggest risk was that injection of the memory gene wouldn't prevent Alzheimer's Disease. That's why he needed a control group who wouldn't get the memory gene injected into their brains. That made a lot of us unhappy. But participating in his trial was the only chance—fifty-fifty—of getting the memory gene."

Susie found more crackers and spread them with jam—Janice's lunch. "Mom and I exchanged letters about her participation."

"And Professor Pearce told us," Betsy added, "that the study wouldn't cost us anything, that we'd be paid for time spent traveling and missing work."

"I wasn't happy about mom's participating. I even discussed it with a political science professor at Wisconsin. He gave me the name of a friend of his in the political science department at the University here who's been studying IRBs." Susie left to find the scrap of paper, returning shortly. "Richard Piper. I should give him a call."

"Did Professor Pearce mention any other risks?" Janice asked.

Mrs. Matthews looked at her blankly. "You mean like leukemia?" she said after a few moments.

"Well, not that specific, but that things could go wrong."

"He mentioned that poor boy Jesse uh,—"

"Gelsinger?" Janice asked.

"Yes, that was his name. He died after getting a gene injected into his blood. But that was because they put the gene in a virus and the virus killed him. Professor Pearce said he wasn't going to use a virus, so not to worry." She thought for a moment. "Maybe he mentioned other risks. I don't remember." She surprised Janice by laughing at that point, repeating,

"'I don't remember.' Maybe that's an early sign of Alzheimer's."

"Oh, I don't think so, Betsy. You've remembered so much, you've given me more information than I could have hoped for."

Janice had finished two cups of tea and too many crackers, and Betsy was looking peaked. She decided not to ask how Betsy might feel if the memory gene was found to play a role in her leukemia; she'd wait and ask after its role, if any, was established. Turning to Susie, Janice handed her the taxi driver's card and asked her to call him. While Susie called, Janice casually asked her mother, "Do you know what happened to the mice, Betsy? The ones that got the memory gene injected into their brains."

"Oh, they remembered how to run the maze to get the cheese."

"But what happened after that? Did they get sick? Did they live to their usual age?'"

The question surprised Betsy. "I don't know," she replied. She thought for a moment. "No, that's not right. He told us that the control mice that weren't injected with the normal memory gene developed changes in their brains just like patients who died with Alzheimer's, but the mice who got the memory gene had normal brains."

"Did he sac—uh, kill the mice to find out or did he wait for them to die?"

"I don't know that he told us that." She thought for a moment. "You don't suppose the mice got sick, like me?"

Janice stood. "It's unlikely, Betsy, but I'll try to find out."

Susie returned. "The cab is on the way."

Janice took both their hands. "Thank you so much for letting me speak with you. If I have more questions I hope it will be all right to get in touch."

"Of course," Susie said.

The cab came within five minutes, just after four thirty, returning Janice to the Medical School where she went once again to the Public Relations office. Evelyn recognized her and asked pleasantly, "Who would you like to see next?"

"No one, but do you know if I need a guest pass to use the Medical School library? I'd like to search PubMed and possibly retrieve some articles."

Evelyn called one of the librarians, repeated Janice's query, gave the librarian her name, and announced smilingly, "It's all set up."

Not having expected that Betsy Matthews would be African-American, Janice wanted to find out what was known about Alzheimer's Disease in blacks. At the library, she searched the PubMed database on "Alzheimer's Disease AND African-Americans" and found two articles in the February 2003 issue of *Archives of Neurology*. The incidence of Alzheimer's among African-Americans was slightly higher than among non-Hispanic whites. Surprisingly, a single copy of the apo-e4 allele was not a risk factor for the disease in African-Americans as it was in whites. One of the papers said the risk of Alzheimer's in African-Americans with two e4 alleles was as high as in whites despite the fact that a single copy did not increase the risk. She paid to photocopy the two articles.

Janice left the library at seven o'clock, famished. She got her room card and ordered supper from room service. She showered, changed into pajamas and when her meal arrived, prepared to eat and enter notes from the day's interviews into her laptop, as well as what she had learned about Alzheimer's in African-Americans. The desk was too high for her to type comfortably until she stacked pillows from the bed on the chair for elevation. She finished her dinner and her notes, planned her interview with Jason Pearce, brushed her teeth, and was asleep by ten thirty.

—∞—

Janice arrived at Professor Pearce's office at five to nine on Thursday morning, taking a seat on a hard metal chair while she waited. Pearce's secretary offered her a cup of tea, which she drank gazing out a window. A red Lamborghini approached and parked alongside the Genetics building. Briefcase in hand, a young man strode out and walked to the front of the building. "Wow," Janice remarked. "I didn't know faculty could afford Lamborghinis."

"That's Professor Pearce's," the secretary replied. "It's the only one on campus."

A few minutes later, Pearce walked in, taking no notice of Janice. "Professor Pearce," the secretary said, "Ms. Polk has a nine o'clock appointment with you."

He turned to her. "Oh yes. The reporter." He flashed a gracious smile and ushered her in. "What can I do for you?" he asked as he stood behind his desk, rifling the morning's mail. Still standing, Janice waited until he finished before answering. His office was plain—bare walls except for photographs on the wall of his wife and two happy-looking children, a girl and a boy.

"I'm here to discuss your gene therapy trial." He looked pleased and asked her to take the chair alongside his desk. "Specifically, about one of the subjects developing leukemia."

His expression darkened. "Oh, that story," he said as he sat down. Resting his arms on the desk, leaning forward slightly, he took note of Janice for the first time.

"Have we met before, Ms.—"

"Polk. Janice Polk."

"Your name is familiar, but I'm sure we haven't met. I remember pretty faces." His eyes trailed down her body. *He would like my legs,* she thought, but she was wearing slacks.

"We talked on the phone a few times in 2002. I wrote a feature story about Alzheimer's and your work."

"Oh yes. Good story."

"Thank you. It helped get me promoted. I follow your work, Professor Pearce, and I was terribly sorry to hear about this potential setback."

"You mean the leukemia patient?"

It bothered Janice that Pearce referred to anyone so impersonally, but then she realized that Pearce might have been trying to protect Betsy's privacy. "Yes. Do you know whether the memory gene activated an oncogene in her hematopoietic stem cells?"

He widened his eyes and she returned his gaze. She had intentionally flaunted her knowledge of the jargon, hoping it would impress him and suggest, too, that she would not tolerate obfuscation. Now avoiding her eyes, he replied in a restrained voice. "That's exactly what happened, Janice." Without emotion, he proceeded to tell her how he and his colleague, Dr. Mittelman, had found that memory gene sequences had disrupted a proto-oncogene in cells they had cultured from her bone marrow.

A knot formed in the pit of her stomach as she thought about Betsy Matthews. *Pearce might as well have been speaking about a mouse as a human being.* "When did you make this discovery?" she asked.

"I reported the findings to an ad hoc committee of the Medical School on Monday," he answered evasively.

"Does the patient know?"

Pearce seemed startled by the question. "I left that up to my colleague, Dr. McAllister; he's a neurologist and is responsible for the medical aspects of our study." Janice did not tell Pearce that Betsy did not know as of 4:30 the previous afternoon.

"Professor Pearce, I'd like to go back to the mouse experiment if you don't mind?"

"Which one?"

"The one where you injected either the memory gene or a blank liquid into the brains of the mice with the mutation in the memory gene."

"Yes. We showed that those who had received the normal memory gene when they were young remembered how to run the maze as they grew older." He paused, looking directly at Janice. "Do you have a problem with our findings?"

"Not at all. It was an audacious, brilliant experiment. I just wondered what happened to the mice who had received the gene."

He let out a sigh of relief and laughed gently. "Well, most of them were sacrificed so we could study their brains and compare them to the controls. The mice who received the memory gene did not have the accumulation of amyloid and neurofibrillary tangles—characteristics of Alzheimer brains—that the brains of controls showed."

"Yes. I read your paper describing those findings. What I wondered Professor—"

"Please, call me Jason."

"What I wondered was whether there were mice that you didn't sacrifice and, uh, what happened to them?"

He sat staring at Janice, furrowing his brow as he fathomed the question. Finally he said, "I don't know." He stood. "But we can find out. Come on, let's go."

In his outer office, one of his graduate students was waiting to see him. "Sorry, Jenny, something has come up. Maybe this afternoon." He told his secretary to cancel his appointments until after lunch. He did not put on his jacket and Janice just had a chance to grab her coat and sling it over her arm as they briskly descended two flights of stairs and strode across the campus to the main Medical School building, taking an elevator down to the subterranean animal quarters. She was surprised to see that security was tighter than in other parts of the school, with a steel door embedded in a heavy gauge steel fence that presumably stretched around the perimeter of the facility, coils of razor wire on top, a cage that contained other cages inside. It occurred to her that the fence was not to prevent animals from escaping but animal rights activists from getting in and freeing the animals.

Pearce pressed an intercom buzzer and a disembodied voice answered, "State your business."

"It's Jason Pearce, with a guest. I'd like to speak to Ollie." The door buzzed and Jason pushed it open, leading Janice down a long corridor. The facility had the characteristic smell of zoo buildings. He stopped at a door that had a name plaque on it: Oliver Katz, Director. Pearce turned the handle without bothering to knock. A chubby, middle-aged, bald man, peering over spectacles, got up from his desk. He was smiling. "Well, what a surprise. I haven't seen you in ages, Jason. What brings you to the bowels of the earth?"

Pearce turned and introduced Janice. "Ollie, This is Janice uh, —"

"Polk."

"Janice Polk. She's a reporter with the uh —"

"*Chicago Sun-Herald.*"

"Really," Ollie said. "Chicago's my home town. The *Sun-Herald* was my favorite paper. Better sports and comics sections than the *Tribune.*"

"That's for sure," she chuckled.

"We came to look at your records," Jason told him.

"Oh, and I thought you were trying to fix me up with this beautiful young woman." Janice cast her eyes down, smiling. Ollie took her hand and *sotto voce* said, "Don't worry Janice, I'm happily married." She took an instant liking to Ollie Katz. *Jolly Ollie*, she thought with an inward smile. His office had no windows; the walls were lined with glass-enclosed bookshelves that held ledger-sized books under lock and key. He turned to Jason. "What records would you like to see? They are organized by species and dates of departure, then by Investigator and experiment."

"Let's see," Pearce said, "we did the experiment in April 2001 when the mice were two months of age. We sacrificed most of them at a year of age, so the ones we kept should have lived——"

"Until fall of 2002," Ollie interjected. He scanned the bindings of the books, took a ring of keys from his desk drawer, unlocked the glass bookcase and pulled down a tome. "September to December, 2002," he read out loud. He carried the tome over to his desk where he and Jason scanned the pages. "Here we go." He ran his finger down the page, counting to eight. "Eight of your mice died, in November and December, right on schedule for this strain."

Pearce took a close look. "Control, control, exptl, control, control, exptl…. twelve in all, eight controls and four who received the memory gene." He looked anxious for the first time. "Let's look at May to August." Ollie returned the ledger and pulled out the one to its left, repeating the process. He flipped the pages until he got to July. "Here we go——" Pearce pushed him aside and examined the entries: "Exptl, exptl, exptl, exptl. Four altogether."

Peering over Pearce's shoulders, Ollie said, "Look at the COD column." Over his spectacles he explained to Janice, "Cause of death."

"Tumors, tumors, tumors, tumors…" Jason read, his voice wavering. "Four out of four. Let's look at the CODs for the ones who died later." Ollie returned to the September to December ledger. "Natural, natural, tumor, natural, natural, tumor…" All the controls and two of the experimentals died natural deaths; two of the four experimentals had tumors. Pearce sat down in Ollie's swivel chair. "Why wasn't I notified?"

Ollie looked at the notations in the May-August book. "You were. By e-mail."

"I never…" Pearce's voice trailed off. He got up. "Thanks, Ollie." Ollie and Janice exchanged smiles. She and Jason walked back hurriedly to the Genetics building, Janice almost running to keep up.

"Damn it!" Pearce exclaimed back at his office. He stood over his desktop computer. "2003 is the first year for which I've saved e-mails." He looked at Janice. "We're only allowed a gigabyte of storage and that's about how much I send and receive in a year.

"Can't you save them on your computer?" she asked.

"Do you know how to do that?"

"No, but somebody at the University must know."

"I was too busy with other things. It never occurred to me that I'd need to go back to check something."

By now it was 11:30. Pearce, who had looked handsome and dapper when he arrived two hours earlier, seemed exhausted. They resumed their seats. This time he studied Janice more deeply. "I suppose you're going to publish what we just discovered."

"Unless you can tell me otherwise, it does represent a flaw in the experiment, whether you knew about it or not, doesn't it?"

He didn't answer. For a minute, he sat silently, staring into space. "Anything else you want to know, Ms. Polk?"

Should she upset Jason Pearce further? Maybe she'd done enough damage to his psyche for one day. But Janice's investigative persona got the better of her.

"There is one question—not about the mice. Are any African-Americans enrolled in your trial?"

He seemed relieved by the abrupt switch. "Yes, eight I believe. We recruited patients partly from the Alzheimer's clinic at City Hospital, which serves the inner city population, a large percentage of which is African-American."

"Is the patient with leukemia one of them?"

Surprised, Jason stared at her for a moment before answering. "I really shouldn't say, but I'm curious why you ask. As a matter fact, yes."

"And you used the same criteria for admission to the trial regardless of race?"

"Yes, of course. They had to have both apo-e4 and memory gene mutations."

From her bag, Janice produced the two articles she had photocopied at the library and slid them across the desk. He glanced at them. "So?"

"The preponderance of evidence, Professor Pearce, is that a single copy of the apo-e4 allele does not increase the risk of Alzheimer's in African-Americans the way it does in whites." He read the abstract of one article while Janice continued. "Some studies show that African-Americans with two copies of the apo-e4 allele are at increased risk of Alzheimer's." He went to a file cabinet jutting out from the back wall of his office and pulled out a folder. Janice could not see the name on it, but would have bet it was Betsy Matthews'. "How many copies of apo-e4 did the subject have?"

He closed the folder and returned it to the cabinet. Barely above a whisper he answered "One," then in a louder voice, "Anything else, Janice?"

In planning the interview, she had wanted to conclude by asking about his support from Ventures Unlimited, Ltd. Heart thumping in her chest, pulsing up to her ears, Janice had uncovered more than she could have imagined and decided to conclude the interview. Mustering all her calm, and her charm, she smiled cordially. "Not for now, Professor Pearce. I might have some more questions later. Goodbye." She

extended her hand. He stared at it and finally shook
it limply.

Janice left the Genetics building and practically
flew across campus back to the Holiday Inn. She had
not yet succumbed to the cell phone craze that was
sweeping the country and wanted to use the phone
in her hotel room to call her editor. As she ran, slow-
ing to a brisk walk as she lost breath, she replayed the
interview with Pearce. *Did he really not know what happened to the mice that were not sacrificed? Had Ollie Katz
notified him? Does Pearce get so much e-mail that he could
have missed Katz's?* It seemed more believable that he
wouldn't know that a single apo-e4 allele was not a risk
factor for Alzheimer's Disease in African-Americans,
but his partner, Dr. McAllister should have known. (She
made a mental note to interview him.) In the mean-
time, she knew she had to go back and interview Ollie
again. She caught her breath before she called her editor, collect.

"I've got something that's front page stuff, a scoop."

"Can you be more specific?"

Janice did not want to give him details but blurted
out, "Looks like scientific misconduct."

"When can you have it?'

"I've got to pin down a few items, then I'll work
on it this afternoon. When do you need it for tomorrow's paper?"

"Today, six o'clock the latest, by e-mail. Try to
keep it under five hundred words."

"I'll do my best."

—※—

Janice ignored the rumbling of her stomach and grabbed a cab back to the main building, taking the elevator down to the animal quarters where she buzzed for admittance, hurried down the corridor to Oliver Katz's office, and knocked.

"Did you come back to seduce me?" Ollie asked with a broad smile.

"Not exactly," she joked, "but I do have something intimate to ask." He looked perplexed. "That is, if you consider your e-mail files intimate."

He was flustered. "I use e-mail strictly for business," he said, offended.

"That's what I thought. I don't suppose you have as much e-mail traffic as say, Jason Pearce?"

"Hardly ever more than ten messages a day, and I send very few."

"If you don't mind can you show me the messages you sent to Professor Pearce in July 2002?"

Ollie went to his computer. "I've got to arrange the messages by 'date sent.'" He scanned the list. "Here we are, July 2002." He showed it to Janice:

From: Oliver Katz, Director Animal Services
To: Professor Jason Pearce, Molecular Genetics
Sent: July 19, 2002, 4:33 P.M.

Professor Pearce:

This is to inform you that four of your mice expired over the last two weeks. Our records indicate that they had lost weight. Two had visible tumors and on dissection the other two showed tumors of internal organs. Two had enlarged liver and spleen, showed internal bleeding, and were anemic. We will retain their carcasses for one month and then destroy them unless you indicate otherwise.

Best wishes

Ollie

Oliver Katz, Director Animal Services

Janice stood up straight. "Did Professor Pearce reply?"

Ollie scanned his inbox from that time. "I can't find a record of his doing so."

"Were the mice destroyed?"

Katz retrieved the ledger. "August 19th. All of them." He put the ledger back. "I was just going to lunch, Ms. Polk. Would you care to join me?"

"Thank you very much, Ollie, but I'm not hungry," she lied.

Janice took the elevator back to the lobby and consulted the wall directory for the office of Dr. Gus McAllister. Rather than call, she went to his office only to learn that he was seeing patients all afternoon and would not be available until six o'clock. Impatient to get back to her room, she did not schedule an appointment.

Back in her hotel room, she ordered a tuna sandwich, a pot of tea, and a slice of apple pie. Waiting for the food, she called the Matthews'. Susie answered. "Have you heard from Dr. Pearce or Dr. McAllister yet?" Susie said no. "Please, Susie, call me if you hear anything. I'll be in my room all afternoon." Janice gave her the phone number and Susie promised she'd call.

Where to begin? Janice thought as she sat propped up on the pillows in front of her laptop. She realized that she was feeling sorry for Jason Pearce. Never had she seen a person change so rapidly in response to her questions. *Was his failure to follow the surviving mice scientific misconduct?* From his response—*taking her along to check the animal records, his consternation at not finding Katz's message, his obvious surprise in learning about the apo-e4 difference*—led Janice to believe that he was guileless. *Guileless, probably, but not guiltless; his 'crimes' were errors of omission, not commission, and not victimless. They might cost Betsy Matthews her life; other subjects in his trial might also face harm.*

Also, at several points in the interview, Janice had gotten the creepy vibe that Jason might be on the verge of seducing her; she had experienced this with other interviewees. *What if he had propositioned her?* She didn't have to think long. *If he thought he could buy her off, he would have been mistaken.* Setting aside these thoughts, Janice wrote as she ate, stretching the tea through the afternoon.

Around four thirty, Susie rang. Dr. McAllister had just called to say that they had found traces of the memory gene in her mother's bone marrow cells, suggesting it had played a role in the development of her leukemia. He had assured Susie that the staff at University Hospital and the medical school would do everything in their power to save her mother. He asked Susie to bring her mother back to University Hospital on Monday morning to start chemotherapy. Janice could tell that Susie was choking back tears as they said goodbye.

Susie's news required a modification of Janice's story. Here's what she sent to her editor:

November 4 2004. Professor Jason Pearce, director of the gene therapy trial at Bates-Bronsted Medical School to prevent Alzheimer's Disease said today that the memory gene injected into the brains of people at risk of getting Alzheimer's Disease played a role in the development of leukemia in one of his subjects. The subject, a 58-year-old African-American woman, said that Dr. Gus

McAllister, a colleague of Dr. Pearce, notified her this afternoon that the memory gene
triggered the occurrence of leukemia. She had
been admitted to University Hospital last week
but was discharged after being transfused. The
memory gene had been injected into her brain
ten months ago.

The story quickly summarized Pearce's previous work
in mice and humans before continuing.

Interviewed in his office, Professor Pearce said
that most of the mice in his study had been sacrificed in order to examine their brains, which
showed that the telltale lesions of Alzheimer's
had been prevented by injection of the memory gene. Unbeknownst to Dr. Pearce, four of
the eight surviving mice that had received the
memory gene developed tumors that shortened their life span compared to all of the control mice. The controls had received a brain
injection but without the memory gene. The
Director of Animal Services at Bates-Bronsted
Medical School, Oliver Katz, informed Pearce
by e-mail of the demise of his animals from
cancer on July 19 2002. Pearce claims to have
no record of receiving the message, having
deleted his 2002 e-mails allegedly because

he was running out of space on the Medical School's server.

In order to be eligible for the memory gene trial, subjects had to have one forgetful allele of the memory gene and one e4 allele of the apolipoprotein-e gene. In whites, the combined presence of these two gene variants increases the risk of Alzheimer's Disease to eighty percent, or eight out of ten. In African-Americans, however, a single copy of the apo-e4 gene apparently does not increase risk, according to a recent article in the journal, *Archives of Neurology*. Dr. Pearce was apparently not aware of this, and his co-investigator, Dr. Gus McAlister, a neurologist, was not available for comment. According to Professor Pearce, of the nineteen subjects enrolled in the trial, eight are African-American, including the subject with leukemia, who has only one copy of the apo-e4 gene.

Interviewed at her home, the patient with leukemia, whose name is withheld to protect her privacy, said that Professor Pearce was very honest in recruiting her and other subjects for the trial. She remembers him saying, "I'm not here to promise you anything," at his first meeting with potential subjects. The patient did not recall his saying that anything untoward had happened to the mice that had received the memory gene.

The Bates-Bronsted Medical School had halted further recruitment to the clinical trial before the relation of the memory gene to the patient's leukemia had been established.

Janice thought the story was as fair to Jason Pearce as she could make it.

—※—

After breakfast on Friday, Janice checked out of the Holiday Inn, leaving her rollerboard in the hotel's storage area. The newsstand nearby carried the Chicago papers. There it was, the lead story on page one of the *Sun-Herald*:

MEMORY GENE INJECTION IMPLICATED IN PATIENT'S LEUKEMIA; SCIENTISTS MAY HAVE BEEN NEGLIGENT

The headline, which she did not write, used a word that she had intentionally omitted; the implication of her story was clear to the headline writer.

To get a better feel for the neighborhood, Janice decided to walk to Mrs. Matthews' house. The day was unseasonably warm, and the sun shone brightly, with only a few high clouds and hardly a breeze. Within a few blocks, the neatly paved walkways surrounded by well-kept strips of grass bordered by chrysanthemums and stylish wooden trash containers every half block, gave way to unadorned sidewalks and old metal garbage cans, some overflowing, waiting to be picked up. As she approached the Matthews' house she saw African-American men clustered on street corners. Here and there, shabbily dressed children too small for school played, unattended, on the sidewalks. In twenty-five minutes, she was at the Matthews' house.

Susie answered the door. "Mama's not feeling well. She vomited the little breakfast she ate, looked like coffee grounds although she hadn't had any coffee."

"Maybe you should call Dr. McAllister," Janice suggested. "It might be too long to wait for Monday."

"I told mama I wanted to, but she told me to wait. Come into her bedroom to say hello."

Betsy looked even worse than on Wednesday. Her hands were cold and clammy.

"Let's call a taxi," Janice said gently, "and get you to University Hospital. I'll pay for it. I think you're too sick to wait until Monday,"

She clutched Janice's hand "If you say so, dear. Susie will have to help me get dressed."

The phone rang. Janice heard Susie tell the caller that her mother was about to go to the hospital. "When I have some time, I'll call you." She came in to help her mother get dressed. "That was Professor Piper, the political scientist who I called after you left yesterday. He said there was a story about mom in this morning's paper and he wants to meet us."

"Maybe you should call Dr. McAllister," Janice suggested, "to tell him you're bringing your mother to the Hospital."

Susie was able to get through to his secretary who told her where to bring Betsy.

By the time Betsy was admitted, it was two o'clock. Shortly afterward, Dr. McAllister entered her room. Janice introduced herself offering her hand.

"The reporter who wrote the story in this morning's *Sun-Herald?*"

Janice nodded.

"I don't know whether to thank you or strangle you," he said equivocally. He turned to Betsy, said some words of comfort, told her Dr. Gilman would see her shortly and then left. Janice followed him out, asking if she could have a few words with him. He looked at his watch. "Of course. Let's go to the doctors' area." McAllister was a tall husky man, considerably older than Pearce, his greying hair in need of a cut. His white coat was immaculate, his name sewn in on the breast pocket with the word "Neuro" underneath. He sank into an armchair, legs sprawling in front of him until he bent them and sat up, feet on the floor. "You've taught me something I should have known, Ms. Polk. If you're going to ask me, did I know that a single copy of the apo-e4 gene was not a risk factor for Alzheimer's in African-Americans before I read it in your story, the answer is no. Should I have known? Yes, certainly I should have known. If you're going to ask 'Why didn't I know?' I could give you several reasons but none of them justifies my ignorance when a human life is concerned."

Janice was taken aback by McAllister's forthrightness and his remorse. She smiled warmly. "You've answered the questions I would have asked, Dr. McAllister. I'm sure you're busy so I won't keep you." As they shook hands, Janice asked, "Can Betsy Matthews' leukemia be treated?"

"Dr. Gilman will see her shortly. We expected the blood transfusion would help her for a longer period. Her leukemia is—" he searched for a word.

"Fulminant?" Janice supplied it.

"Yes. Exactly. We'll have to hear what Dr. Gilman has to say."

Janice returned to Betsy's room, intending to say goodbye, then pack up and head to the airport for her seven o'clock return flight to Chicago.

Susie was just hanging up the phone. "I've arranged to meet Professor Piper at three o'clock in the hospital cafeteria for coffee. Maybe you'd like to join us?"

The word 'cafeteria' reminded Janice that she had not eaten since breakfast. "Sounds great. Actually, I'm starved. I'll head down now, get something to eat and meet you there."

Chapter 12

THE RACE QUESTION

D r. Gilman stopped by Betsy's room shortly after Janice left. Susie was sitting uneasily in a lounge chair at the foot of her mother's bed.

"I'll be frank with you, Mrs. Matthews. The kind of leukemia you have is not like any other, undoubtedly because no one else has ever had a leukemia induced by injection of a foreign gene. In addition to the presence of segments of the memory gene, your bone marrow showed other chromosome abnormalities that signal that your leukemia will be difficult to treat. Usually the benefits of transfusion last more than ten days, but you're almost as anemic now as when we first admitted you. On the bright side, though, you're younger than most patients with the type of leukemia that resembles yours, and the younger you are the better the chance of a cure." He paused, turned to Susie, who was listening intently. She nodded and Gilman continued. "Here's what I'd like to do. First, we'll transfuse you again. Then, tomorrow, we'll start chemotherapy with daunorubicin, which we'll give you intravenously. We'll keep you in the hospital for a couple of days. You might experience nausea and vomiting, but we can give you another drug to counteract that. Also, your urine will appear red for a couple of days; that's not blood but an effect of the drug. Your hair might start to fall out. It's also possible that you'll be more susceptible to infection, and it's more likely you'll get an infection that's hard to treat if we keep you in the hospital." He turned and smiled at Susie. "As long as you've got your daughter to help take care of you, I think you'll be better off at home. We'll test your blood frequently to see if the drug is working."

"Is there a less toxic alternative?" Susie asked.

"Not really. We could try lower doses, but we may be racing against time, so I'd like to start with a full blast."

"Well, mom, are you game?"

"I don't think I've got a choice."

In the cafeteria, Janice went to the grill counter and uncharacteristically ordered a cheeseburger smothered with onions, plus French fries; then she dispensed a large Coke, justifying the high calorie meal as probably the last one she would eat that day. She took her tray and found a table midway between the entrance and the windows in the rear, taking a seat facing the entrance of the almost-empty cafeteria.

As she finished her burger, a man with brown curly hair and a dark beard entered, looked around, gazed at his watch and just stood there. Janice got up, leaving her unfinished Coke on the table, emptied her tray, and walked over to him. "Excuse me, but are you Professor Piper?" He nodded. "Susie Matthews said you'd meet her here." As an afterthought, she offered her hand, "I'm Janice Polk, a reporter for the *Chicago Sun-Herald*—"

"The one who wrote the story about the mouse gene?"

"That's me."

Just then, Susie hurried into the cafeteria and spotted Janice talking.

"This is Professor Piper, Susie. He's just arrived."

"Sorry I'm late. Reverend Johnson stopped by to see mom just as Dr. Gilman was leaving. I invited him to come down here to meet the two of you when he's done talking with her."

Janice pointed to the empty table with the solitary cup of Coke. "I was just finishing my lunch." They each ordered coffee and joined Janice at her table.

"They're going to start mom on chemotherapy tomorrow," Susie began. She pried open the lid on the little plastic cup of cream and poured it into her coffee. "Dr. Gilman's not very optimistic. If the leukemia doesn't kill her, the therapy might." She wiped her eyes. "I should have insisted she not participate in the experiment."

"Were you thinking of doing that?" Richard asked.

"I thought a lot about telling mom that she shouldn't participate. But then I asked myself, what if she listens to me and then develops Alzheimer's? The risks seemed small. So I said, 'mama, you've got to decide.'" She started to cry.

"Look, Susie," Richard began tentatively, "I was at the meetings of the IRB"—he glanced at her. She nodded, indicating that she knew what he was talking about—"where the protocol was discussed very thoroughly. None of the scientists on the panel asked what happened to the mice that had received the memory gene. The mice seemed so remote—I'm not sure I can fault them on that." *Still,* Richard thought, *Jason should have followed the surviving mice.*

"What about the apo-e4?" asked Susie, who had read Janice's story. "The IRB just took Pearce's word on it?"

"Well, if a reporter," Richard smiled at Janice, "could dig out the differences between whites and blacks, I suppose somebody at Bates-Bronsted should have."

"Don't you think Pearce had an obligation to look into it more thoroughly since eight of the nineteen subjects were—" Susie stopped to wave at someone, and shortly Henry Johnson, in his clerical collar, approached holding a cup of coffee.

"Hello Henry," Richard said. Susie was surprised. "Henry sits on the IRB we've been talking about. That's how I know him."

Susie introduced Janice to Reverend Johnson.

"That was quite a bomb you dropped on Bates-Bronsted in your paper this morning." Reverend Johnson smiled as he said this. Janice took it as a compliment.

Richard jumped in. "Yes, it certainly was. You may have brought the University to its knees."

"That wasn't my intention. I was just doing my job."

"What was in that package you just brought mom, Reverend Johnson?"

"A cake the church ladies baked for her. On the icing they wrote, 'Get Well Soon, Betsy.' I hope it will raise her spirits."

"With that personal touch, maybe she'll eat it, but she doesn't have much of an appetite. Thank you very much, Reverend." Susie sipped her coffee. "Last year, did you speak to mom about joining the clinical trial?"

"Yes, I did."

"Did you advise her to participate?" Susie asked.

Reverend Jackson laughed. "I only give spiritual advice. I left it up to her, and she was certainly well informed." Henry turned to Richard. "We thought we had covered all the bases, didn't we Richard? Did the IRB drop the ball?"

"The system's imperfect, Henry, but as Susie was just asking, did Jason Pearce have an obligation to look more closely since eight of his subjects are African- American?"

"Pearce is not an M.D.," Henry said. His Co-PI, Dr. McAllister is a neurologist; he should have known."

"I spoke to Dr. McAllister a few hours ago," Janice interjected. "He admits he should have known."

"The doctors don't really know much about us, do they?" Susie asked rhetorically. "As long as we're there for them to practice on."

"That's an overstatement, Susie," Henry said. "But if we're going to be disproportionately drawn into experiments, it is incumbent on the Medical School, if not the doctors, to make sure that we are not exposed to extra harm."

"How would they do that?" Richard asked.

"I've thought about that since I read your story this morning," he smiled at Janice. "The proportions of African-American medical students and medical school faculty have to be increased."

Susie pulled out a pocket calculator from her handbag. "Forty-two percent of the patients in the trial are black," she reported.

"And a third of the city's population is black," Henry remarked. "Nowhere near that percentage of medical students or faculty is black."

"I can find out the exact percentages," Richard offered.

For a moment, Reverend Johnson was pensive. Then he grew animated. "Betsy's misfortune might accomplish something I've tried to do for a long time, without success: end discrimination at Bates-Bronsted. Johnson pulled out his appointment book. "Let's see. Today is Friday November 5th." He paged ahead. "November 14th. Rich, if you can get those percentages to me next week, I can preach a sermon to rouse the community on Sunday November 14th."

"I'll do my best," Rich replied. No one spoke for a moment, then Rich said, "What's the step after the sermon?"

"I'll ask to meet with the President of the University," Reverend Johnson said firmly.

"And if he doesn't budge, then a demonstration," Susie added.

Reverend Johnson turned to her. "Candlelight vigils would be more appropriate.

We can keep them up until the President responds."

Janice glanced at her watch. "I'm afraid I've got to excuse myself. I've got a seven o'clock flight back to Chicago."

"And I should be getting back to mom," Susie said.

"Can I give you a lift to the airport?" Richard asked Janice.

"I'm sure you've got better things to do with your time."

"Well, I am approaching a deadline, but another hour out of my day is not going to hurt."

"I have to pick up my rollerboard from the Holiday Inn."

"No problem. It's on the way." The four of them shook hands in the hospital lobby, then Janice and Richard went to his car. As they approached it, Rich apologized. "I hope you don't have a lot of luggage." The car was a two-seat Mazda Miata, faded red. "I bought it second-hand when I took the job here. The nice thing is it fits into small parking spots. I'd put the top down but it would be a little chilly." Janice was relieved the top would stay up. He waited in front of the Inn as she retrieved her luggage. Richard popped the trunk; the rollerboard fit in easily.

"What's the deadline you're working toward?" Janice asked.

"A book on IRBs. I'd like to see it published by the spring so I can use it when I come up for promotion. Right now, I'm finishing a case study of what happened to Betsy Matthews to include as an appendix."

"How'd you get interested in IRBs?"

"I took a course in bioethics, learned about the Tuskegee syphilis experiments, forced feeding of hepatitis virus to retarded children, and experiments on prisoners and soldiers without their consent. That's what led me to become interested in the role of government in protecting human subjects in research."

"Sounds fascinating."

"The first regulations were issued in 1967," he continued, "but they weren't enforced until a whistle-blower revealed what was happening at Tuskegee. It took until 1979 to provide stringent operating procedures for IRBs."

"Your interest doesn't sound like that of most political scientists."

Richard thought for a while; he was turning onto the interstate and merging into high-speed traffic. "I probably have my parents to thank for that."

Janice looked at him, puzzled. He had a handsome profile—straight nose, bushy beard, and ruffled curly brown hair.

"I was conceived in Mississippi during Freedom Summer, 1964. My parents, both physicians, volunteered with the Medical Committee for Human Rights to provide medical care to students who came down to help register black residents to vote, as well as to black residents.

"I marched alongside my parents in anti-Vietnam war demonstrations when I was three, passed out leaflets for George McGovern when I was seven, and only when the boycott ended was I allowed to eat grapes." Extending his right arm behind the stick shift, he put his hand on Janice's knee, his left staying firmly on the wheel. She stared at his hand, surprised. "You know, Janice, I sometimes wonder if my parents hadn't been progressive, would I have been? Would society's emphasis on sports, stardom, and sex been too much of a distraction." Returning both hands to the wheel, he turned off at the airport exit ramp, noticing that Janice was gazing at him intently. "Did you get assigned this story or did you pursue it on your own?" he asked. "It doesn't sound very sexy."

"My grandmother has Alzheimer's, so I've had a longstanding interest, sexy or not."

Richard double-parked in front of Departures, climbed out, and retrieved her rollerboard from the trunk. He wheeled it to the curb where she was standing, searching for the airline ticket in her purse. "Thanks so much for driving me here and telling me about your work and background." They stared at each other for a few seconds and then hugged. After security, on her way to the gate, she thought, *Richard is a very tactile person. And maybe I am too.*

Chapter 13

NADIR

Jason left early on Friday November 5th to meet with the contractor and architect at the new house. With the frame completed, siding going up, and roof installed, much of the work had moved inside. Audrey had a hairstylist's appointment at ten so Hannah took Rachel and David to school. As Audrey was getting ready to leave, the phone rang.

"Is Jason there?" an unfamiliar male voice asked.

"I'm sorry, he's not."

"Is this Audrey?"

"Yes."

"This is Donald Sharp, Ventures Unlimited. I tried Jason's office and his secretary said he might still be home."

"No, he's not. He's off inspecting some property we bought."

There was an awkward silence. Finally, Sharp said, "I don't suppose you've seen a *Chicago Sun-Herald* this morning?"

"No."

"There's a front page story in the *Sun-Herald*. Wait a second, I'll read you the headline, 'Memory Gene Injection Implicated In Patient's Leukemia; Scientists May Have Been Negligent.'"

Only when her mother had phoned to tell Audrey her father had died suddenly had she had the same sinking, gasping feeling, the air knocked out of her. She sat on the sofa next to the phone.

"Audrey, Mrs. Pearce, are you still there?"

"I'm here," she said weakly.

"You realize this is a disaster. I've called an emergency meeting of our Board. Jason is on the Board and I thought I should notify him, but I don't want him to come. He and his work will be the subject of the meeting."

"Isn't that all the more reason to have him there?"

"I don't think so. The story seems pretty airtight: Jason was negligent. The purpose of the Board meeting is to decide how and when Ventures will terminate its support." No apology or humility tinged his voice. "Besides," he continued, "he'll have his hands full explaining his mistakes to the FDA." Audrey was silent. "I'm sorry to be the bearer of this news, Mrs. Pearce. I hope you'll pass it on to your husband. Goodbye."

She sat there with the receiver on her lap until it started to beep and she heard the familiar, "If you'd like to make a call, please hang up..." She obeyed. *What should she do? Jason was unreachable by phone. She could miss her stylist appointment and drive out to the site. No, she should get hold of the story and read it first.*

~

The stylist kept Audrey preoccupied with her chatter, first about how beautiful her hair was without any color, "really amazing." Then she asked if Audrey knew a string of so and so's and what had happened in their lives; some of them Audrey knew, some she didn't. Tipping her generously, Audrey left, wondering whether her stylist would soon be asking other customers if they knew Audrey Meacham and what had happened to her. She bought a copy of the *Sun-Herald* at an international newsstand, found a public bench near where she had parked and read the full story. Donald Sharp was not exaggerating. She could blame Sharp for leading Jason away from his basic research and down this path, a path that ended at an abyss, but Jason had walked down the path himself. *How could he escape blame? How would he handle it when he reads about his mistakes? How should she respond? Should she be like the dutiful wife who stands by her politician husband when he's caught cheating on her? Should she say, Jason darling, I warned you? No, that would do no good. And what about the stigma? Rachel was old enough to understand that her father's failure to do something had hurt another human being. Should they tell her, "Daddy made a mistake and he's very sorry about it?"*

Realizing she was hungry, Audrey went to a bistro nearby and while she waited for a table, Laura Mittelman walked in. Under the circumstances, Audrey would have preferred to eat alone, but she could not refuse Laura's invitation to share a table. As they waited to be served, Audrey handed Laura the *Sun-Herald*. "Did you know about this?" Laura shook her head and read quietly, turning pale as her eyes moved down the page, her breathing shallow and rapid. The waiter took their orders. "Oh, Audrey! I feel partly to blame."

"You? How?"

"I wondered what had happened to the mice Jason had injected that he didn't sacrifice, but I just assumed he was too good a scientist not to follow them." When the soup and salad they both had ordered arrived, they ate in silence for a few minutes.

"Jason's changed, you know, Audrey."

"Yes. I think so, but what do you mean?"

"He seems less interested in his work. Last week, when he asked me to look for the memory gene in

Mrs. Matthews' bone marrow cells, he was more interested in talking about his—yours and his—new house and how he was going to build a swimming pool, and invited me out for a swim when it was finished. And after I spoke to you on the phone last Sunday, and Jason came to the lab he——" Laura stopped abruptly.

"Go on."

Laura looked down at her plate. "He did something he never did before."

"Did he try to——"

"I'm sorry, Audrey. I chided him, told him he was in enough trouble and didn't need a sexual harassment case on his hands."

Audrey smiled wanly. "Good for you, Laura."

—∗∗∗—

Audrey gave Laura a lift back to the campus, parked, walked to the main medical school building, and took the elevator to her office, glad that she hadn't met anyone on the way. Shortly after she arrived, Gertrude Brierly came in and saw the *Sun-Herald* on Audrey's desk. "So you know," she said, taking the seat across without being asked. "The President and the Dean have called an emergency meeting today at five o'clock. Reporters are demanding to know the University's response. FDA called to say they are likely to investigate; they're just waiting to see what the University says. I passed that along to the Dean."

Audrey listened calmly, forcing her face to remain impassive.

"Where's Jason? Nobody's been able to find him," Gertrude asked.

"He went out to visit our house under construction this morning."

"Did he tell you about the interview with the *Sun-Herald* reporter yesterday?"

"He mentioned it casually when he got home from work, then went to play with the kids as if nothing was wrong." *Was Jason in denial? Did he think it would blow over, the way he thought Betsy Matthews' leukemia would blow over while we went to dinner with the President?*

"Do you think Jason's seen the story?"

"I don't know." Now Audrey was beginning to worry about where Jason was.

"He's expected to be at the 5 P.M. meeting," Gertrude said, "but I think the Administration's mood is such that the meeting will go ahead whether he's there or not. The Dean's been looking all over for him. His secretary has no clue."

"I'll try to track him down," Audrey promised.

After Gertrude left, she called home. The phone rang five times before Hannah picked up. "Is Jason there, Hannah? I need to speak with him."

"Uh, he's here but he's in the shower."

"Please have him call me as soon as he gets out. And you'll pick up Rachel and David later, right?"

"Yes of course."

In the shower? Didn't he shower this morning? *Why is he showering again? And how does Hannah know he's in the shower?*

A half hour later Jason called. Audrey had decided not to question him about how he had spent his day. "All hell's broken loose, Jason. That reporter who interviewed you yesterday—her story's on the front page of the Chicago *Sun-Herald.* I heard it first from Don Sharp. He's called a meeting of the Ventures Board and doesn't want you there. And Gertrude just told me the Dean's called a meeting for five o'clock. The situation's not good. I hope you're prepared to explain your mistakes."

"Mistakes?"

"Yes, Jason. Not following the mice who weren't sacrificed and not knowing that a single copy of the apo-e4 gene is not a risk factor in African-Americans."

Jason seemed more worried about Ventures Unlimited than about the University. "What do you think Ventures will do?"

"They can cut off your funding, if not immediately then at the end of the year, but that's less than two months away. It depends how the contract is written."

"Well, I guess I'll have to go back to NIH."

"Are you out of your mind?"

TONY HOLTZMAN

"I discovered the memory gene, didn't I? I've shown that people who have a mutant version are more likely to get Alzheimer's. Nobody in the scientific world disputes that."

"Oh, Jason!"

⁂

Jason did not go to the Dean's meeting and Audrey was not invited. When she got home from work that evening, Jason was playing happily with his kids, managing to get both of them to tell him what had happened at school that Friday; Audrey could seldom get a word out of them about school. In the kitchen, Hannah was preparing the children's supper. "Hi Audrey," she said, as if nothing had happened.

"Hello Hannah. Is everything all right?"

"Why shouldn't it be?" Clearly Hannah had not read the newspaper, and word of Jason's blunder had not yet circulated among the neighborhood nannies.

"No reason." Audrey felt stupid probing, but still she asked, "What time did Jason come home today?"

"Let me think... I had just finished straightening Davy's room. That boy can certainly make a mess. Must have been about one o'clock, not long before you called."

"Did he say where he'd been?"

"He took a hike around your property—I can't wait to see it—got his pants dirty near the stream at the far side, he said, and then climbed up the hill. He tracked mud all over the kitchen floor I had just washed. He had mud on his face too."

"I'm going to take Jason out for dinner tonight, Hannah. He doesn't know yet. He's playing with the kids and I don't want to disturb them; they're having such a good time."

Upstairs, Audrey found Jason's khaki pants, the ones he'd worn that morning, lying in front of the laundry chute, caked with mud. His face towel also was streaked with mud, and his shoes, lying on their sides, had mud around the rims. Relieved, she changed into a black sheath dress, the same one she'd worn on their first date.

Jason was on the floor with the kids, helping David assemble a wooden puzzle. He looked up. "Are you going out?"

"I thought it would be nice for us to go to that quiet French restaurant near the University. We haven't eaten out for a while. Hannah will take care of the children."

"Shall I make a reservation?"

"It's Friday. Probably a good idea." He went off to phone. Awkwardly in her tight dress, Audrey bent down to help Davy finish the puzzle.

They drove down in the Lamborghini, one of the few times Audrey had agreed to ride in it; Jason drove too fast for her comfort.

As they waited for their table, Jason asked, "This is the same restaurant where we had our first date?" She smiled appreciatively. "Probably too early for the *Nouveau Beaujolais*," he said after they had been seated. "How about a *Pinot Noir?*" He had learned something about wines in the last eight years. After he ordered the wine, he took Audrey's hands and said, "Sorry about the mess I made this morning. I had never hiked around the edge of the property before and hadn't taken a close look at the stream near the far property line. Imagine owning our own stream. Might even be some fish in it. The kids will have great fun."

"Yes, you did make quite a mess," she laughed. They sipped their wine without speaking. *It would be nice,* she thought, *to believe that after eight years of marriage Jason and I can sit quietly in a cozy restaurant, so confident in our relationship that conversation isn't necessary to enjoy each other's company.* After the waiter delivered their entrees, she began. "Jason, you're—we're—in serious trouble." He had already started to eat.

"What do you mean?" he said, speaking with his mouth full.

"Unless you can explain your error of omission— you know what I'm talking about—the University is going to desert you. And so will Ventures. And so might FDA and NIH."

"You don't believe they all will, do you?"

"You're playing a high-stakes game. Ventures is not going to risk losing investors by supporting a project in which people might be needlessly killed."

"Killed?" he said with surprise.

"Killed. If Betsy Matthews dies, people will say that you—well, your clinical trial—killed her. And the University, Jason, will not have its reputation besmirched for the sake of one faculty member who overshot the mark."

"Overshot the mark?"

"Yes, overshot the mark. Ventures was so eager to sell the memory gene that—"

"You mean the test for the memory gene?"

"The test for the memory gene, but mainly the memory gene therapy. So eager that they snookered you into the clinical trial before you knew how the memory gene exerts its effect. They seduced you, Jason, and now they will drop you."

"But the IRB approved the trial."

Audrey put her fork down, trying to swallow past the lump in her throat. "The IRB trusted you as a scientist. I can't fault you too much for the apo-e4 problem; Gus should have known about that. But not to check your mice? The IRB must have assumed you had, as any good scientist would have."

"If anything went wrong with the mice, Ollie Katz should have called me."

"You haven't read the story, have you?" Jason stared at his wife, waiting for her to continue. "The story gives the exact date that Katz e-mailed you that your mice died with cancer. Apparently, you didn't read it before deleting."

"I get a hundred e-mails a day. I can't read all of them."

"Do you at least look at who sent them?"

"I try."

"How many do you get from Katz?"

"Not many," he admitted.

Exasperated, Audrey changed direction. "I'm afraid that Gertrude Brierly is going to have to pay——" Containing herself no longer, she added, "Another one of your victims."

"FDA will exonerate me."

"What makes you think so?"

"We conducted the trial in accord with all the IRB's caveats——"

"That may be, but did you show conclusively that injection of the memory gene was safe?"

"Don't you think the IRB's partly to blame? Why didn't *they* ask what happened to the mice?"

"I told you why. Maybe they should have. But it's your study, Jason. You initiated it. You're responsible."

Jason had cleaned his plate and the waiter collected it, then looked at Audrey inquiringly. "You can take mine," she said. "It's very good, but I'm afraid I don't have much of an appetite."

"How about dessert, Audrey?"

"You can have something."

Jason turned to the waiter. "I'll take the check."

On the way home, they did not speak. On arriving, they headed straight to bed. Jason had no trouble falling asleep. Audrey read for a long time before turning out her light.

"At first I thought the horses were pulling my Lamborghini. I saw them far off down the winding driveway that leads to our new house. I was standing on the front portico. 'What's wrong with my car?' I wondered." Audrey put her arms around Jason who was shivering in his sweat-soaked pajamas. "As they drew closer, it wasn't my car at all. It was a beautiful, gilded carriage, gleaming in the noonday sun. The panels were vermillion, like my Lamborghini. The horses were a curious pair, a gleaming black stallion on the right who seemed more to be dancing—showing off—rather than pulling, and an old gray mare on the left who was doing most of the work. There was no coachman; the horses, especially the mare, seemed to know where to go. They stopped on the graveled driveway in front of our portico. I stood there admiring the coach. Over its door was the Latin saying that graces the entrance of that old building on campus, '*Ad virtutem per sapientiam.*'"

Still hugging him, she murmured, "To virtue through wisdom."

"Then, slowly, the door of the carriage opened from the inside and a man stepped down. He looked up at the house and finally at me. At first I didn't recognize him. He was wearing a dark sharkskin suit, almost threadbare. His face was pale, like the ghost he was. As soon as he spoke, I knew who it was. 'Jason Pearce, what have you done?' Professor Chapman seemed to be looking through me. I couldn't stand his stare and averted my eyes back to the coach. A curious thing was happening. The bright gilt was tarnishing; the vermillion paint on the body began to peel off. Chapman repeated his question. With that he turned around, got back into the coach and slammed the door. At that instant the black stallion stepped out of his traces and galloped off down the driveway. A terrible grinding noise came from the coach. The old mare turned around to look, struggled to pull the carriage, but got nowhere. Sweat glistened on her flanks. Slowly, the coach crumbled to the ground, the mare with it. In a few minutes nothing was left. 'Professor Chapman' I cried. That's when I felt you holding me."

As Audrey hugged him, he buried his face in her hair, sobbing. "What are we going to do?" his muffled voice asked.

Audrey stiffened. *We?* "Worst case scenario, Jason. *We*"—she emphasized the plural, putting herself in Jason's boat—"we lose everything."

Chapter 14

RICH AND AUDREY HAVE LU NCH

Richard Piper thought that Audrey could get the information Reverend Johnson wanted for his sermon. He also wondered how she was dealing with the news of Jason's apparent negligence.

"Oh, Richard, it's so nice of you to call," Audrey said when Richard phoned her "You've seen the *Sun-Herald* article. It's not been easy around here."

"I bet. How's Jason taking it?"

There was a long silence. Finally, she said, "It's a long story."

"How about lunch sometime?"

Again a long silence. "How about today?" she asked.

Richard was taken aback. "I have class from eleven to one but I could meet you after that."

"Great!" She suggested the bistro near campus. Richard decided to wait until he saw Audrey to ask about the data for Reverend Johnson.

In the long silences after Richard's questions, Audrey had been asking herself, *Do I want to confide in Richard?* Then she quickly reviewed their relationship. In a matter of seconds she made up her mind and suddenly talking to Richard assumed great urgency.

She had met Richard soon after Davey was born when she started to work at the medical school and became an ex-officio member of the IRB. A few months later, Gertrude had invited her and Jason to a small dinner party at which Reverend Johnson, his wife Anita, and Rich were the other guests. At the table Rich was at one end, Audrey sitting caddy-corner to him.

After Gertrude served the soup, Audrey turned to Richard. "If you don't mind my asking, what made you interested in studying IRBs?"

He savored a spoonful of the soup before answering. "I have a general interest in inequality; it hasn't been studied much in biomedical research."

The reverend joined in. "I'm surprised you think so. Look at Tuskegee; that's been well studied and has led to reforms in research."

"No question about that, Henry, but a lot of inequality remains. With Gertrude's permission, I've been going over the proposals and final reports submitted to the IRB on the ethnic background of the subjects enrolled in research here at the Medical School. A much larger proportion of subjects are African-American than in the general population."

"I suppose that's the reason the federal IRB directive put a community representative on the Boards." Henry paused. "You know, Richard, I am the first African-American to serve on the Board at Bates-Bronsted."

"Better late than never," Richard said cynically, putting his soupspoon down. "That's not the only aspect of inequality that interests me. There's the tremendous inequality in knowledge between the doctors doing studies and the subjects, an inequality of knowledge. Maybe *asymmetry* is a better word than *inequality*."

"Yes, that's true," Henry replied. "I often feel uncomfortable voting on whether to approve a proposal that I don't really understand."

Gathering empty bowls, Gertrude responded to the Reverend. "The IRB doesn't

expect the community representative to analyze the scientific merit of a study. That's up to
the scientists on the Board." She headed off to
the galley, followed by the Reverend who had
offered to help serve the main course. Richard
and Audrey continued the discussion, while
Jason and Anita had one of their own.

"Do you question the ability of the scientists on the Board to convey the scientific merit
to the lay members?" Audrey asked Rich.

As he responded, Richard put his hand just
above Audrey's knee; the hem of her skirt had
slipped upward and he was touching her panty
hose. He squeezed slightly and she blushed,
glancing at Jason. Busy talking to Anita, he
noticed nothing. Richard was gazing at Audrey
intently, moving his face closer to hers and lowering his voice. She noticed a tiny breadcrumb
in his beard and had an intense desire to flick it
off. *Is he flirting with me or just emphasizing the point
he wants to make?* His hand remained on her knee.

"I do, Audrey," he said. He moved his face
back an inch. "Science has become so super-
specialized that even one's supposed peers may
not understand it." He slid his hand off her
knee, and it emerged on the table.

Audrey had made no effort to move her
thigh; his grasp was not unpleasant. *I wonder*

whether he touches people when he speaks to them.
If we had been sitting in the living room and he had
done it in plain sight of everyone, I would have hardly
given it a thought, but under the table—

Gertrude and Henry returned with the
main course. Gertrude asked Audrey to serve
portions as she went to fetch a basket of bread
and a bottle of Cabernet.

At the IRB meetings after the dinner
party, Audrey often sat next to Richard.
Occasionally, he would lean toward her, touch
her arm lightly, and whisper something about
the proceedings. They often chatted briefly at
the conclusion of the board meetings. Despite
his beard, he seemed younger than Jason, his
brown hair just curling over his ears and collar,
his cheeks smooth and ruddy above his beard.

—————

"So you want to know how Jason's taking it," Audrey
began after they ordered lunch at the bistro. Audrey's
hair was slightly out of place and her eyes were red.

"And you too," Richard replied.

"I'm not sure Jason's even read the story in the
Sun-Herald."

"But Janice Polk did interview him?" Audrey nodded. "Does he deny what she wrote?"

"He maintains he was never notified that most of the mice who received the memory gene died of cancer."

"The story said the Animal Director has a record of notifying him."

"Yes, I pointed that out to him. Jason doesn't seem to realize the magnitude of the problem, Rich. He's not an M.D., you know, and the thought that someone might die as a result of something he did, or didn't do, never entered his head." Their food was served. "Yesterday," Audrey continued, "the President announced he is setting up a faculty committee to investigate the handling of the trial. Jason shrugged it off. He thinks the committee will exonerate him." She picked up her fork to start her salad, "That's not going to happen, Rich." She sipped her water, trying to calm down. "Do you know what Jason did on Friday—the day after he was interviewed by that, that uh, reporter?"

"Janice Polk?"

"Yeah. He went out to the property we bought last year, about ten acres, to talk to the architect about our new house—a mansion I'm embarrassed to say—and then tramped around the perimeter, getting his feet wet in the stream on the far side. That property's become the most important thing in his life. He doesn't realize he's going to lose it all, Rich. He's going to lose his precious Lamborghini as well."

"You mean you, uh, he, borrowed to get all that?"

Audrey nodded and bent her head down toward her plate as the tears welled up.

Richard didn't say anything for a few moments. "Did you try to bring him to his senses?"

"I did." She ate a few forkfuls before continuing. "Jason and I had dinner out Friday night. I was blunt... as much as said if Mrs. Matthews died he would have her blood on his hands. That night, he had a dream, nightmare is more like it, that Professor Chapman—you remember him?" Richard nodded; he had never met Chapman but knew he had opposed the University's securing patents for profit. "Jason dreamed that Chapman told him he was destroying the University. Jason woke up in a sweat, crying, in my arms, 'What are **we** going to do?' I don't know what more I can do, Rich." The waiter came to clear their plates. "I'd like some coffee, black," Audrey told him and then explained to Richard, "I haven't slept much lately and I need to get through the afternoon."

"I'll have coffee, too, please, with cream," Richard told the waiter.

"I didn't mean to dump on you, but there's nobody else I can talk to."

Richard was surprised that Audrey felt close enough to be able to "dump" on him. He put his hands over hers and said, "You can stand by Jason."

Audrey turned her palms up and held Richard's hands. "Jason's changed. It's money that's seduced him, not other women—although I worry about that, too," she said, thinking about what Laura had told her on Friday. "The CEO of Ventures Unlimited called on Friday, looking for Jason, but he told me in so many words his company was going to drop Jason."

"Maybe that's a good thing," Richard said quietly. "The bad thing was when Jason took their money in the first place."

"I agree. I thought he'd be immune to that sort of fiscal seduction but I was wrong." She set her cup down. "Gertrude Brierly told me yesterday that the FDA, NIH's Recombinant DNA Advisory committee," she smiled wryly, "whose acronym appropriately enough is the RAC, and the federal Office of Protection from Research Risks are likely to investigate Jason's research. Depending on the findings, he may be barred from conducting clinical trials. That's what happened to the P.I. at Penn after a death in a gene therapy experiment in 1999. NIH could suspend all research grants until the University improves its review of human research. That happened at Johns Hopkins after a subject died in a 2001 clinical trial."

"And I suppose under those circumstances the University is not going to stand by him."

Audrey picked up her cup. "It's planning its own investigation and won't lift a finger to help Jason if he's found to have been negligent. The University might face a suspension of all its grants if Jason is not exonerated."

"Can your family live on your salary?"

"Maybe, but it would be a blow to Jason's ego. We'll let our au pair go, manage with one car, but what's he going to do, cook and clean house?"

"What's the alternative?"

"He can get another job, I suppose. He's occasionally talked wistfully about teaching high school science."

Twice, Audrey asked the waiter for refills of coffee. With the third, he brought the check. As Richard reached for his wallet, Audrey said, "I'll pay. You're cheaper than a shrink."

"No, let's split it. Lunch was my idea." They each put in some cash.

Outside, Audrey thought to ask, "Did you call just to see how I was doing or did you want to talk about something else?"

"As a matter of fact, I did have a small favor to ask of you, but it might only disturb you and I can get the data some other way."

"Let me be the judge. What did you want?"

Richard told her about his meeting in the hospital cafeteria with Mrs. Matthews' daughter and Reverend Johnson, and what Henry planned to do. He added, "It might make Jason feel even worse to know that his uh, mistake, is what sparked this protest against the University."

They were walking side by side and when Audrey responded she did not face Richard but continued to walk toward the campus. "I honestly don't know, Rich. Jason and I never talk about race or discrimination—he grew up in Nebraska—or politics for that matter. I doubt he even voted last week. It's a little strange because his mother is a feisty activist. When Jason realizes the University has abandoned him, this might be a way to channel his anger. He might feel better knowing that something positive could come from his mistake." She glanced at Richard. "What exactly do you want?"

"The percentage of African-American medical students and the percentage of African-Americans on the Bates-Bronsted faculty."

"The Medical School has to file that information with the Federal government. I think I can get it for you."

They reached the turnoff to Richard's building. Audrey gave him a hug and kissed him lightly on the lips. "I'm glad we had lunch, Rich. I feel better."

⸙

Despite the three coffee refills, Audrey dozed off at the weekly meeting of University Hospital's Risk

Reduction Committee, something she'd never done before. She hoped no one had noticed. When she returned home, Jason was playing with Rachel and Davy. The kids hugged Audrey, while Jason continued to assemble Lego pieces. The kids quickly resumed playing with him. *Should she tell Jason about her lunch with Richard? Did she want to arouse jealousy?* She decided against it. Besides, Richard had given no sign of affection, other than putting his hand on hers, which Audrey took as a sign of sympathy, not desire. She knew very well that she had initiated the hug and kiss as they parted after lunch. For years, Richard's hand on her knee under the table at Gertrude's had baffled her.

Jason was not in a talkative mood at dinner. Audrey prodded the kids about their school day, but mostly they ate in silence. Afterward, Audrey proposed playing Chutes and Ladders, a game that Davey was just able to grasp and that was not too boring for Rachel. Jason said he'd rather take a walk. When the kids begged to go with him, he looked at Audrey and said, "Mommy would rather you stayed home and played with her. Besides, it's dark already; the days are getting shorter and the nights are cold."

Audrey didn't have any objection to the kids going as long as they wore their coats, but Jason gave her a stern look that seemed to say, *I did my share of playing. I want to walk by myself.*

"Come on," she said to David and Rachel, "we'll have a fun game and when Daddy gets back we'll make popcorn." The bribery worked, and the three played together, but it seemed less fun than the four of them playing. Audrey began to worry that she and Jason were competing for their children's affection.

He was still not back when they finished, but she made popcorn anyway, leaving a small bowl for him while she got the kids ready for bed and read to them, something Jason usually did. By the time they were asleep, Audrey was ready for bed. A few minutes later, she heard Jason come in and climb the stairs. "Did you have a good walk?"

"I decided to take the Lamborghini for a spin; drove out to the new property, walked around, and came back."

This news brought Audrey fully awake. "Jason, we've got to talk."

"Really? What more is there to say?"

The question deflated her. Overwhelmed by exhaustion, she sank back on the pillow and was asleep before he got into bed.

The rest of that week, Jason divided his time between the lab, going over all his notebooks, talking to Laura about her experiments, reviewing the literature on Alzheimer's, and driving out to the new property, where the builder was trying to get the windows and doors installed before winter struck. On

Thursday, a team of FDA investigators and a representative of the RAC and NIH showed up on campus with subpoenas to examine Jason's and Laura's labs, as well as the animal quarters' records. After Jason acquainted them with the layout of his lab and the locations of his notebooks and those of his fellows, they excused him until the following Tuesday when they would question him. The NIH suspended all its grants to Bates-Bronsted pending the outcome of the investigation.

The day after she had lunch with Rich, Audrey phoned him with the percentages. "I dug a little deeper and looked at trends, Rich. Admissions of blacks to Bates-Bronsted Medical School have fallen fifteen percent since 1998 and last year they comprised only five percent of the first-year class. I was surprised that the graduation rate for black medical students the last few years has been higher than for whites."

"Very interesting. What about faculty?"

"I couldn't get trend data but total black faculty here is three percent and tenured faculty only one percent."

"This is a great help, Audrey. Reverend Johnson will be grateful for the data."

"I told Jason about the protest you and Reverend Johnson are planning. He didn't seem much interested, Rich. He's like Nero. He can't face up to losing his Lamborghini and the ten-acre estate. He still drives out every day to see the progress." She paused. "Jason is going to meet with the feds next Tuesday. He's optimistic he can persuade them that the clinical trial is an important step in preventing Alzheimer's despite the harm that's happened. 'We have to find a better way to prevent the memory gene from crossing the blood-brain barrier before we inject it,' is the way he puts it." Another pause. "I'm not optimistic, Rich."

"Hang in there and thanks again for getting the data."

Richard passed the information on to Reverend Johnson, mentioning Pearce's wife as his source. Henry called Richard on Thursday to read a draft of his sermon and to tell him that, as a courtesy, he had notified Gertrude that he was going to release Mrs. Matthews' name. "Will you be at my church Sunday, Richard?"

"I wouldn't miss it, Reverend."

Susie called Richard on Friday, six days after Betsy started chemotherapy, to report that she had been admitted to University Hospital for the third time. "She eats very little and vomits most of what she does eat. Her hair is falling out, and this morning she awoke short of breath and feverish. I'm calling from the hospital, Richard. The x-rays show she's got pneumonia." Susie stopped. Richard heard a catch in her throat. "She's not expecting to come home again, Rich; before she got into the cab to the hospital she threw a kiss at the house and said 'amen.' She never did that before."

"Reverend Johnson told me you and your mom had given him permission to use Betsy's name in his sermon this Sunday."

"Yeah, we told him if it would help the protest, then by all means. Will I see you there Sunday?"

Again, Richard said, "I wouldn't miss it."

Chapter 15

THE SERMON

The congregation was finishing a hymn when Richard arrived and took a seat as inconspicuously as possible toward the back of the packed church. Reverend Johnson's preaching voice was a more resonant baritone than in conversation; he held his audience's attention, his remarks punctuated by shouts of "that's right," or "yessir," or "amen."

Brothers and sisters, as we approach the holiday season our hearts should fill with joy. We give thanks everyday for what God has given us but our joy is heightened at Thanksgiving, and again at Christmas when we celebrate the birth of our savior, our savior who led us to recognize the good in every man and woman, to love thy neighbor and bear no malice.

And while we as a minority have much to be thankful for, we are still oppressed. Yes, our ancestors suffered more as slaves but we are still not accorded the dignity of a free and equal people. I mean right here in this city. Some of you put on the only dress or suit you owned, worn and out of fashion, and walked here with holes in the soles of your shoes because you couldn't afford either a car or the bus fare, or the shoemaker. Some came without a coat to protect you from November's chill and fearful of the coming winter. Some of you stood in line for a job last week, turned away not for the first time because there are no jobs. Some of you stood in another line, at a soup kitchen, or sought shelter because you had lost your home. Some of our congregation has not come to pray at all this morning because they are too sick, sick because they could not afford healthcare in time to prevent serious illness. And at least one I know is not here this morning because she joined an experiment in which she should never have been enrolled. (He paused here.)

Many of you know Betsy Matthews. [The congregation gasped, expecting the worst.] She has been a member of this congregation even before I arrived. Her daughter Susie is with us this morning, but Betsy lies in a bed at University Hospital with pneumonia. Pneumonia as a complication of leukemia or its treatment, either of which can prove fatal. The leukemia is a consequence of Betsy's participating in an experiment at Bates-Bronsted. You may have read about this in the newspapers, although Betsy's name was withheld.

The doctors who are caring for Betsy, first at City Hospital and now at University, are good doctors. They are doing what they can for her. The doctors who enrolled Betsy in their experiment are good doctors. They thought it likely that by injecting a gene into her brain they could prevent Alzheimer's Disease.

None of these doctors is black. In the 2000 census, one-third of the population within the city limits was African-American. Only three percent of the faculty at Bates-Bronsted Medical School is black and only five percent of the medical students are black. Had a black scientist been on the research team it seems to me he or she would have looked in the medical literature, finding that one copy of a gene that increases the risk of Alzheimer's Disease in white people does not increase its risk in us. Betsy Matthews had only one copy of that gene and she should not have been in the clinical trial. In that case, she would be sitting in a pew here today.

One other piece of data: Eight of the nineteen people enrolled in this experiment are African-Americans. That's forty-four percent of the enrollees, more than our percentage of the City's population. When it comes to participating in a potentially dangerous experiment, the color of our skin does not disqualify us, but that color almost always disqualifies us from becoming medical students or faculty at Bates-Bronsted.

Sometimes, we are able to get jobs at the City's hospitals and the University. Not high-level jobs like scientists and doctors, but low-level, menial jobs—janitors, orderlies, nurses' aides. As the biggest employer in the City, the University is often the key to our wellbeing. But even those of us fortunate enough to get the low-paying jobs the University offers are still poor.

When is this system of double values going to stop? Double values in education. Double values in employment. Double values in health. We continue to provide the subjects for experiments designed and implemented by white scientists and doctors to benefit mostly white and rich patients who can afford the expensive treatments. The United States has trained

more African-American doctors and scientists
in the last thirty years, but not enough—not in
the proportion we represent in the population.
Or anywhere near the proportion that blacks
serve as research subjects. This discrimination
has got to stop.

The murmurs of approbation that echoed the
Reverend's remarks crescendoed at this point and
almost everyone was saying "That's right," and "amen."
Henry lowered the volume and announced quietly that
he was going to request a meeting with the President of
the University to point out the disparities, suggesting
in his request that Betsy Matthews would never have
been enrolled in the experiment and would never have
developed leukemia had Bates-Bronsted trained more
black medical students and recruited more African-
Americans to serve on its medical and scientific staffs.

And I am serving notice here and now that
we will speak, we will protest, we will stand
watch until justice is done. Let us pray for
Betsy Matthews.

After a minute of silence, he signaled that instead of
the usual closing hymn, the audience sing *We Shall
Overcome.* Richard felt tears well up.

A summary of Reverend Johnson's sermon, along with other sermons in the city, appeared in the local paper the next day, Monday November 15th, but it did not attract other attention. Richard called Audrey to thank her again for the data, to tell her about the sermon, and to let her know that Reverend Johnson had secured an appointment to present the community's demands to the University President the coming Thursday. "How are things going?" he then asked Audrey.

She brought him up to date: "The FDA inspectors are on campus, examining Jason's laboratory notebooks and the animal records, talking to his fellows and colleagues. Tomorrow, Jason, Gus, and Gertrude are scheduled to appear before the investigators." She paused. "I really don't know if Jason is going to put his best foot forward or shoot himself in it. He vacillates. Sometimes I think I've convinced him to be contrite. Other times, he just walks away from me."

Chapter 16

THE HEARING

Gus had lunch with Jason on the Friday before they were scheduled to appear in front of the FDA panel. Afterwards, he called Audrey and asked if he could come to her office. When he arrived, he settled into a chair opposite Audrey at her desk. "I invited Jason to lunch today," Gus started, "to tell him that I was prepared to take full responsibility for failing to recognize that a single copy of the apo-e4 allele is not a risk factor for Alzheimer's in African-Americans and, consequently, that Betsy Matthews should not have been admitted to the trial."

"What was Jason's response?"

"Frankly it surprised me," Gus said. "He smiled and said 'Thanks, Gus. That should lay the case to rest. I never thought they had much against us.

"Oh no!" Audrey groaned.

"'What about the surviving mice getting tumors?' I asked."

"'If Betsy Matthews hadn't been enrolled because she didn't have two apo-e4 alleles we wouldn't be in this bind today,' Jason said. I pointed out what he well knew, that because of the mouse tumors, and Laura's discovery that the injected memory gene had triggered Mrs. Matthews' leukemia, everyone who received the memory gene, regardless of race, was at risk of cancer. 'Maybe,' he said. 'We'll have to wait and see.'"

Audrey was incredulous. *How could her husband take such a cavalier attitude? Was he crossing his fingers that no one else would get cancer? Didn't he realize that until the memory gene could be effectively prevented from crossing the blood-brain barrier and shown that it corrected the memory defect in mice without causing cancer that no further trials would be done? Did he realize that FDA, NIH, and the University might not take his error of omission so lightly that they would let him find better ways of proceeding? This was not the meticulous Jason she knew, the Jason who did not cut corners in his research on gene regulation.* She simply didn't know what to say.

"Audrey," Gus said after a few moments when she failed to speak. "I don't know what's got into Jason, but he's riding for a fall. Unless he changes his attitude he's going to be pilloried. And that might destroy him."

"I've tried telling him that, Gus. Sometimes he grasps what I'm saying." She told Gus about Jason's nightmare. "Other times he acts as if what's really happening is a dream, and he doesn't believe it. Right now, he's hardly talking to me and certainly not listening."

Gus stood. "It must be hard for you, Audrey." As he reached the door, he turned. "He's not drinking, is he?"

"I don't think so. I never smell alcohol on his breath and he seems sober. Jason has never had his integrity questioned and doesn't believe he ever would."

"Unless he changes before he meets with his inquisitors he's likely to get burned at the stake," Gus said as he left.

At dinner that evening Audrey mentioned to Jason that Gus had come to see her. "He thinks you're riding for a fall."

"What do you think?" he asked, his mouth full of food.

Audrey put her fork down, looked him in the eye, and said, "I think Gus is right." They continued the meal in silence.

At breakfast on Saturday, Jason asked her what she thought the FDA might do. "I assume that the University will take its cue from the Feds," he added. The kids had finished eating and were playing in the living room.

"FDA can forbid you from applying for an Investigational New Drug again."

"In that case what would the University do?"

"Worst case: fire you for conduct unbecoming a member of the faculty."

He flashed his boyish smile. "Is that all?"

"Actually, no. You could be criminally prosecuted for negligent homicide and Mrs. Matthews' family could sue you for wrongful death. Neither seems terribly likely, but you never know."

"If that happens, will you be my lawyer?"

"It would be highly unusual for a wife to represent her husband, or vice versa. For negligent homicide you'd want to hire a criminal lawyer. As for the federal agencies and the University, I think your own testimony is the best defense. These agencies are most concerned with preventing something like what happened to Betsy from happening again. They are not out to get you. Besides, if I represented you against the University, I'd have to quit."

Jason thought for a minute. "Let's talk in the living room," he said. Audrey asked Hannah to take the kids out to play. Still in their pajamas, they sat on the sofa. Audrey stepped out of her slippers and tucked her legs beneath her, facing Jason. "You know, Audrey, it's very hard for me to believe that I contributed to someone's death."

"That would be true of anyone who didn't act with malice aforethought."

"Our lives seemed to be going so well. You happy with your work; me on the verge of preventing

Alzheimer's Disease; the kids a joy to be with; our living standard rising. Then *poof*! A woman gets leukemia and it all starts to crumble. It doesn't seem fair."

Audrey resisted saying, *To you, to us, or to Betsy Matthews?*

"Am I to blame? What about Don Sharp and his blandishments, his booze and money? What about the University for giving me everything I wanted as long as I brought in money? What about the IRB failing to put a brake on the trial? If I had been able to answer the one question that really intrigued me when I joined the faculty, I wouldn't be asking any of these questions. That's where I *am* to blame."

And what about the mice you failed to track, Jason? Unsure whether he was struggling to understand how, and why, he had failed, Audrey hesitated to ask. The bruise under her eye had healed but she worried that her husband was a tinderbox, waiting to ignite, rather than a lost boy looking for Audrey to watch over him. She took a deep breath. "And your mice, Jason?"

He looked straight at her, sighed, and got up. "We'd better get dressed before Hannah brings the kids back in."

For a moment, Audrey wanted to take his hand, pull him back down, and bury her face in his chest. For a moment, he had seemed the innocent young man she had fallen in love with eight years earlier.

Later that morning, Jason insisted they drive out with the kids to look at the new property. When Audrey questioned whether it was a good idea, he responded, "Why not? Might be the only time they'll get to see what they almost had." *Maybe he was finally facing the calamity.* Davy wanted to stay home and ride his new tricycle, only agreeing to go when they put it in the back of the SUV, promising he could ride it at their new house. Jason drove. It was a perfect autumn day, oak and maple leaves fluttering to the ground in the gentle breeze. Low in the sky, the sun lent a mellow glow to the multi-colored hills that in other seasons came only before sunset. Audrey had not been to the property since construction of the walls and skylighted roof. Inside, the oak flooring planks were stacked on joists in one corner. "They're going to lay the floor next week," he told her. In her mind, she placed the furniture from their small house, then thought, *No, Jason will want everything new, not the old stuff I inherited.*

From the back of the house, the meadow stretched gently upward to a crest and rolled down to the creek. Heavy forest rose on the other side of the creek and in the distance the mountains seemed to touch the cumulus clouds at the horizon. With the kids running ahead, Jason and Audrey climbed to the crest and then hiked down to the brook that formed the far boundary of their property. The kids loved dropping sticks in and racing downstream to pull them out. It was idyllic.

They hardly spoke on the way home. Even the kids were quiet, dreaming perhaps of what living in the country might be like.

They had no further discussion that weekend about how Jason would respond to the investigators on Tuesday. She agreed to accompany him and he took her suggestion that he wear a jacket and tie. She saw to it that his slacks were sharply pressed and his shoes shined.

※

On the eleventh floor of the Medical School's main building, the elevator opens on a small windowless corridor, with an oak-paneled door to the Dean's offices on the right wall, and a similar door to his conference room on the left. When Audrey and Jason emerged from the elevator on Tuesday afternoon, Gus McAllister, Gertrude Brierly, and Oliver Katz were sitting side by side on straight-backed chrome chairs in the corridor. They smiled weakly at the two new arrivals as they took the empty chairs. Little conversation ensued. The five of them sat like delinquent children waiting to be called into the principal's office. The door to the conference room opened and one of the FDA officials in his three-piece suit stuck his head out and called in Oliver Katz. Fifteen minutes later Ollie emerged, the door shutting silently on its hydraulic closer behind him. Again, like school children, the others looked expectantly at Katz hoping he would yield some wisdom that would enlighten the others when their turn came. Katz did not sit down. "Everything's being recorded," he started. "They covered what I expected: handling dead animals, record keeping, communicating with faculty about their animals. They seemed to know the answers before I said a word. I guess they were giving me a chance to correct errors, but they didn't make any." He pushed the button on the elevator and a moment later disappeared, leaving one chair empty.

Gertrude was called next. They kept her for forty-five minutes and when she came out, clutching her handkerchief, her hair was a mess. She collapsed into the chair and wept openly. Gus gave her a hug, but almost immediately he was called into the conference room. Given Gertrude's state, Audrey knew better than to try and extract from her what had happened. Soon she stopped crying, blew her nose and in a weak voice said, "I can't imagine they can do anything worse than what they did to me." She stood and Jason and Audrey stood with her. She took Audrey's hands. "Please, Audrey, call me later."

Gus was in for about twenty minutes. It was clear from the brief intervals between the calls that he was not going to be able to tell Jason what had transpired. "It's no picnic," was all he said before the door opened and Jason was called. Audrey and Jason both stood. The official quickly said, "Only Professor Pearce, ma'am."

"But——" Jason started to say.

Audrey resumed her seat, smiling at her husband as if to say, *It's all right, you'll do fine.* Jason ventured into the room. Before the door closed Audrey noticed that the heavy mauve drapes had been drawn; the harsh fluorescent ceiling fixture was all that illuminated the room.

Gus sat down next to Audrey. "They asked me to explain my duties as Chief of Neurosciences. 'Did I run the Alzheimer's clinic at University Hospital?' I used to, I told them, but I had too many responsibilities as head of the department. 'Why did I agree to become co-P.I. with Professor Pearce?' Because I had considerable experience directing clinical trials and still saw patients, including those in the early stages of Alzheimer's. 'How did I become aware that a single copy of the apo-e4 allele was not a risk factor for Alzheimer's Disease in African-Americans?' I admitted that I learned it from the news story in the *Chicago Sun-Herald*. 'I should have known it from the literature,' I told them, 'and my ignorance was a fatal flaw in my responsibility as co-P.I.' They wanted to know if commercial interests funded any of my work. I told them that although Ventures Unlimited funded part of the clinical trial, neither I personally nor Neurosciences received funds from the corporation. 'If Ventures withdraws its support for the trial, how will it affect my department?' Not at all, I had to say." He had been speaking to the space in front of him. Now he turned to Audrey. "I'm afraid Jason can't say that." They were silent for a moment. Then Gus continued. "Finally, they wanted to know what I thought would be fair punishment for my—, for my, sin. Those weren't their exact words, but you know what I mean. 'It's for you to decide,' I told them, not wanting to beg for mercy. They thanked me for my candor and dismissed me."

After thirty minutes, Jason exited looking no worse than when he had entered, and the three of them went down in the elevator. They said goodbye to Gus and headed for the Lamborghini. "Well, how did it go?" Audrey asked.

"They wanted to know why I didn't check on the mice that weren't sacrificed. I told them we were so excited by finding that injection of the memory gene markedly reduced the amyloid plaques that we forgot."

"We?"

Jason turned to Audrey as he drove. "'We—' Did I say 'we'?" Audrey nodded. "I meant to say, 'I.' Gee...I must have said 'we' to them too. I guess that's why they asked me who else was responsible for following the mice." He turned back to the road. "I told them the animal keepers. Then they wanted to know when I erased the email message Katz had sent notifying me that the mice had tumors. I guess I got a little defensive at that point. I said I couldn't say for sure I ever got Katz's message. I deleted all the messages from 2002 in 2003 because I was running out of space on the University server. They seemed to think I should have saved all those old messages on my computer. I told them no one ever told me that or showed me how to do it."

Jason turned on to the highway from downtown and continued to describe the interrogation. "They knew, of course, that part of my salary was being paid by Ventures. I told them I had also received a bonus from Ventures as well as stock and stock options."

"Did you volunteer that information, or did they ask?"

He thought for a moment. "They asked. They also wanted to know if we had informed potential research subjects that the trial was partially supported by Ventures. I told them we hadn't. 'Could I have done the work without support from Ventures Unlimited?' I told them that NIH did not believe I was qualified to study Alzheimer's Disease and turned down my grant. So I had no choice."

Immediately, Audrey recognized the irony that Jason failed to see, although NIH's concern about

Jason's qualifications probably did not extend to the possibility that he would not examine the cause of the mice's deaths.

Jason turned off the highway and waited for the red light to change. "Their next question really got my goat. 'Do you think your failure to follow the mice might have been influenced by Ventures Unlimited's largesse?' Certainly not! I replied. Then they wanted to know what would happen if the company withdrew its support. I'd have to apply elsewhere, I said, to NIH for instance. 'What if NIH turns you down?' they asked. I said I didn't see how they could after what I've demonstrated in mice as well as showing that humans with a forgetful memory allele are prone to develop Alzheimer's Disease. They reminded me that I had made a serious error of omission that resulted in a possibly fatal illness in at least one subject. I told them I'd never make that mistake again.

"Finally, they wanted to know what I thought would be fair punishment for my error. I thought for a moment and told them that I'd learned my lesson."

Arriving home, Jason got out, but Audrey sat in the car, trying to calm down. When she didn't follow he came over to her side and opened the door. "What's the matter?"

"Jason, I don't know if they were intentionally setting traps for you, but you walked into every one of them. You alone have to take responsibility for not following your mice. You alone put people at risk for cancer. I think they'll throw the book at you." He stormed into the house and she followed at a safe distance.

———

That evening, Audrey and Gertrude talked. "The FDA thinks the fault rests with the IRB," Gertrude told her. "They thought that I should have invited outside experts familiar with gene therapy experiments to review the project. And the Board should have listened to the one member who suggested that the experiment be conducted in primates first. That the Board didn't is apparently my fault. They got really angry when I pointed out that the proceedings of the IRB in approving the Phase I trial were sent to the FDA and that the agency approved them when it issued the IND." Her voice rose as she described what happened. After a moment of silence, she concluded in lower tones, "They as much as told me they're going to recommend the University fire me."

"Oh, Gertrude. I'm so sorry. I don't think Jason will fare much better."

"Were they harsh with him, too?"

"I'm not sure, but from what he told me, they hold him responsible for not examining the surviving mice, and I doubt his defensive responses, as he described them, endeared him to the committee."

On Wednesday, the FDA and RAC people were still deliberating on campus, preparing a report to deliver to the University the following day.

———

As he announced in his sermon, Reverend Johnson promptly scheduled an appointment with the University's President. It was arranged for late morning on Thursday, November 18th. Richard called Henry Thursday afternoon to find out how the meeting had gone. Henry was fuming. "The President's secretary told me that the President was in meetings with the FDA and was preparing for an emergency meeting with the Board of Trustees on Friday. She said the President apologized for having to cancel our meeting and asked to reschedule it the week after Thanksgiving, the next time he would be available. I had to decide, Richard, whether to leave the letter with our demands or wait more than a week. I handed the letter to the Secretary and wrote "URGENT" on the envelope, urging her to make sure he read it before he left for the weekend."

———

Later that Thursday afternoon, the Chief Attorney for Bates-Bronsted came into Audrey's office as she was about to leave, and collapsed into one of the soft chairs in front of her desk. "Things couldn't be worse, Audrey." Ventures Unlimited had officially notified him that the company was going to terminate its contracts with the University for Jason's work. "We have to decide," the Chief Attorney continued, "whether to contest premature severance or whether it's in the University's best interest, in view of what triggered it, just to let it go." He paused and sighed, "But it gets worse. A few hours ago the President met with the FDA and NIH representative and it's clear they are going to throw the book at us." Audrey resisted interrupting him to ask specifically about Jason. "And to make matters still worse, when the President got back to his office, he found a letter from Reverend Henry Johnson demanding that the medical school admit more African-American students and appoint more African-Americans to the faculty. Of course, the letter mentioned the plight of Betsy Matthews. Reverend Johnson's letter notified the President that the local community would hold weekly candlelight vigils in front of University Hospital until the Medical School admitted more African-Americans." He stopped after this summation, perhaps waiting for a response. Audrey felt helpless. The Chief sighed again and told her, "The President's called a special meeting of the Board of Trustees for tomorrow." She was beginning to feel that this summation was a prelude to the Chief wanting to tell her something unpleasant. After a moment of silence he came out with it. "Audrey, I've relied on you a lot, especially on matters related to faculty-industry relations, but in view of your relation to Jason Pearce I can't have you involved any longer." Still she did not speak, adding to the Chief's discomfort. "Perhaps you should, uh, uh, take a leave of absence."

"Are you asking me or telling me?"

He stood up, his mission accomplished. "I'll leave it up to your good judgment," he said and closed the door behind him.

She sat behind her desk, doodling with pencil and paper. The Chief was right. Jason's error of omission not only jeopardized him but the Medical School and University as well, not to mention Betsy Matthews. It was logical for the Chief and others in the Administration to believe that she would defend her husband. And doing so could put her in conflict with the University, which would want to distance itself from Jason and his error. Still, she felt that in her nine years working for the University she had protected its interests, including faculty-industry relations. She had not always been listened to and now some of her greatest worries were being realized; a private company could turn the spigot off when the flow no longer served its interests, the University be damned.

Jason and Audrey had hardly spoken since their trip home in the Lamborghini on Tuesday. As they were finishing dinner on Thursday, she told him about the visit from the Chief Attorney. "He asked me to take a leave of absence, but he'd be happier if I quit."

"What are you going to do?"

"I really don't have a choice, Jason." She got up, headed for the door and, barely audible, said grimly, "And neither do you." She got her coat and went out in the cool autumn air.

She liked the Chief and wondered if the President had put him up to suspending—really firing—her. She was angry: at Jason, at the Chief Attorney, at the University. *It's guilt by association. I've done my best for the University despite what my husband has done to sully its name.*

The following Monday she informed the Chief that she would take her accrued vacation time starting immediately—it amounted to a month—and expected full pay as was her due. The Chief agreed. Audrey knew it was only a delaying tactic.

—※—

On Tuesday November 23rd, two days before Thanksgiving, Audrey opened the front page of the local newspaper. Two headlines struck her with full force. The headline for the first read, *Leukemia Victim*

of Gene Therapy Experiment Dies. The story summarized
the events leading to Betsy Matthews' death the previous day and announced her name and the time and
place of her interment. The second struck even closer
to home: *NIH Suspends All Grants and Contracts to Bates-
Bronsted Medical School Until Reforms Instituted.*

Jason's name first appeared toward the bottom of
the second article, reporting that FDA had rescinded
his license to investigate the safety or effectiveness
of the memory gene, designated as a New Drug, or
any new drug, in humans for five years, at which
time his eligibility would be considered. "In addition," the article continued, "the National Institutes of
Health announced that Pearce would be ineligible for
grants involving human subjects for five years." The
final blow: "The President of the University said the
Board of Trustees had recommended dismissing Jason
for 'conduct unbecoming a member of the faculty.'"
Ventures Unlimited, Ltd. was not mentioned.

Seeing it all in print shortened her breath and left
her fingers trembling. "Conduct unbecoming a member of the faculty" drew her wrath. *The President is as
likely to buck his Board as I am to retain my job; he probably urged them to make the recommendation.* She could
not recall that a charge of unbecoming conduct had
ever been raised for a scientist at Bates-Bronsted.
Physicians who were incorrigible alcoholics or drug
users, and for whom treatment had failed and who

proved, finally, incompetent had been dismissed, but the charge of misconduct was never leveled on them. And she knew of "unbecoming" sexual conduct on the part of several faculty members who had never been punished. She was not exonerating Jason; his mistakes had proved fatal. From what he had told her, she doubted he had been contrite before the investigators. *But contrition would not have saved him*, she realized. *FDA, the RAC, and NIH had to protect human subjects and ensure the integrity of human research. The University had to follow suit, but did it have to show its contrition by condemning a faculty member—one who had made major contributions to science and medicine—to loss of his livelihood? And what of Gus McAlister? Neither story mentioned him. Jason and I will have to find new jobs. It won't be easy.*

The story also reported that the Bates-Bronsted IRB would be placed under new leadership, Audrey shuddered as she read that; Gertrude was right—she was the scapegoat. In addition, the number of scientific and community members would be increased, and human research involving minorities would receive extra scrutiny by the IRB and, whenever possible, members of the group in question would be consulted. She left the paper for Jason, who had slept late, as he had been doing the last few days, kissed Rachel and Davey goodbye, and drove to Bates-Bronsted.

She went straight to Gertrude's office where she found piles of books and memorabilia in stacks on the floor, ready to be put into cartons that Gertrude was assembling as Audrey entered. "You're not wasting any time," Audrey said as lightly as possible. "Did they give you a deadline for vacating?"

"I'm not waiting around to find out. Jason and I are the sacrificial lambs and, in my case at least, no appeal will work. I leave with a clear conscience, I'll tell you that. In our system, especially when the media gets hold of a mistake, the institution that holds the power will succeed in absolving itself from blame. This time, at my expense."

"What will you do?"

"I've kept my medical licensure up to date. I'll need a refresher course, but I think I can get a job practicing medicine. I might even earn more than I have here. I'd like to write up my views on the strengths and weaknesses of the IRB system. Whether any reputable journal will publish them is another matter." She had finished assembling one carton and stooped to place a stack of books in it. "What about Jason? It's not going to be easy for him to find another job as a scientist; he's effectively blacklisted."

"Honestly, Gertrude, I don't know. I don't know. We haven't spoken about it. And the Administration wants me out." Depression was rapidly replacing Audrey's anger and she turned to leave.

Having deposited her load, Gertrude stood. "I thought I'd go to Betsy Matthews' funeral tomorrow," she said. "The least I can do is pay my respects."

Audrey brightened. "That's a wonderful idea. Why don't Jason and I pick you up and we can go together." Gertrude agreed and they made arrangements for the following day.

Jason was not home when Audrey returned. "He played with the children for a while," Hannah reported, "gave them both a big hug and a kiss, and left without saying a word." Audrey had put a note for him on the kitchen table, reminding him to pick up the free-range turkey she had ordered from the organic foods market. The note was still there. Audrey called the market; he had not picked up the turkey. He did not come home Tuesday night. On Wednesday morning, Audrey picked up Gertrude in her Lexus SUV and they drove to the cemetery.

PART II. AFTER THE INTERMENT

After Betsy's interment, Janice arrived back at the airport around 1 P.M., taking the shuttle to the terminal from the rental car return in the slackening rain. The terminal was crowded with people whose clothes exuded dampness. She stood in the ticket line and signed up to fly standby back to Chicago, then bought a sandwich and Coke in the food court, which she ate while waiting at the gate for the first flight; they never called her name. Waiting for the next flight, she thought about Richard Piper's remark in Betsy's hospital room that Janice "had almost brought the University to its knees." *I never expected that my investigative journalism could have an impact on people and institutions. It's hard to think of myself in the same category as Woodward and Bernstein, but my story certainly brought down Gertrude Brierly and Jason Pearce.*

She felt sorry for Gertrude Brierly. The flaws in the IRB system were not her fault and she seemed totally committed to protecting the people who were subjects of University-sponsored research. She also felt bad about Jason Pearce who had been open and honest with her.

She finally got a seat on the 7 P.M. flight, arriving back in her Chicago apartment a few minutes before 10 P.M. She called her mother to let her know she was back. Her mother told her that Grandma Bertie had died the previous day, two days after Betsy. At Thanksgiving dinner the next day with her mother, her cousin, her cousin's husband, and their two kids, they observed a moment of silence for Bertie.

Chapter 17

VENTURES UNLIMITED, LTD.

On Black Friday, Janice phoned Donald Sharp's office at Ventures Unlimited. As she expected, he had taken the remainder of the holiday week off and his secretary was not authorized to make appointments with the media without his permission. Janice decided to go to his office on Monday morning, prepared to camp out until he agreed to see her.

The carpeting, leather upholstery, and paintings of the reception area had changed from Janice's last visit three years earlier; even the Chicago skyline view was altered by the ubiquitous cranes and new construction. The internal changes, making the room still more affluent, suggested the company's increasing success—at least until Janice's story appeared.

Janice didn't have long to wait. Sharp took off his camel hair coat, revealing his turtleneck, tooled boots, black hair tied in a long ponytail—his trademark appearance. "Ah, Ms. Polk! It's good to see you again after— what has it been, two, three years?" Janice nodded. "Your career has come a long way. I read your stories regularly in the *Sun-Herald* so I know you've maintained an interest in Alzheimer's Disease." He stood behind the chair he intended for her until she was seated. "And that's why you've come to see me," he said as he walked casually to his imposing chair on the other side of the desk. It was a statement, not a question, and she nodded. She had thought hard beforehand about her first question, phrasing it so that he would have to answer 'yes' or 'no': "Is Ventures Unlimited going to cut off its support of Professor Pearce?"

"What do you think, Janice?"

She was ready for that reply. *He's trying to get me to wheedle the answer out of him and I'm not going to play his game the way I did three years ago.* "I have no opinion on the matter," she replied, waiting.

"Yes."

"When?"

"When?" Donald Sharp looked just a little uncomfortable. Janice was feeling in control. "Do you mean when did we initiate cutting off support or when will the cut go into effect?" Janice smiled coyly, but didn't answer. "Ah, you mean both, don't you?" Janice nodded with a smile. "Our Board of Trustees met shortly after it became known that the leukemic patient's—"

"You mean. Betsy Matthews?"

"Yes. That her marrow cells were infected with segments of the memory gene." He smiled accusingly. "Your story. Our Board unanimously approved the cut."

"And when will it go into effect?"

"Ventures Unlimited honors its contractual obligations, Ms. Polk. The current contract ends in December. We are not proceeding with a renewal."

"Are you continuing to support Professor Pearce's research that does not involve human subjects?"

"All of Pearce's research that Ventures supports involves human subjects."

"So after the year ends, Professor Pearce will no longer receive any funds from Ventures Unlimited, Ltd.?"

"That is correct."

"For the record, Dr. Sharp, what prompted Ventures Unlimited to make this decision?"

"You know very well, Janice, having discovered the fatal flaw in Jason's research yourself." She didn't say anything, wanting him to be explicit. Finally, he continued. "Professor Pearce's failure to follow-up on the surviving mice who received the memory gene was inexcusable. Ventures Unlimited will not be a party to shoddy research."

Janice shifted gears. "Ventures and Bates-Bronsted Medical School are constructing a facility for testing people for variant memory genes. What will happen to that work?"

"Since gene therapy for Alzheimer's Disease has been put on indefinite hold, Ventures Unlimited sees no point in continuing with that endeavor. I doubt the University will continue on its own."

"Let me go back to Professor Pearce for a moment, Dr. Sharp. Your company gave his research an enormous jolt after NIH did not renew his grant on gene regulation. With hindsight, do you think you made a mistake?"

He sighed. "Let's talk off the record for a minute." Janice nodded and put her pencil and notepad on the edge of Sharp's desk. "Jason Pearce was, and still is, a brilliant innovative researcher. His work on gene regulation was so meticulous that cutting corners was not a concern. Ventures Unlimited knew, as did Jason, that the injected memory gene could go astray and be harmful. What we did not know, and perhaps Jason did, was that it had gone astray in his mice."

"Are you suggesting that Professor Pearce knew the surviving mice had tumors?"

"Hasn't that occurred to you? Do you believe he simply destroyed all his email for 2002 simply to make space in his email account on the medical school's server?"

Sharp's accusation stunned her. Never for a moment did she think Jason Pearce had been disingenuous when he told her why he had erased his email from 2002. "You're accusing Professor Pearce of deliberately lying, Dr. Sharp. Have I got that right?" He nodded. "Do you really think he would do that?"

Sharp relaxed, sat back and smiled, clearly relishing having finally put Janice on the defensive. "Come now, Ms. Polk, are you that naïve?" Janice didn't answer. "Jason Pearce was on the verge of preventing Alzheimer's Disease. He was also on the verge of making a vast fortune. Ventures stock was rising steadily and he still had stock options he had not exercised. He had borrowed to buy an expensive car and ten acres of land and to build a mansion. He was smart enough to know that if something untoward happened to the surviving mice the whole edifice of his human research would crumble."

Janice thought for a moment. "I checked this morning and Ventures Unlimited stock has fallen since my story broke. If your theory about Pearce's avarice is correct wouldn't he have exercised his options?"

Sharp smiled. "Maybe he has. I don't keep track of that. You'll have to ask him." He stood.

Sharp's accusation had so unsettled Janice that she never asked to go back on the record. They shook hands and she left.

Chapter 18

VIGILS

When Janice got home after her interview with Sharp, there was a message from Susie Matthews on her answering machine. "Thought you'd be interested to know that the first candlelight vigil will take place tomorrow, Tuesday, November 30th at 5 P.M. in front of University Hospital. Richard and I both hope to see you there. So long." Janice had been thinking about Richard on and off throughout the long weekend, wondering if he was married, if he would keep in touch. So she was pleased to hear that he joined Susie in hoping she'd return for the vigil.

Confident her editor would agree—her stature at the *Sun-Herald* had risen further as her dispatches about the Bates-Bronsted debacle scooped other papers—Janice immediately made a round-trip reservation, and booked a room for Tuesday at the Holiday Inn returning to Chicago the next day. Not only did her editor agree, he also arranged to have a local photographer take pictures of the candlelight march for the paper.

Janice took a cab from the airport and checked into the Holiday Inn—they were getting to know her—and walked the short distance to University Hospital in the brief twilight, gusts of cold wind slapping her in the face. The sky was overcast but the forecast of sleet had not materialized. Rounding a corner on to the main avenue, she saw the points of light moving in procession along the sidewalk opposite the entrance to University Hospital. The candles were held by people—black, white, Hispanic—separated from each other by about five feet. They were spread over a distance of about fifty yards but as more people joined, the procession lengthened. Some of the candles were going in one direction, others in the opposite, forming an oval of moving lights. The marchers simply held their candles, managing to shield them with their free hand against gusts of wind. None of them spoke. As many police as marchers were in the area; a bunch stood at each end of the oval and across the street, making sure the entrance to the hospital was not obstructed.

Janice was tempted to join the vigil—a young woman was handing out candles—but knew she had to maintain an appearance of objectivity. She joined the group of bystanders that had gathered inside the oval. A young man gave her a flyer.

AN UNNECESSARY DEATH

We mourn the death of Mrs. Betsy Matthews who died tragically in University Hospital, November 22, 2004, in an experiment for which she should never have been recruited.

* **African-Americans were over-represented in the experiment in which she took part**
* **But no black doctors or scientists conducted the experiment.**

WHY WERE THERE NO MINORITY DOCTORS CONDUCTING THIS EXPERIMENT? WHY ARE THERE SO FEW AFRICAN-AMERICAN MEDICAL STUDENTS IN THE BATES-BRONSTED MEDICAL SCHOOL? PROTEST THIS UNFAIR DISCRIMINATION!!

There followed in smaller print announcement of a rally to be held at Reverend Johnson's Church the coming Friday, and a plea to write or telephone the President of the University (address and phone number supplied) and Dean of the Medical School urging them to increase the number of black faculty and medical students.

As she stood and watched, first Reverend Johnson passed, then about five candlelights behind him, Susie Matthews, and about ten lights behind her, Richard Piper. Each of them saw Janice and smiled.

An hour after Janice arrived, Reverend Johnson, leading the procession, halted and snuffed out his candle. As the marchers reached the spot at which he did this, they snuffed out their candles. They stood around for a few minutes and led by the Reverend, sang *We Shall Overcome,* then quietly dispersed.

Richard came up to Janice and invited her for a drink. She told him she had to file her story immediately so it would make Wednesday's paper—before the wire services got hold of it. "I understand," he said, "but there's something else you should know." She looked at him quizzically. "Jason Pearce has disappeared."

"What?" Her journalistic instincts took hold. "Since when? How do you know?"

"Look, Janice, you have to write the story about the vigil. Why don't you call me when you're done? If it's not too late I can come over to the Inn, we can have a drink, a bite to eat, and I'll tell you what I know."

She agreed. Her curiosity got the better of her and she did not spend as long as usual preparing the report on the vigil.

───※───

They met in the Holiday Inn lobby at nine o'clock and went to a quiet lounge where they sat on bar stools opposite each other with a small, round high table between them. A waiter came by and they both ordered Chardonnay and some bar food. "What did you think of the vigil?" Richard asked.

"Very impressive. In my report I emphasized the silence and the orderliness; the trouble anticipated by the police never materialized. 'As the group dispersed,' I wrote, 'they sang *We Shall Overcome*, a 'some day' dream still unfulfilled more than forty years after it was sung in the civil rights movement.'"

Richard got off his stool, walked around to her, hugged her and then kissed her cheek lightly. "That's beautiful."

Richard is a very tactile person, Janice thought again.

"I hope you'll stick around to cover the rally on Friday," Richard added.

"That depends what the story is with Jason Pearce. Tomorrow at noon I have an appointment to interview the President of the University. I want to get his opinion on your demands. I'm scheduled to return on the seven o'clock to Chicago." Their wine and food arrived. "All right, Richard, don't keep me in suspense about Jason Pearce."

He took a sip and put his glass down on the round table between them. "My source is Audrey Meacham, Jason's wife."

"I met her briefly a few weeks ago."

"Audrey and I sit in on the IRB meetings and we've gotten to be friends. She called me on Thanksgiving morning, the day after Mrs. Matthews' funeral, to say that Jason had not come home the past two nights. He was supposed to pick up a turkey for their Thanksgiving dinner, but never did. On Wednesday evening, she drove out to their new house, still under construction. His Lamborghini was parked in front. She found Jason sitting on the floor of the living room, dark except for light from an old table lamp on the floor next to him, a few empty beer bottles at his side. 'What do you want?' he asked gruffly. Audrey reminded him that they were planning a Thanksgiving dinner the next day. 'You'll have to do it without me.'

"She had anticipated Jason might refuse to come home, and brought some blankets, a few changes of clothing, a heavy sweater, and his toiletry, including a safety razor and soap to supply him until he was ready to come home. 'This is home,' Jason yelled at her. Audrey tried to reason with him but he dismissed her. 'I have to work this out by myself.' She was at the door when he asked about the kids. She told him that they missed him. 'Tell them I miss them, too,' he said and waved her out."

"That's terrible," Janice commented.

"When Audrey called me, she asked my opinion on bringing the kids out to visit Jason. Her mother had advised her not to; it would be too upsetting all around."

Janice interrupted. "Do you have kids, Richard?"

"Me? No. I'm not even married." He paused. "I guess Audrey asked me because she confided in me a couple of weeks ago about Jason's behavior."

"So, what did you tell her?"

"I asked what she had told the kids about Jason's absence. She had explained to them that he had a setback in his work and he needed to be by himself to figure out how to deal with it. The older one, Rachel, she's seven, seemed to grasp it. She's not sure about David, who's four. Rachel told her mother that she thought she could make her father feel better."

"And?" Janice asked.

"I told Audrey I agreed with her mother, and suggested that she go ahead with the Thanksgiving dinner. 'It might give a semblance of calm to the kids,' I suggested. She accepted my advice and asked if I'd like to join them. I said sure and she gave me their address and the time. After I hung up, I thought about it, deciding it wouldn't be a good idea. I didn't want to give any of them the idea that I was a father/husband substitute. And if Jason should happen to return, my presence might be upsetting to him. I called her back and explained to her why I wouldn't be coming. Instead, I took Susie Matthews out to dinner. I think she was grateful not to sit alone at home. She's going to stay in town until the rally, then go back to Madison.

"On Friday," Richard continued, "I called Audrey. Still no Jason. She asked if I would do her the favor of driving to their property and make sure Jason's Lamborghini was still parked in front. I wanted to finish the Betsy Matthews' case study for my book, go over my entire manuscript once more, and mail it to the publisher on Saturday. With luck," he explained to Janice, "the publisher will return the proofs before the Christmas break and I can send them back early in January. So I asked if I could wait until Saturday. 'Okay,' she said.

"On Saturday, I mailed the manuscript and after lunch followed the directions Audrey had given me to their property. The Lamborghini was parked in front. The house is quite large, the wood frame finished but the windows on the second floor were yet to be installed. It looked like a typical construction site with dirt all around and scraps of building material on the uneven ground, equipment under a tarp, a port-a-pot on one side. I drove past and turned around.

Okay, I thought, *Jason is still there, but is he alive?* I asked myself. Turning around again, I parked in back of the Lamborghini, sitting for a minute to figure out what I would say. I intentionally slammed the car door and stamped the mud from the unfinished walkway out of my shoes as I climbed up the steps. As I reached the top Jason came out. He had a three-day beard and uncombed hair. He was wearing a white dress shirt streaked with dirt, its tail hanging haphazardly out from his jeans, and dirty sneakers. 'Did Audrey send you, Rich?'

"I was surprised he recognized me. 'She's worried about you, Jason. She wants you to come home.'

"He ignored my remark. 'Come on in, Rich, lemme show you our new home.'

"How could I refuse? He took me on a tour. There was no furniture, and no equipment in the kitchen: no sink; only two output valves on the pipes coming up from the floor. No stove, only a hotplate plugged into an uncovered wall outlet. No refrigerator, but an ice chest in the living room where an oak floor had been partially laid; plywood subfloor elsewhere. A couple of blankets were strewn in one corner of the living room. Near them on the floorboards, an unlit table lamp, the ice chest, and some scattered beer bottles. 'I've got electricity and cold water,' he said. 'The refrigerator and water heater will be delivered next week.'

"Our voices echoed in the empty house. He was proud of the house, showing me the kitchen and where the dining room, and game room (with a billiard table, he announced proudly) would be and pointing up the raw stairs, 'five bedrooms and a Jacuzzi in the master bathroom.' We walked around the outside, standing on the site of the swimming pool, not even a hole in the ground. He invited me back in, offering me a beer from the ice chest, bottles lying in a pool of water, the ice long melted. He was going to get cleaned up after I left and go into the village to get a meal, some ice, and replenish his food supplies. In this he seemed rational but when I asked about his plans or how long he was going to live alone out there he became evasive. I asked if I could get him anything or whether he had a message for his kids or Audrey. 'No to both,' he said, and I left."

"So Jason's still out there?" Janice asked. The waiter cleared their plates and Richard ordered another Chardonnay. "No thank you," Janice said when he asked if she wanted a refill.

"Audrey called me on Sunday," he continued. The state police had called, asking to speak to Jason Pearce. Audrey told them he wasn't home. They had found his Lamborghini abandoned on the side of the road leading to the little village two or three miles from the house. The officer told her that unless Mr. Pearce moved his car in the next two hours, they'd have it towed and impounded at considerable expense. Audrey told me she had found a spare set of car keys in Jason's night table drawer. Would I meet her at her house so we could drive out to pick up the Lamborghini, which I would drive back to her house? Of course, I said. On the way over I wondered why she hadn't told the police about Jason's strange behavior. I concluded, and she confirmed it when we drove out together, that she didn't want to involve the police as long as she knew Jason was alive. We drove past their new property and about a mile farther we found the Lamborghini on the right shoulder, aimed toward the village. It would not start and the gas gauge registered empty. We drove to the village to call AAA from a payphone, and then returned to the Lamborghini to wait. The tow truck came within an hour and poured enough gas into the tank and carburetor to get us to the village where we filled the tank. On the way back, we decided to stop at the unfinished house." Richard paused to sip his second glass of wine. "Jason was not there."

Janice shook her head sorrowfully.

"I spoke to Audrey this afternoon," he continued. "Still no sign of Jason. He did not show up to teach his graduate class this morning. She's ready to call the police."

Janice drank the last drop of wine and beckoned the waiter when he passed through. "I guess I will have a refill." Listening to Richard tell the story, she realized she faced an ethical dilemma, which she conveyed to him. "You realize, Richard, that you're speaking to a reporter. I could call the *Sun-Herald* with what you just told me and the headline might read: 'Censured Scientist Disappears.'"

Upset, Richard gazed at Janice. "Don't you think you should talk to Audrey first?"

Janice put her hand on Richard's. "Of course. I don't want to expose her to the hounds of the press—myself excluded—while her husband's fate, or more precisely his whereabouts, is unknown." Her wine came and she took a sip. "What do you think has happened to Jason Pearce?"

"The worst is that he's taken his life." Neither of them spoke for a moment as if they were already in mourning. "Another is that Jason has fled; he may want to start a new life, maybe under a new identity." Again, they were quiet.

"Any other ideas?" she asked.

"When he ran out of gas he took a shortcut back to the house and got lost."

"Have you discussed these possibilities with Audrey?"

"Actually, she had thought of all of them and told me."

Janice's brain was whirring. "You know, Richard, I interviewed Donald Sharp, the CEO of Ventures Unlimited, yesterday." Richard looked puzzled at this diversion. "Sharp told me that Jason Pearce has stock options in Ventures Unlimited." She took another sip of wine. "But after the fiasco, Venture's stock is falling rapidly. If Jason has fled, he might have sold his options to get cash while there is still cash to be gotten."

"I'm sure Audrey's thought of that, but I'll pass your suggestion along."

Janice swirled her glass, considering what to say next. *Her story was responsible for Pearce's disappearance. The least she could do was console his wife. To hell with the latest story.* "I'd like to meet Audrey to convey my concern to her. Maybe I can help."

"I'm not sure she'd be keen to meet you," he said, "after what you've done."

They had both finished their second glass of wine and when the waiter came by, they both ordered a third, talking for a while about other matters. Janice told him that her grandmother with Alzheimer's had died two days after Betsy Matthews. Richard elaborated on the manuscript, which he had gotten off to the publisher. "I am something of a troublemaker for the University—"

She gave a little laugh, "That makes two of us."

"But having a published book should more than offset that."

"Even if it's critical of the University?"

"Most of it deals with the protection of research subjects in general. Only the case study deals with

Bates-Bronsted Medical School. And, in addition, my Department has recommended me for tenure but when it gets to the Appointments and Promotions Committee in which the Administration wields power, anything can happen."

"What do you mean?"

"If the Committee does not second my Department's recommendation, I am, in essence, denied tenure. The University is under no obligation to renew my contract." He held his right hand palm up in front of his mouth and blew. "Poof. I'm out of a job."

They talked about their pasts and finally the conversation returned to Jason's disappearance. "Does Audrey know that you and I are ——" she hesitated "——friends?"

"I don't think I've mentioned that we're acquainted."

"Would it be awkward for you to tell her I'd like to meet her, help in any way I can?"

"Why would it be awkward?" He thought for a moment. "Conspiring with the enemy?" He put his hand on Janice's. "I'll assure her you want to help, not dig for a story."

"That puts it about right."

By now it was eleven-thirty. Janice insisted on paying for her wine. They settled with the waiter and walked to the lobby. Richard offered his hand. Impulsively, Janice threw her arms around his neck and kissed him. It seemed an eternity to her before she felt his arms encircling her and he responded to her kiss. They agreed that he would pick her up the following morning.

Janice had trouble falling asleep. Richard's embrace elated her and she wondered where it would lead. And Pearce's disappearance bothered her deeply. She decided not to return to Chicago the next day. Well after midnight, she called the airline to extend her stay. She had to pay a penalty but there was a seat on the seven o'clock flight out on Friday. It was past one before she fell asleep. On Wednesday morning, she called her editor to tell him there were "new developments" and she was going to extend her stay through Friday. On her way out to meet Richard, she went to the front desk and arranged to keep her room.

The sleet that had threatened the vigil stormed into the city on Tuesday night. When Richard's old Miata stopped in front of the Inn Wednesday morning, Janice ran out, with a plastic kerchief covering her brown hair. He leaned over to give her a kiss as she climbed into the passenger seat. "I called Audrey before I left home to tell her I was planning to bring the reporter who had written the story."

"How did she react?"

"Stony silence. 'I'm bringing her as a friend, Audrey.' She was distrustful that the reporter who blew the whistle on Jason now wanted to help, but she agreed to let you in."

"Understandable reaction," Janice replied.

Audrey opened the door for them, hair in disarray, eyes puffy, no makeup. Her plain white blouse was not tucked into her jeans. The children were in school and the au pair was not around. Richard introduced Janice who offered her hand. Audrey simply looked at it.

"Mrs. Pearce, I know my story has caused you and your husband grief. If I hadn't asked him about the mice who weren't sacrificed he would still have his job. Frankly, I feel guilty about what's happened, but if I had it to do over again I would ask the same question." Janice dropped her hand. "But I want to tell you now—maybe because of what I've done—that I am genuinely concerned about your husband, and although I have enough information for a front page story I promise that I am not going to write a word without your permission." Audrey glanced at Richard, as if asking whether Janice could be trusted. He nodded.

"Janice learned from Ventures Unlimited, Audrey, that Jason had stock options. If he's exercised them in the last few days, it might give us a clue as to what he's up to." They had been standing all this time and

Audrey motioned them into the living room where Richard and Janice took seats at opposite ends of the sofa. Audrey sat in a lounge chair facing them.

"Jason left managing the stock options entirely to me," she began. "I exercised some of them and sold the stock at a good price, helping us meet constructions costs of the new property. We still have some options left, but I doubt they're worth much after what's happened. I can call our broker to find out." She paused and then threw out gratuitously, "I don't have any love for Donald Sharp or Ventures Unlimited." She glanced at Janice who was looking at Richard, *adoringly*, Audrey thought.

Janice turned to Audrey. "Do you have a joint credit card and bank accounts?" she asked.

"We do. I checked the balances this morning." They looked at her expectantly. "He made two withdrawals of $500 each over the weekend."

"He could have withdrawn a thousand bucks to meet expenses, maybe a bit extravagant," Richard commented. "On the other hand, a thousand could get him out of the country."

Do you know where he keeps his passport?" Janice asked.

"I'm not sure," Audrey replied. "He's invited abroad quite often so he may keep it with him. I keep mine and the kids' passports together." She excused herself, returning a few minutes later to say she couldn't find

Jason's passport, and that their broker had just told her their few remaining stock options had not been exercised.

"Maybe it's time to call the police, Audrey," Richard said.

"What should I tell them?"

"That your husband has been missing since Saturday."

The police, of course, had a record of finding the Lamborghini late Saturday night. They also had a record of picking up a young woman midway between the Lamborghini and the village, walking barefoot toward the village, her shoes in her hand. She refused to say where she had come from but said she had to get back to the bar on Main Street before midnight to meet her sister; the police gave her a lift. After Audrey notified them on Wednesday that Jason was missing, they put the two unusual findings together and a police detective visited the bar where the bartender recalled that a young woman and an older man, neither of whom he knew, had left together around ten o'clock that Saturday night. The detective reported this to Audrey two hours after she notified them of Jason's disappearance. He added that he was trying to find the young woman and would keep Audrey posted.

Now I've got a new worry, Audrey thought. Then she thought about Laura's telling her about Jason's attempted embrace. *He has changed. Does he no longer love me?*

Do I no longer love him? That depends. If his changes are irreversible I cannot live with him. She realized that *irreversible* could also mean that he had taken his own life. In that case, she would love him for what he had been, not what he had become.

The slap, the sexual transgressions; can I trust him even if he promises to be better?

⸻

After leaving Audrey's, Richard offered to give Janice a lift to her interview with the President. On the way, he asked if she had plans for that evening. "Only to write up the interview and maybe make some notes about Jason Pearce's disappearance."

"Well, then, how about dinner?"

She turned to look at him. He was driving intently. "I guess I'll have time this afternoon to complete my professional responsibilities—"

"You're not going to file a story on Jason's disappearance, are you?" Richard asked.

She laughed. "I made a promise to Audrey not to break the story. I just can't keep all the information in my head—in case there's a future story."

Richard turned to her and found a smile. "I'd love to have dinner with you, Richard. And maybe a movie afterward?"

Richard dropped Janice off in front of the building that housed the President's office shortly before noon. At the appointed hour, the President came out of his inner office and welcomed Janice graciously, asking if she'd like to join him for coffee. She declined. He poured himself a mug, and with his free hand, escorted her into the office. It was as grand as Donald Sharp's with a more pastoral view, facing away from downtown and out toward the hills and mountains twenty miles distant. He was in shirtsleeves, wearing a tie with repeated caps and gowns in black on a pale blue background.

"I'm glad I have the pleasure of meeting the journalist who saved the University from disaster," he said disarmingly. "Think what might have happened if you hadn't been so alert. We could have had an epidemic of cancer if the clinical trial continued and more subjects received the memory gene." He gulped his coffee, then set the mug down. "What can I do for you today, Ms. Polk?"

"Let me begin by asking you about the letter you received from Reverend Johnson. I'm sure you know he made the letter public. Have you arranged to meet with him?"

"I plan to respond to his letter, of course."

"But will you meet him face to face?"

"If it's one-on-one, without his congregation stamping into this office"—he swept his arm around the luxurious furnishings as if to say *these items are much too precious to be exposed to, uh, an uncouth herd*—"of course it can be arranged." Then he added gratuitously, "It's too bad that junior faculty members have got themselves mixed in this. They don't understand what a delicate position we're in."

"Delicate?"

"Well, yes," he reiterated tentatively. "We try to maintain good relations with the community. We don't need faculty members trying to ignite them."

"Do you think Reverend Johnson's sermon two weeks ago, in which he related the death of an African-American in the clinical trial to the very small numbers of blacks on the Bates-Bronsted faculty, was instigated by junior faculty?"

"No, of course not."

Janice dropped the question of faculty involvement, although she was sure the President had been referring to Richard. That was not why she was interviewing him.

"Do you think there is a relationship between Betsy Matthews' death and the small number of African-Americans on the Bates-Bronsted faculty?"

"The answer involves a lot of 'if's,' Ms. Polk. *If* we had more blacks on the medical faculty, and *if* one of them happened to be a neurologist, and *if* Jason Pearce had asked him to be co-investigator, and *if* the African-American neurologist was aware of the difference in risk factors between blacks and whites, which Dr. McAllister wasn't, then, yes, there might be a relation."

"Let's go back to your first 'if.' From what I've learned, only one percent of the Bates-Bronsted tenured faculty is African-American. In this city, a third of the population is black. Do you think that's fair?"

"No, I don't. If the country had more African-American medical school graduates we'd have a larger pool to recruit faculty from. In the 1980s and 1990s we did increase the percentage of African-American students admitted to Bates-Bronsted—"

"—to six percent," Janice interrupted, "in 1998, the peak year."

"We would have admitted more if they had been qualified."

"I've dug a little deeper, sir. And it turns out that for the last four years the dropout rate among white medical students at Bates-Bronsted has been higher than blacks. By that measure, the African-Americans you've admitted are more promising than the whites. Nevertheless, the percentage of black medical students admitted to Bates last year was only five percent."

"I'd like to see the data, Ms. Polk, but you know the University must tread lightly on affirmative action, lest we get sued by white students who are turned down, as happened at the University of Michigan."

"But if blacks are doing better in medical school, it's not a question of affirmative action. Besides, last year, the Supreme Court held that a narrow use of race to obtain the educational benefits of a diverse student body is not prohibited by the Constitution."

"If you can give me written copy of what you just told me, I will send it along to the Bates-Bronsted Admissions Committee, although I'm sure they're aware of the Supreme Court ruling. But even if the pool of African-American candidates for our faculty is sufficient—I'm not saying it is—I don't have a free hand in their selection, you know. The chairman of a department seeking a new faculty member makes a recommendation and I can tell you that I seldom have received a nomination of an African-American."

Janice could not resist interjecting. "I guess you wouldn't expect much more when the vast majority of faculty in every department is white males." The President did not respond.

"Just two more questions about faculty members, sir. The story in the local paper did not mention Dr. McAllister, yet he was the co-investigator on Professor Pearce's project. Is the University contemplating any action regarding Dr. McAllister?"

Staring into his empty coffee mug, the President took a moment before answering. "Dr. McAllister has served this University in many capacities and has built one of the finest neuroscience departments in the country. Neither the FDA nor the RAC investigators recommended any action against Dr. McAllister, and the Board of Trustees saw no reason to censure him in any way. I believe he has censured himself. The Board asked me to convey to Dr. McAllister that it had every confidence in his wisdom and abilities and looks forward to his serving the University for many more years." He glanced at his watch again. "Are you finished, Ms. Polk?"

"One last question. The Political Science Department has recommended Richard Piper for promotion to Professor with tenure. Will you support that recommendation?"

"Whether I do or not is irrelevant. It's up to the Appointments and Promotions Committee to approve his department's recommendation."

"But isn't it your responsibility as President to make the appointment?"

He rose from his chair, visibly irritated. "Let's cross that bridge when we come to it, Ms. Polk." Janice stood. "But let me say this. If Richard Piper's service to the University had been as exemplary as Dr. McAllister's, I'd have no hesitation."

Janice thanked him, said she'd send him the data he had requested (although much of it originated within his administration), and offered her hand. Limply he shook it and showed her out.

She was sorry she had asked her last question. For one thing, she had let her personal affection for Richard interfere with her journalistic judgment. For another, the President's response dismayed her. He made it as clear as he could that he did not approve of Richard. She knew she could not keep that news from Richard.

They had dinner at the same French restaurant Audrey had taken Jason to a couple of weeks earlier. After ordering a bottle of wine, Janice asked if Richard had heard from Audrey. He shook his head. "How about your interview with the President?"

"He's not very well informed about the status of African-Americans at the Medical School. I know more about the current situation and the law regarding affirmative action than he does, and I don't know much." Over the meal, Janice tried to imitate the President's pomposity and how she had deflated it. While they waited for coffee, she looked at Richard hesitantly. "Richard," she began, "as long as he's President, you're not going to be welcome at this University."

"What are you talking about? He doesn't even know who I am."

"Oh yes, he does." And she proceeded to tell him what she had learned.

He looked forlorn and didn't speak for a few minutes. Suddenly he brightened. "Well, if that happens, I'll move to Chicago and beg you for a job sharpening your pencils."

After dinner, they saw *Sideways*, fitting since a bottle of pinot noir had lubricated their meal. Then they drove back to Richard's apartment.

Chapter 19

WICHITA

After Richard left, Jason opened the cold-water valve on a pipe in the kitchen, filled a pot with water, and heated it on the hotplate. He had purchased the pot, hotplate, a stack of paper plates, and plastic utensils on a foray into the village the previous Wednesday when he realized he would need more than he had brought from home if he was going to spend the holiday at his unfinished house. He dipped the soap Audrey had brought into the hot water, lathered his face and neck, and shaved as best he could without a mirror. Then he stripped and used the rest of the water to wash his body with the T-shirt he had been wearing, rubbed himself with his pants to dry off, and made a mental note to buy some towels in the village. He dressed in one of the changes of clothing

Audrey had brought, giving no thought to his wife's kindness or concern in having delivered them.

In the village he stopped at the bank lobby to withdraw $500 from the ATM. Folding the spewed wad of twenty-dollar bills into his two remaining twenties and pocketing them, he went first to the village's general store where he picked up a bag of ice, two cold six packs, orange juice, a loaf of bread, some packaged cold cuts and cheese, two frozen dinners, and two face towels from the dry goods aisle. In the village, Jason was not known by name, only as 'the guy with the Lamborghini" and now he lifted its front boot into which his ice chest just fit. He filled it with the ice, beer and other perishables, putting the dry goods on the passenger seat.

About eight o'clock, he parked in the dirt lot of the one bar on Main Street, wedging the Lamborghini between a pickup and an SUV. A few pickups had slain deer wedged in their beds, while some of the sedans and SUVs had them lashed to their roofs. The deer explained the distant shots he had heard while camping out at his house.

Jason was more familiar with bars from movies that Audrey had dragged him to than from actually frequenting them, so he used his silver-screen sensibilities to navigate the bar. Most of the customers sat at tables, dressed in heavy woolen plaid shirts and cargo pants or jeans, talking loudly. In his sport jacket and white shirt, clean-shaven Jason stood out. A few middle-aged women, dressed not unlike the men, were sprinkled through the room. The bar itself was relatively empty. He took a seat at one end, his back to the tables. "What'll you have?" the bartender asked.

"Lemme have a shot of Jack Daniels."

"Neat?"

Jason was not sure exactly what 'neat' meant, but he didn't want to appear a novice.

"Yeah, neat."

The bartender filled a shot glass from the bottle and plunked it down in front of him. A little surprised that nothing followed, Jason asked the bartender for some pretzels. The bartender reached under the bar and pulled out a snack bowl of pretzels with mixed nuts. Cold sober, Jason contemplated his drink. Invoking his vast vicarious experience, he knew what he had to do, and so chucked the bourbon in one gulp, plunking the empty glass on the bar. His wedding band clinked against the glass; Jason removed it and slipped it in his jacket pocket. As the burn tracked the liquor all the way to his stomach, he reached for the snack bowl, trying not to show discomfort while the sting slowly dissipated into radiating warmth. Casually gathering another handful of nuts, he turned to watch a party of four men take seats at the other end of the bar. The bartender was serving them when a young woman with long blonde hair entered, stood for a moment scanning the scene, and glided sensuously but gingerly in stiletto heels to a barstool a couple of seats away from Jason. A momentary hush fell over the crowd. Jason began to wonder if he actually was in a movie. She let the coat slip off her shoulders, revealing the contour of her breasts through a high-necked beige blouse. Embarrassed to be staring at her, Jason turned away but as he did so, he thought she smiled at him. He turned back; she was still smiling. *This really could be a movie.*

"Hi. Are you a regular here?" she asked.

"No. First time."

"Mine too." Her voice blurred into the background noise.

"Sorry. I didn't hear you. Why don't you come closer?"

She lifted her coat off her stool and slid into the one next to Jason's. While she arranged her coat on the back of her new seat, he noticed she was wearing a miniskirt; her legs and thighs could not have been more perfectly shaped. "My first time too," she repeated when she was finally seated. Close up, he was aware that she was heavily made up; very red lipstick smeared on thickly, eye shadow too prominent, cheeks powdered, hiding any blemishes.

"Can I see your ID, miss?" the bartender asked. She fumbled in her purse and looked at Jason inquiringly.

"She's a friend of mine. I'll vouch for her," Jason said. He turned to her. "What would you like?"

"Uh, a Martini?" she asked uncertainly. Jason nodded. With more sophistication she added, "Make it dry, please."

"And I'll take a refill—with a chaser this time." The bartender looked dubiously from one of them to the other, shook his head, went to the far end of the bar where he prepared her drink and refilled Jason's glass. Jason wondered whether she knew what 'dry' meant any more than he had known 'neat.' When the bartender returned they clinked glasses and said, "Cheers" simultaneously. "So if you're a friend of mine, you should tell me your name."

"Kimberley." She took a few of the pretzels from Jason's dish. "What's yours?"

"Jason."

"You from around here?"

"I'm building a house a few miles down the road."

She took a sip and thought for a minute. "Not that big mansion on the left side as you head toward the city?"

"Well, it's not exactly a mansion, but it's probably the one you're thinking of."

"Awesome! We live in a shack on the dirt road that leads to the town dump." She corrected herself. "Lived."

Jason posed his question on top of Kimberley's last word. "You and?"

"My mother and her boyfriend. I'm in the process of moving out."

Relieved that the boyfriend was her mother's, he exclaimed, "Really?" A plot was forming in his woozy brain.

"It's not a pretty picture. I've smacked him a couple of times but he doesn't take 'no' for an answer. I can't wait to get out of here."

"Where will you go?"

"Any place but here." She drained her Martini and plucked the olive from the bottom of the glass. Taking hold of the edge of the bar with both hands to steady herself, she sighed, "Phew! I shouldn't have drunk that Martini so fast. I'm a wee bit dizzy." Jason shoved the pretzels and nuts in front of her. He thought about a third shot, but with Kimberley already dizzy, he didn't want another round only to have her get sick in his Lamborghini or on the hardwood floors. Concerned about slurring his speech, Jason listened carefully to himself as he asked, "How about I show you my new house, Kimberley?" *I sound articulate,* he thought.

"When?"

"Right now. The cold air will do you good. I can't mix you a Martini but I've got some cold beer."

She scowled. "I told my older sister—she dropped me off—to pick me up here at midnight." Kimberley giggled. "No, I'm lying. Sis insisted it couldn't be any later."

Again, Jason listened to his own words. "If we go now you'll be home before midnight." With a flourish he added, "Cinderella."

Ignoring the tag, Kimberley pouted, "Not home, here!"

"Okay. Here." He settled with the bartender for both of them and started to climb off his stool. Kimberley looked up at him dubiously. His best warm smile had the desired effect. She got up, put her coat on and, wobbling on heels, grabbed his arm and together they tottered out of the bar.

"Cool!" Kimberley said for the second time when he unlocked the passenger door of the Lamborghini, swept the few dry goods onto the floor and helped her slide in.

"You rich or something, mister?"

"Remember, my name's Jason," he said as he started the car, and backed out carefully. "Not really. I'm a scientist, Kimberley. I made an important discovery and I've been handsomely rewarded."

"What kind of discovery? A bomb or something?"

They were out of the village and Jason flicked up his brights. They passed a "deer crossing" sign. "Nothing like that. A gene that prevents memory loss."

"You mean like old people get? I've heard about that. What is it?" She thought for a minute. "Alzheimer? Isn't that it?"

"Yeah," he said, not wanting to dwell on the subject. He glanced at her. She had taken a tissue from her purse to wipe off her lipstick, and then flipped down the visor, using the illuminated mirror to reapply it. "How old are you, anyway, Kimberley?"

"Eighteen. January 19th, 1987."

Concentrating hard, he did the arithmetic. "Seventeen. You're still seventeen."

"What's the difference, I'll be eighteen in a couple of months." From the fuzzy recesses of his brain, Jason recalled that the law branded adults who had sexual relations with minors criminal predators for life.

He looked at her again. "You look," he hesitated, "and act, much older."

"I try. How old are you?" she asked.

"Forty-three."

"You're older than my father." Quickly, she added, "But you look much younger."

Jason pulled into his driveway. Instead of turning the car parallel to the entrance he parked with the headlights illuminating the front door and the dirt path to it. Kimberley opened her door, starting to get out. "Would you mind carrying these few things?" He handed her the items he hadn't put in the ice chest. I'll leave the lights on so you don't trip and I'll get the ice chest from the boot."

"Boot?" She was treading carefully to the door, her heels sinking into the soft earth.

"The trunk. In Europe they call it the boot." Carrying the ice chest to the front door, he got there in back of Kimberley. He opened the door, flicked on the entrance hall light, a bare bulb suspended from its wires, and invited her in. "I'm just going to turn off the headlights. I wouldn't want a dead battery to strand us here." When he returned, she was standing in the hall with her coat wrapped around her.

"Uh, Jason, I need the bathroom."

"You're not sick, are you?" he asked with a look of concern tinged with disdain.

"No," she said, looking down. "I just have to pee."

"The best I can offer is a Port-a-Pot the construction workers use. It's around the side. I don't have a flashlight, but I'll turn the headlights back on and point you in the right direction." He stood a few feet away as she used the Port-a-Pot and walked her back to the house, then turned off the car lights again. Before entering the finished floor in the living room, both he and Kimberley took their shoes off. Jason turned on the small table lamp sitting next to the blankets, spread out one of his new towels, retrieved the ice chest from the door, and set it on the towel. "How about a beer?" He looked at her for the first time since the car. She had not repowdered her face and now he could see some pimples on her cheeks and that her brown eyes, were much darker than her hair. He sat on the floor and invited her to sit beside him. She hesitated but soon enough sat down. "Don't you want to take your coat off?"

"I'm still cold. Don't you have any heat?"

"No heat, no furniture." He pointed to the blankets. "This is my bed."

She shivered and he put his arm around her. She did not draw closer to him. He started to stroke her hair. Still no response. Gradually, Jason realized that whatever had attracted Kimberley to him at the bar, sustained or enhanced by the Martini, was wearing off. Still he persisted. He turned his body to face her and put both his arms around her and kissed her. For an instant, her lips parted slightly and pressed his. Abruptly, she stood up.

"Please bring me back to the bar."

He looked at his watch. "It's only ten thirty. You've got plenty of time."

"That's not it. I just want to get out of here."

"You don't like my house?"

"When you get it finished, I'm sure it will be very nice. Your kids will like it, I'm sure."

Jason was stunned. "What makes you think——"

"You have kids? There's a tricycle leaning against the side of the house near the potty. And why would a bachelor have such a big house unless he's got a family?"

Kimberley headed to the front and put her shoes on. "Please, Jason." She shrugged him off when he put his arm around her to guide her to the car.

A half moon had risen over the distant mountains, providing faint illumination, but the road was closed in by forest on both sides.

About a mile from the village the engine sputtered. Jason managed to drive on to the shoulder before it went dead. The starter turned over but the engine did not catch. "This has never happened before."

"Are you out of gas?"

Jason couldn't remember the last time he had filled the tank. He peered at the illuminated gas gauge. EMPTY. "Good thinking, Kimberley. We're out of gas." She took off her shoes, opened her door, got out in her stockinged feet, and started running toward the village.

"Wait! It's dangerous. Let me help you." She was beyond a bend in the road and did not respond. "Be careful," he added, although there was little chance she could have heard him. He turned off the lights, locked the car, and headed back to his house on foot.

By the time he arrived, his head had cleared and he realized that he could not sink any lower: masquerading as a wealthy bachelor rake, seducing a schoolgirl. *What was he thinking?* He knew he could not blame it all on the alcohol. He had gone into the bar cold sober. He had smiled back at her. He invited her to sit next to him. *And what if she had let his kiss linger and he had slipped off her coat and unbuttoned her blouse?* He got up and banged his head against the wall. *He should be grateful to her.*

He dozed that night, waking up once, sure he had heard sirens. He visualized Kimberley lying by the side of the road, her stiletto heels a few feet away, the medic pulling a sheet over her head.

He finally fell asleep about five. and dreamed they had taken Kimberley to the morgue, laid her on a slab next to another woman. The coroner asked him to identify both of them. One was Kimberley. The other was Betsy Matthews.

⟞⟝

The nightmare awakened him about nine o'clock on Sunday morning, the sun streaming through the uncurtained windows. *I've got to get out of here!* he thought.

Where are you headed? an inner voice intoned. Then he remembered Kimberley's answer: *Any place but here. I can't go back to Bates-Bronsted, to ridicule.*

What about Audrey, Rachel, and David? the inner voice asked.

I've caused them enough grief.

You're not ready to face up to it, are you? the voice taunted.

He stuffed all the clothes and his toiletries into two plastic grocery bags that had held his purchases from the general store and headed toward the village. After passing the Lamborghini, he paid careful attention to the road's shoulders, looking for skid marks, trampling of weeds and shrubs, traces of clothing, shoes, dried blood. Nothing. At about ten thirty he reached the village. The general store was open and he bought a cheap vinyl overnight bag—the only luggage the store had—into which he crammed his belongings even before he had paid for it. He had pulled out his credit card, but then decided cash was better—*in case anyone will be looking, I don't want to leave a credit card receipt trail.* As he doled out the twenties, he asked casually, "Anything new in town?"

"Since you were here yesterday?" the clerk asked. Jason hadn't paid much attention to the lad's face yesterday or today—just a teenager taking a part time job. He wondered if he knew Kimberley. "Nope. No bank robberies, murders, kidnappings. Not even a car theft. Nothing ever happens here," the kid said. Jason didn't ask, *What about rape?*

"Is there a bus station in this town?"

"Yeah. In front of the Walgreens up Main Street. I think you can buy tickets there."

"Thanks," he said, heading out the door.

"Bon voyage," the clerk shouted after him.

Jason stopped at an ATM and withdrew another $500.

Inside the drugstore, he picked up a timetable. Only two buses stopped in the village: one, later in the day, going to the city down the road; the other's final destination, Chicago, departing in one hour. He started to pull out his credit card, then remembered to pay cash. "Chicago, one way, next bus."

"I'm not sure any seats are left," the agent replied, typing into his computer keyboard. "Sunday after Thanksgiving. Lots of kids going back to college." He studied the computer screen. "You're lucky, sir. You got the last seat."

Peeling off more twenties from his wad, he took the ticket and went to the lunch counter, bought two eggs over easy, hash browns and sausage, toast and coffee—the biggest breakfast, in fact the biggest meal he'd had since Tuesday.

The bus was packed. Jason took the last empty seat, on the aisle almost at the rear. A young African-American man was sitting next to the window, a senior at Northwestern, he told Jason. With nothing to read and having to crane to look out the window, Jason fell asleep, exaggerating his slouch tendency with his head sometimes resting on the shoulder or arm of the young man, who quietly extricated himself without waking Jason. He dozed on and off throughout the day, getting up for restroom breaks or to buy a sandwich or a magazine, which he read without really paying attention. He kept asking himself what the dream meant: Kimberley and Betsy Matthews lying side by side. So far as he knew, Kimberley was alive. Betsy Matthews, he remembered, died the day before he last drove out of the city to his property. *I didn't kill her any more than I killed Kimberley,* he told himself. Mrs. Matthews was old. She would have died from something else, maybe even Alzheimer's if she hadn't been in the trial. The flaws in his logic gnawed at his mind but he kept repressing them. And as for Kimberley, he had done her a good turn, teaching her to beware of older men who try to hide their connubial state. That reminded him—he patted his jacket pocket— the wedding band was still there, and he put it on.

At two in the morning the bus arrived in Chicago jarring Jason from a deep sleep. The cold stung his face and in the terminal he pulled the heavy sweater out of his bag, put it on under his sport jacket, and read the departures schedule. The only bus leaving in the next hour went to St. Louis. All he wanted was to go back to sleep. A bus seat would be more comfortable than a hard bench in the terminal. At the ticket counter, he purchased another one-way ticket using cash, climbed on the outbound bus, falling back asleep quickly and not awakening until eight A.M., when the bus arrived in St. Louis.

After putting his overnight bag in a locker, he walked out of the terminal into a grey, blustery Monday, spotting a twenty-four hour restaurant across the street. Coffee and a steak with eggs warmed him, but the cold stung when he went back out on the street; he needed a warm coat.

At the height of rush hour, plenty of people were out. A bent black woman in a threadbare coat and carrying a shopping bag approached him, walking in worn sneakers. "Excuse me, ma'am." She passed him, but he turned and caught up alongside. "That bag looks heavy. Can I help you carry it?"

She stopped, looked him over, clutching the bag more tightly. "You're not gonna run away with it, are you?"

He stared at her, incredulous. *My god! What do I look like?* He stroked his cheek and realized that he had not shaved since Saturday. "No," he replied, "You look tired and since I'm not going anyplace in particular, I thought I could give you a hand."

People were passing in both directions. Still suspicious, the woman shrank further into her coat. "And why aren't you going anyplace in particular?"

Jason laughed. "You sound like my mother." Now they were walking side by side, the woman still clutching her bag. "I just got off the bus from Chicago and I'm trying to get my bearings."

"Well, if you tell me what you're looking for, maybe I can help you."

I wish I knew popped into his head, but what he said was, "I'm looking for a used overcoat."

She thought for a moment. "There's a Salvation Army store on the block after next. If it's not open by the time we get there, it will be in a few minutes." She stopped and faced him. "You got enough money to buy it? I can help you out if you don't."

Jason laughed and pulled out his wad of twenties, thinner but still substantial. "How about you? Can you use a twenty?"

Offended, she said emphatically, "I don't take handouts." They continued to walk together silently, then she stopped again and turned to him. "But it would be nice if you would carry my bag until we get to the store," and she handed him her bag.

Jason spotted the sign, turning up his collar as they crossed the second street. She stopped in front of the store and he handed over her bag. "Thank you very much, young man. I hope you find what you're looking for."

———

He bought an overcoat for forty dollars and counted his remaining money, five hundred and sixty dollars. *Now what?* Jason asked himself as he turned up the collar of the overcoat and plunged his hands into its slash pockets. *Find a job?* He remembered passing a restaurant with a "Help Wanted" sign posted on the bottom of its plate glass window. Retracing his steps, he realized that he wouldn't get a job until he shaved and cleaned up. He passed the restaurant and returned to the bus depot where he retrieved his bag from the locker. In the men's room, he stripped to the waist, shaved with soap and hot water, rotated the hot air hand-blower up to dry his face, pulled the last clean T-shirt from his bag, and put it on followed by his last clean shirt, sweater, sport jacket, and overcoat. Again checking his bag in a locker, he returned to the restaurant.

A middle aged African-American woman wearing an apron stood behind the counter. Three customers sat separately at the counter, the empty stools topped with cracked black leather, the inner foam cushioning exposed in several places. Jason leaned toward the counter between two stools.

"What can I get for you?" the woman asked.

"I'd like to apply for the job."

She looked surprised. Jason gestured to the sign in the window. "That job?" He nodded. She moved slowly, as if in pain, down a short hall to the kitchen and shouted to someone.

An older black man came out. Wiping his hands on his apron, he strode toward Jason. "We're looking for a dishwasher. Washing dishes and pots, maybe some bussing." He looked at Jason suspiciously. "Why you want a job like that?"

Why do I want a job like that? Jason didn't answer.

"You're not an alky or a druggie are you?"

"Oh no! Nothing like that." The proprietor waited for Jason to say something else, but he remained silent.

"Mister, lemme look at your hands." The man took Jason's hands in his own, turning them over.

Jason felt and saw the hardened, swollen, reddened flesh of the boss's hands. The man dropped Jason's hands. "Mister, this ain't the kind of work you're used to. Your hands will be bleeding and raw after a day scrubbing in almost boiling, soapy water. Your hands weren't made for dishwashing."

"Does that mean you won't hire me?"

"For your own good, mister. Try something else." He returned to the kitchen. Jason politely thanked the woman behind the counter and left.

With people at work the streets were quieter. The sun occasionally peeked through a heavy layer of cloud, but still it was cold. He went back to the bus terminal, retrieved his bag from the locker, and scanned the departures. He could continue south to New Orleans. *But then, why did I waste forty dollars on an overcoat?* Besides, the bus to New Orleans didn't leave for another four hours. The next departure was to Wichita via Kansas City. Seemed like the easiest thing was to keep moving. The ticket cost Jason another eighty dollars.

He changed buses in Kansas City, MO and quickly the bus crossed the Missouri River into Kansas. *Bloody Kansas.* The two words echoed in Jason's brain. He dredged his memory... *bloody Kansas, bloody Kansas.* Both his parents' ancestors had settled in Nebraska and were staunch supporters of a free state. Even before he was in high school, he remembered his mother lamenting the sad state of civil rights. "But at least we're not Kansas, bloody Kansas," she had said.

⸻

"Whaddya mean, mom?" he had asked. Reminding young Jason that his father taught history in Kearney before he went to Vietnam, she told Jason about the influx of free settlers into the Kansas and Nebraska territories in 1855 so that they could vote against slavery in both territories. "Slaves never were brought to Nebraska in large numbers, but Kansas was another story. Ruffians from Missouri packed elections in Kansas to allow slavery. The fighting between the groups led to deaths on both sides. 'Bloody Kansas' they called it. Do you know," she went on, "that the case that ended separate but equal schools for Negroes was brought in Kansas? Can you imagine? You might have thought it was only in the Deep South, but until 1954 the schools were segregated by law in Kansas, bloody Kansas."

Jason's parents married while still students at the University of Nebraska in Kearney. In 1965, more to support his family than to display patriotism, his father volunteered for the Air Force, went to Officer Candidate School in Alabama, and in 1967 became a pilot in Vietnam. Years later, Jason's mother told him that his father was angry and depressed about spraying Agent Orange from his C-123 transport plane. The Air Force never told her the full circumstances of his death; she wondered if he had committed suicide by crashing his plane. With his death benefit and her part-time work, she had enough to keep her son fed and clothed, supplementing his formal education with her own renditions of history and social justice. After her husband died, she became an anti-war and civil rights activist.

⸺

Jason wondered what his mother would think of him now. *Running away is a cowardly response to adversity.*

But what am I running away from? Forgetting to examine the mice did not seem a terrible crime in itself. Only when it contributed to a faulty clinical trial in which a person had died, did it become horrendous. *Does that mean I killed her?* Jason shook his head; he couldn't buy it. *I never wanted to work with humans. It led to my downfall.*

Jason had loved the physical and biological sciences, possibly because they didn't involve human contact. He hadn't been interested in other people's problems and he didn't expect others to be interested in his. In St. Louis, he was surprised when the woman whose shopping bag he offered sensed his predicament and offered to help. *And that restaurant owner wouldn't give me a job for my own good.*

His bus terminated in Wichita, at eight o'clock in the evening, Jason then faced the choice of taking a bus north to Salina—it left at one in the morning—or a bus south to Oklahoma City, but that one didn't leave until eight in the morning. Again, he preferred sleeping on a bus than on a hard bench in a cold, dingy waiting room. It would be his second night on a bus. He bought his ticket to Salina, found an all-night restaurant across from the bus terminal, returned to the terminal around eleven o'clock and took a seat on a long wooden bench in the waiting area. Across from him, he watched as an attractive, young white woman carrying a small suitcase sat down near a young African-American man. He was wearing a windbreaker over a white dress shirt, open at the collar, neatly pressed khaki slacks, and polished loafers. The woman turned to him and asked, "Do you have the time?" The man looked at his watch, told her, and asked where she was heading. Jason heard her say Kansas City and then in response to her reciprocal question, the man said

"Salina." They continued to chat amiably and Jason's attention wandered.

A grizzled man, with two or three days of beard, sat down on Jason's bench a few spaces way from him. He, too, observed the conversation of the two people on the opposite bench and began to mutter to himself. Finally, he got up, strode to the African-American, gripped his windbreaker at his throat and pulled him up. Their faces were very close. "Whatcha doin' boy? Botherin' this nice young lady!"

The woman said, "Really, he isn't bothering me."

The African-American did not say a word. The grizzled man started to push him to the nearest wall. Instantly, Jason stood and grabbed the man's shoulders, forcing him to let go of the black man. "You heard the lady," he said. "He isn't bothering her. Get your hands off him." He continued to hold the man by the shoulders.

A policeman standing near the entrance sauntered over.

"Tell this man to get his goddam hands off me," the grizzled man said to the cop. Jason let go.

"He accosted this young man for no reason," Jason said, pointing toward the African-American, who had resumed his seat.

"He was botherin' that woman," the grizzled man said, nodding at the woman. The cop looked at him and at the young woman. He turned to Jason. "You should mind your own business, mister."

The grizzled man and Jason returned to their bench, a few feet apart. After a few moments, the man slid closer to Jason, turning to him. Jason could smell alcohol on his breath. In a low growl he said directly into Jason's ear, "You know, mister, it's still easy to kill a nigger."

Jason stared silently at him, then stood up and took a seat next to the African-American; the woman was on his other side. "I heard you're headed to Salina. That's where I'm going."

The African-American smiled. "Thanks for pulling that guy off me." He paused. "Is Salina your final destination?"

The question surprised Jason. "I doubt it. What about you?"

"No. I'm heading to Kearney, Nebraska."

"Kearney? Really? I'm from Kearney. Haven't been there for years. What's bringing you to Kearney?"

"I'm interviewing for a job at the University."

"What kind of job?"

"Math. There's an opening for an Assistant Professor. I just got my Ph.D. in Mathematics."

Jason offered his hand. "Congratulations. What are your chances?"

"There were over a hundred applicants and they've narrowed the field to five, so my odds have improved considerably." Shaking Jason's hand, he added, "My name's Alex."

"Jason. Jason Pearce." He thought for a moment. "Can you get to Kearney from Salina?"

"It's not easy. You've either got to go west to Denver or east to Kansas City. With transfers it takes almost twenty-four hours. I'll take my chances hitchhiking. A brother might pick me up."

The loudspeaker interrupted their exchange. "Bus to Salina leaving in five minutes from pier two."

"Well I guess that's us," Alex said. He and Jason stood. They smiled goodbye to the young woman and Jason turned to grin impishly at the old man.

They sat next to each other on the bus, Alex by the window, staring into the darkness.

Jason turned to him. "You know what that old man said to me?"

"The one who accosted me?"

"Yeah. He said, 'It's still easy to kill a nigger.'"

Alex chuckled, then went silent for a moment. "He's right, you know."

Jason's surprise must have shown.

"Maybe not lynching," Alex continued, "but killing by neglect, killing by abuse, yeah, and sometimes by murder." He stopped, reflecting. "These days police violence is more frequent than mob violence."

And suddenly, Jason saw the truth. He grasped Alex's upper arm. "You're right, it is still easy," he exclaimed. "I know. I know because I killed one."

Alex stared at Jason. "You? You killed a"—he couldn't repeat the 'n' word. "You killed a black man."

"No. A black woman." More animated than he had been since the start of his journey, Jason quickly explained what had happened—how he did not start out working on Alzheimer's, how he stumbled on the memory gene, about the mice he didn't sacrifice, the clinical trial, Betsy Matthews, his dismissal and his running away.

Jason thought Alex pulled away from him, but any actual movement was imperceptible. Somehow, his confession relaxed him and he fell asleep as the bus motor droned on, driving them through the dark night; only the muted interior safety lights provided illumination. *He was back at the Wichita Bus Terminal. Repeatedly, the old man was banging Alex against the wall while the cop was doing the same to Jason.* He awoke with a start and was shocked by the bus jerking back and forth, finally coming to a complete stop in total darkness.

"Are you all right?" Alex asked quietly. "You were shouting 'Stop, stop' as the bus started to shake.

"I must have been dreaming," Jason replied. "I'm fine."

Sitting toward the back they could not hear what the driver had said, but eventually the message filtered back that the bus had broken down; the driver had radioed for help and they should try to stay warm; the electrical system had failed.

For long minutes they were both silent. The temperature began to fall. Jason took off his coat and spread it over both Alex and him. Assuming that after his confession Alex would be prosecuting him in his mind, so he was surprised when Alex asked in a very low voice, "Are you still running, Jason?"

The question startled Jason. He had to think. "I was until we started talking. You've explained a lot to me, Alex." Again, he was quiet for a few minutes. "I can't go back to Bates-Bronsted, even if they wanted me. But I can stop running." He thought for a few moments and turned to Alex. "If I rented a car to drive to Kearney could I give you a lift?"

"That would be fantastic," Alex replied. "Do you still have relatives there?"

"My mother, that's all. I think I'll surprise her. In fact, you can stay with us tonight."

"You're too kind. Can I chip in for the car?"

"No, I've got plenty of cash. Come to think of it, I'm not running any longer, so I can use my credit card." This seemed to settle matters and they both fell asleep under Jason's coat.

The sun was already up when a replacement bus pulled alongside. Groggily, the passengers transferred to it, then waited while their checked luggage was moved. They were deposited safely in Salina around eleven o'clock. They had a late breakfast and then Jason called a cab to take them to the Hertz Car Rental, too far away to walk with their bags. From there they drove to the Central Mall, leaving their luggage in the trunk, agreeing to meet back at the car at about three o'clock. Jason went on a mini-shopping spree at Dillard's, outfitting himself with underwear, socks, shirts, a pair of slacks, shoes and a heavier weight sport jacket than the one he was wearing. Alex was waiting at the car. "I'm going to the Mall men's room to shave, wash, and put on my new clothes," Jason told him. "Mom would not like me showing up looking and smelling like a bum."

It was close to five when they left Salina, heading north on US-81, Jason in a new sport shirt and jacket, slacks and shoes—clean-shaven and hair combed. They stopped for a leisurely dinner at an inn outside of Minden, Nebraska, a small town that sparkled under its newly installed Christmas lights and decorations. It was almost ten o'clock when Jason, after a few wrong turns, finally found his old neighborhood in Kearney. The streets were dark and deserted, far different than the part of town nearer the University. He parked in front of his mother's house; no lights were on in the front windows. Leaving their bags in the car, they walked up to the front door. Jason rang the bell, they waited; he rang once more. No response. "Mom must be asleep. Wait here, Alex, I'll go around back. That's where her bedroom is."

As Jason rounded the corner of the house, a patrol car turned onto the street, pulling up behind Jason's car, the only one on the street. A searchlight mounted on the passenger side flashed on, illuminating the front and side of the house. The light caught Jason and then swiveled back to illuminating the front door where Alex stood waiting, blinded like a deer in headlights. The patrolmen were out of their car in a flash, one with his revolver in one hand and a bullhorn in the other, headed for the front door, where Alex stared blindly into the bright light. "Drop whatever you're holding and come out with your hands over your head and walk toward the patrol car."

"I'm not holding anything," Alex said, slowly regaining his vision as he emerged from the intense circle of light.

"Don't be a smart ass, mister." The first cop came up behind Alex when he was a few steps away from the car and slammed him hard against its side.

The other cop, flashlight in one hand and revolver in the other, headed around the corner of the house. As he did, Jason, having heard the bullhorn, came toward him, his hands also over his head. He saw the first cop push Alex against the car. "Hey, take it easy. He's not armed and he did what you asked him."

Jason felt the muzzle of the second cop's gun in his back. "Another smart ass," the second cop muttered. "Good thing you're white or I'd slam you twice as hard."

While the second cop watched, the first patted Alex down roughly. He went easier on Jason. They were both handcuffed and pushed into the back seat of the patrol car. The second cop radioed that he had apprehended two men, "one white, the other a, uhh, a Negro, attempting a burglary. Possibly also a car theft." The headlight of the patrol car illuminated Jason's car, which had Oklahoma plates. They copied the license and punched it into their computer.

"I can save you the trouble," Jason told them. "I rented the car in Salina."

"Well if you don't mind, sir," the cop said facetiously, "we'd like to get an independent verification."

The commotion disturbed the neighborhood and lights came on in a few nearby houses, but Jason's mother's house remained dark.

At the police station the two men were brought into a holding pen, surrendering the contents of their pockets and their belts. A half hour later, a detective interviewed Jason. "Are you Jason Pearce?" he asked, holding Jason's driver's license in his hand, matching the photo with Jason's face.

"I am."

"You're a missing person, Jason. Did you pull off a job back east?"

Audrey must have reported my disappearance to the police. "Nothing like that, I—"

"What are you doing in Kearney? You got plenty of cash. Did you pull off another job tonight?"

"The house at which you apprehended us is my mother's."

"What's her name?"

"Pearce. Carol Pearce."

The detective took out the local phone book and found her name listed at the address where Jason and Alex were picked up.

"Was she expecting you?"

"No. I haven't seen her for a few years and I thought I'd surprise her. Either she slept through our arrest or she wasn't home."

The detective handed Jason the phone from his desk, rotating the phone book so Jason could read it. "Call her."

"I know the number," Jason said as he dialed. *Please mom, answer the phone.* She picked it up on the third ring. The detective put the conversation on speakerphone.

"Mom, this is Jason."

"Jason? Why are you calling so late? It's the middle of night where you are. Is everything all right?"

"I'm in jail."

"Is that what you called to tell me? Were you in a demonstration? I've been arrested a few times, too, you know."

"Nothing like that I'm afraid."

"What then?"

"The police thought I was trying to break into your house."

Trying to absorb her son's answer, she did not answer right away. "Where *exactly* are you?"

"In the Kearney police station."

Again, a short pause. "I'll be there in fifteen minutes." She hung up.

Jason allowed himself a smile.

"What about your uh, "accomplice? Is he your brother?" the detective laughed.

"No. Alex has a Ph.D. in mathematics and is a finalist for a professor's job at the University here. He's scheduled for an interview with the math department tomorrow." Startled, the detective glanced at his watch; obviously too late to get corroboration from the University. He walked Jason back to the pen and motioned Alex to come out. "You'll have to wait in here until your mother comes." Jason entered the pen and the detective locked him in.

"I don't mind," Jason replied politely.

Alex corroborated what Jason had reported about him and he was soon locked in the pen with Jason who told him that he would call the math department first thing in the morning and explain Alex's predicament." If the chair of the math department first hears about your incarceration from the police, you'll never get the job. After I explain the situation, I expect he'll call the police who will release you, and I'll come by and pick you up, assuming they let me out tonight. You can return to my mother's house to freshen up before your interview."

When Jason's mother arrived, the police asked if she wanted to press charges of attempted burglary against her son. She laughed. "He could have used his key." She had to sign various papers before they would let him go.

"I didn't know you were such a heavy sleeper, mom," Jason said as she drove back to her house.

"Don't jump to conclusions. I was at the movies with one of my friends and didn't get home until five minutes before you called."

"Have you talked to Audrey lately?"

"It's been several months." She glanced sideways at her son. "You've left her? Is that why you've come home?"

"'Don't jump to conclusions,' mom," he chuckled, and then realized that technically she was right. "It's a long story, it's late, I've had a long day, and I've got to be up early to help Alex. I'll tell you tomorrow."

"Who's Alex?"

"A friend I met in Wichita; we drove up together from Salina. He's still in jail. I hope the cops don't beat up on him."

"Why should they?" They arrived at Carol's house and parked in back of Jason's rental car.

"He's black."

Carol Pearce stared at Jason. "Why didn't you tell me when we were at the station? He's not safe."

"Mom, this is Nebraska not Kansas. You told me that sort of stuff wasn't likely to happen up here."

"Oh, Jason! I don't know any more. The whole world is a dangerous place."

Chapter 20

BACK EAST

The phone woke Audrey at seven-thirty on Thursday morning.

"Mrs. Pearce, we've located your husband." She recognized the detective's voice and was instantly alert. "The police in Kearney, Nebraska arrested him last night for attempted burglary."

"Burglary?" *That doesn't sound like Jason.*

"The police had his driver's license and the photo identified him beyond a doubt."

"Is he all right? Has he been wounded?"

"I've told you all I know, ma'am."

Kearney. Did he flee home to his mother? Is he sending me a message?

Audrey had a good relationship with her mother-in-law, although they had relatively few contacts, none since the summer. So far as she knew, Jason hadn't spoken with her either. The time in Kearney was an hour earlier; she had better wait to call. Besides, she had to help Hannah get the kids ready for school and then drive them. It was nine thirty before she was able to call. The line was busy. Maybe Jason was trying to call her. Her phone did not ring. Fifteen minutes later the line was still busy. Finally, at ten o'clock she got through. Carol Pearce answered. "Carol, this is Audrey." Dispensing with pleasantries, she asked. "Is Jason there?"

"He's out now. I picked him up at the police station last night." As if that was not unusual she asked, "How are Rachel and David?"

"They're fine. Well, not exactly. They miss their father." After a brief pause, "The police here told me he was arrested for attempted burglary last night."

"If Jason still carried his key to the house he grew up in, he could have let himself in while I was at the movies." Continuing in her peppery voice, "News travels faster west to east than east to west. Maybe you can tell me what's going on, Audrey."

"Hasn't he told you?"

"We got back here very late. He's promised to tell me everything today." Neither spoke for a moment, then Carol started, "You two aren't—"

Audrey interrupted, not waiting for Carol to finish. "I hope not! I haven't seen or heard from Jason for over a week. Yesterday, I notified the police that he was missing. Is he all right?"

"Seems okay to me!"

"Please ask him to call me."

"I'll do that," Carol replied.

Immediately, Audrey called Richard to tell him the news. Starting to leave a message on his machine, she was surprised when Janice cut in, "He's just left for class. Is Jason all right??"

Audrey was stunned to hear Janice's voice; she didn't have to wonder what sort of relationship she and Richard had. "Just tell him I called," she said and hung up. *Why didn't I tell Janice? She's been trying to help me.* She knew why.

As soon as she put the phone down, it rang. "Audrey——"

"Oh, Jason. Are you okay? I've been worried."

He didn't answer right away. "I told you I had to work things out for myself. It wasn't until yesterday that I did." The line was silent for a moment.

"What happened yesterday?" she asked. *Has he run off with another woman?*

"I'll tell you when I see you—soon, I hope.

"Maybe you should tell me now." He did not answer right away. *Have I antagonized him again?*

"I realize now the magnitude of my mistakes and I take full responsibility."

Relieved, she asked, "When are you coming home?"

"I'd rather you and the kids joined me out here, at least until we can figure things out. What I did—or didn't do—was criminal negligence and Bates-Bronsted was right to fire me and there is nothing left for me there. I'm sorry for everything I've put you through.""

"Oh, Jason, I hoped you would come to your senses."

"I have. I should have listened to you, Audrey." Changing the subject, he asked, "How are the kids?"

"They miss you, Jason."

"I miss them too, and you."

"When are you coming home?" she repeated.

The silence lasted so long that finally Audrey asked, "Are you still there, Jason?

"I'm here." In a subdued voice he answered, "I told you I'm not going back."

"I understand you're not going back to Bates-Bronsted," she paused, swallowing the lump in her throat. "What about the kids? What about me, Jason?"

"I'd rather you all came out here. Mom can put us up for a few days until we decide what to do."

Audrey vacillated. *Does he think we still have lots of money?* She took a different tack. "What about the house, Jason, and the new property, and your Lamborghini? We've got to decide what to do with them." Marshaling her argument she added, "And the kids, Jason. I don't want to pluck Rachel out of school in the middle of the year. How would we explain it to Davey?"

"Look, Audrey, my friend is waiting for me to get him out of jail. Let me think about it. We can talk some more when I get back here, okay?"

"Okay," she replied.

"Goodbye," Jason said and she heard the phone click off.

ACKNOWLEDGMENTS

I've been working on *Blame* on and off for ten years, overlapping with my first three novels, A*dirondack Trilogy,* which I completed in 2013. *Blame* should have been easier to write because it was based on my professional experience as a physician and geneticist, but I wanted to make it as accurate as possible without losing the drama of a good novel. That took a lot of help.

As a student at New York University, I spent electives and summers working in the laboratory of the late Charles Gilvarg from whom I learned critical thinking and experimental design. After my residency in Pediatrics at Johns Hopkins I enrolled in a Ph.D. program in Biophysics at the Medical School where Howard Dintzis and Michael Naughton furthered my scientific education. The Chair of Pediatrics at the time, the late Robert E. Cooke, invited me to join the faculty and start my own lab before I completed the Ph.D. I don't know if it was an offer I couldn't refuse, but I didn't. The colleagues with whom I worked and learned from are numerous, but special appreciation goes to the late Barton Childs, as well as Michael Kaback, Haig Kazazian, Barbara Migeon, and David Valle. Toward the close of my active career, Aravinda Chakravarti, who came to Hopkins to head the McKusick-Nathans Institute of Genetics, gave me new insights into genetics.

On the literary side, sharing my work with the Desert Writers of Las Cruces New Mexico under the tutelage of Kevin "Mac" McIlvoy, then Professor of English Literature at New Mexico State University, improved my writing immeasurably. Recently I reread Mac's tightly handwritten two pages of comments on an early draft of *Blame*. (I called it *A Conflict of Interest* back then.) I was surprised at how many of his gentle criticisms I had responded to over the years without remembering where they originated.

Many of the Desert Writers were put off by the jargon and couldn't see where I was going with an early draft. After a few years' hiatus, filled mostly with completing *Adirondack Trilogy*, I returned to *Blame* with a better idea of what I wanted to say, but less clear on how to say it. Participating in an Advanced Novel Workshop with Lynn Stegner in Stanford's

Continuing Education Program helped me see the light. This talented group carefully dissected several chapters. Afterwards, Lynn did a fantastic substantive edit of *Blame* followed, after a revision, by a line edit, both vastly improving the novel and teaching me a lot more about writing fiction. Friends whose critical honesty I trusted, Maryhelen Snyder, Tom Schneider, Lori Andrews, gave me their insights as did two of my children, Deborah and Steven, who had the time and patience to read at least one draft. Deborah, who once worked as an editor, did two masterful edits as well as proofreading. Steven pointed out extraneous material, which I excised, and his wife, Eva Cohen, did the very appropriate cover design.

My wife, Barbara Starfield, died suddenly and unexpectedly in 2011 while I was completing the *Adirondack Trilogy*. She and I had preliminary discussions about this novel and *Blame* would have been a better story had she lived. She has left an irreplaceable void in my life.

Made in the USA
Charleston, SC
14 October 2016